WILLOW GLEN HEIST

ALEC PECHE

ISBN:978-0-9987768-1-1

ACKNOWLEDGMENTS

Many thanks to my first reader and my editor for improving the quality of the story and my writing! Thanks to Liza Paolini for doing another review of this manuscript.

Thank you for reading my book. If you enjoyed it, won't you please take a moment to leave me a review at your favorite retailer?

Thanks!

Alec Peche

1 CHAPTER ONE

Solve a nine year old bank heist? Retired detective Natalie Severino sent Damian Green an email detailing the crime. He vaguely remembered hearing about it in the news a decade ago. The SJPD had hired her as a consultant to close some of their two hundred cold cases. He'd already helped Natalie solve a couple of cold cases involving murder; a bank heist should be easier. Natalie was the detective, Damian was the computer whiz, able to break into any system or analyze any complex set of data. It was a great partnership as he wanted to sit quietly on the sidelines feeding Natalie helpful information but he absolutely wanted his name kept out of the press. Damian stared out to sea thinking about the variables involved in such a case.

Damian, Ariana and Hermione were seated on the deck of the catamaran, anchored off of the Australian Barrier Reef. They'd taken a private charter to Madang in Papua New Guinea, stayed overnight and then picked up the boat and loaded it with provisions for a week of sailing and scuba diving. Ariana's dog, Miguel had also joined them.

It had taken a while to get used to the noise of water slapping against the hull. When out in the open sea between the two countries, it sounded like a drum beating constantly. Damian had slowed the boat down just to lessen the noise. It had taken a day and a half to reach their destination as they made detours to snorkel or scuba dive in a few majestic places along the way. Once they got to the reef they moved south along it, never diving in the same place twice. It had been a magical week with no worries that any of them might be under attack. This lunch was their last meal before they would head to Cairns and the plane ride home to California.

"This was the most wonderful vacation," sighed Hermione and then she wistfully added, "The only thing missing was Mom and Dad."

Damian and Ariana looked over at the thin, wiry fourteen year old with short cropped black hair. Her natural hair color had been a shade of red and with lots of sunblock, she'd avoided getting sunburned this past week.

"We've found not a clue to their whereabouts," mused Damian. "Are you interested in telling me more about your parents so I can find them?"

Hermione paused weighing the pros and cons of telling Damian about her parents and as she'd decided multiple times before, she shook her head 'no'.

The three of them had created a little family over the past four months. Hermione lived with Ariana, but visited Damian's home on Red Rock Island located inside San Francisco bay several times a week. He'd found her asleep in his dinghy when he returned late one night to his home. She'd been on the run from a group of men that had broken into her family home and either kidnapped or killed her parents.

Damian had created a new identity for her and enlisted Ariana's help in caring for the teenager. They knew they were substitute parents until the fate of her parents was determined. They hadn't contacted the authorities as they didn't want her lost in the foster care system; and frankly Damian thought he could be as good as the police in finding her parents. So far, despite coming to know Ariana and Damian very well, Hermione had failed to break her silence on her parents.

"Okay, you know you can tell me whenever the mood strikes you," Damian said trying to lighten the air between them. He was over six feet tall, and sun and grief had etched lines into his forty-something face. Like Hermione, he was heavily muscled from swimming, as well as running on his treadmill. His hair had never looked whiter than after the week in the South Pacific sun.

Hermione looked a little relieved and nodded.

Just then, Miguel whined as he'd done the past week indicating he wanted to go overboard for a swim. The dog was a Portuguese Water dog who loved the water, and it was so much warmer here than at his home in San Francisco. Damian opened the gate to the stairs at the back of the boat and the dog dived in. They had a ball that floated, so he was the luckiest of dogs playing fetch off the coast of Australia.

"I'm happy we didn't have any middle of the night interruption like we did in Cozumel," Ariana said, keeping an eye on the dog. "Damian, your plan of landing at that small airport in Papua New Guinea, and the rental of this boat has kept us safe. I'm also glad we're not returning to Madang; I didn't enjoy the noise of the waves hitting the hull. You're a brilliant vacation planner."

"We could have been hit by pirates leaving Madang, but I had our weapons ready," Damian said with a smile.

Pirate attacks in this region of the world were rare, but still happened. Damian used his engineering smarts to devise a self-defense system for the boat. He had a motion detector on the boat that could sense another boat approaching from a mile away. He brought a drone, water balloons, and three power washers, all containing his signature pepper juice. It would have blinded any pirates that got close. Still, if they shot enough holes in the catamaran, they could've sunk. He was even prepared for that with scuba sets ready to go at all times each packed with an inflatable life raft. If all else failed they'd leave the ship and go underwater for a bit, swim away and then resurface with life rafts. He'd also fashioned a mask and breathing apparatus harness for the dog and he was glad he hadn't had to put that to the test.

Damian was a modern day MacGyver, capable of building anything to meet his needs. He owned many patents and collected hefty royalty checks based on his ever expanding list of inventions. Even during this vacation, he'd been experimenting with wave and solar energy to power the catamaran. He was returning the boat with nearly full gas tanks as they had been able to generate their own power about four hours into the voyage.

He also set up a satellite communication system that protected their location. It bounced from server to server around the world before hitting a server in Iceland which was a long way away from their current position.

Ariana sought to change the subject and asked, "You said you received an intriguing email from your detective friend. What new case does she want you to work on?" Her brunette bob was drying around a face remarkable for its dimples that appeared when she smiled. Shorter than the teenager and the man, she was a compact figure.

"It's a nine year old bank heist."

"A bank heist? I thought the robbers never got away with robbing banks and doesn't the FBI solve those kinds of cases?"

"That's a good question; you're right about the FBI. I'll ask Natalie why this is the local police's case."

"What did they steal?" Hermione asked.

"Sixty million in cash and jewelry. They got both the money in the vault and they opened some safe deposit boxes that people stored expensive things in."

"Wow that's a lot of money and double wow that they have never been caught," said the teenager.

"Fortunately, they robbed the bank after hours, so no one was hurt."

"Yeah, that's good," Hermione replied. "So why weren't they caught? I thought they took your picture every time you entered a bank. Wouldn't it be easy to figure out who you are?"

"These guys drilled underground so there were no cameras on them until they reached the vault and they had something with them that caused the vault camera to fail."

"How about serial numbers?" Ariana asked. "I thought that banks kept track of serial numbers."

"I thought so too, but that must not be the case," Damian replied. "Once we return home, I'll have a lengthy discussion with Natalie about the case and get all of those details."

"Aren't you going to be working on your new company?" Hermione asked.

"I just do what Ariana says I need to do in regards to the company. She has the lion's share of the work getting it going. So I'll still be able to give Natalie some time for her cases."

"How about me?" Hermione asked. "I thought you were going to teach me how to play water polo so I could try out for the team."

"We could do that right now if you want. We'll use the back steps to represent the net. You have to hit the first or second step. Anything higher is higher than a water polo net and is out of bounds. We'll use Miguel's toy ball as the ball. Ariana will be one team and you the other. So whoever has the ball is playing offense with the other person playing defense. I'll defend the stairs as goalie to both of you."

Soon they were having a raucous time playing the game along Damian's guidelines. Damian gave them some tips between each ten minutes of play time and he could see improvement by both women. Hermione had stamina from her training as a swimmer, but Ariana was slyer, and in the end, she won.

They decided to have one more dive, and then shower and clean up the boat for their journey to Cairns. Their plane was to leave at seven in the evening and would arrive home the next day in San Francisco.

Later that night all three of them were asleep on fold-out beds as the plane journeyed back to the United States. They all had challenges ahead once they arrived home. Damian had a company to get up and running with Ariana's considerable help and Hermione would start school in two days.

2 CHAPTER TWO

Damian entered the limousine that would carry them to their respective homes. He rarely ordered a limo for anything, but because of the dog and the scuba gear, they had a large amount of luggage and gear. He'd had an acquaintance check on his cats in his absence, making sure they had sufficient kibble to eat. It was the longest he'd ever been away from them and he would have to get back in their good graces.

He escorted Ariana and Hermione into their house making sure there were no strangers inside and bringing their luggage in. He continued the journey across Marin County and south across the Richmond San Mateo Bridge to his home on Red Rock Island. They'd landed in the middle of the day on a Friday, just missing the worst of the commuter traffic where a forty minute journey could easily become a two hour journey. As he crossed the bridge, he could see his island in the distance and he was happy to be home. This was the longest he spent away from the island since moving there nearly seven years ago.

His wife and two girls had been murdered by a convict that was mistakenly released from prison over seven years ago. Natalie had solved the case and killed the convict during his arrest when he tried to kill her. His first six years had consisted of two visitors to his island - Natalie and Mike, who provided water taxi service and parcel delivery for him.

Since Hermione arrived in his life, both she and Ariana had been to his home multiple times as well as Natalie's son and his fiancée. Angus Walsh, an employee of his new company had also visited. His first six plus years had been quiet and productive, but since Hermione entered his life, he found himself doing things for her that he might have done for his youngest daughter if she'd survived.

The final hurdle was in getting Hermione to trust him and Ariana. Damian might be one of the top ten computer geniuses worldwide, but he had been unable to trace her parents to determine if they were dead or alive. Like Hermione, he'd seen the security footage that captured her parents struggling, then being taken out of their home in canvas bags, but it was unclear as to whether they were dead or alive. Hermione's name had been changed from Hannah to Hermione, and they had done what they could to change her appearance. She knew some secrets about her parents that she hadn't shared with him, and he'd been unable to trace them or even identify who they really were. He could only hope that someday she would trust him, as he had her hidden so well that her parents would never find her.

As usual, he sighed with frustration that he couldn't figure out the mystery of Hermione's parents. Oh well, it would come someday; unless her parents were dead and not looking for her. She went back to school on Monday and would try out for the water polo team after school that day. He and Ariana would be in attendance to cheer her on. Over the weekend they planned to play two more games in the bay with a proper net and ball and wetsuits as the water was too cold to stay in for long even if you were working hard staying afloat.

Jet lag began to catch up with Damian as they'd crossed eighteen time zones on their way home. He'd take a short nap, and then go fishing to get Bailey and Bella their first fresh fish meal in some eight days. He also wanted to finish the construction on Hermione's room. He knew it could have been built quickly if he'd just hired a team but he couldn't stand having strangers on his island as he didn't trust them to keep their mouths zipped about his home. The room was small and windowless and in the back of his lab, but he used a plasma screen to simulate a real window. He had a camera on the side of the island that was the source for the screen so she'd see a lot of fog, a little sun, and the darkness of night. She'd have to use his bathroom upstairs, but she wouldn't stay here that often and really all she needed was a bed and some privacy. She'd picked the paint color and it was called 'evening peace', a sort of light purple-silver color. All that was left for him to do was paint the room and install the door. He had a bedroom set that she chose from IKEA all ready to be installed once he finished painting. By Sunday, he thought in the middle of a big yawn, she could stay overnight with him in comfort or just have some place to go when she visited.

He laid down for that quick nap with thoughts of everything on his to-do list. When his cell phone alarm chirped an hour later, he was groggy but ready to tackle some of the stuff on his list. Then his cell rang with an incoming call from Natalie.

"You're back! How was your scuba diving trip?" Natalie asked.

"It was great. The coral reefs are very beautiful. Now I'm trying to shake off an eighteen hour time zone change."

"What do you think about the bank heist cold case? It would be a real feather in my cap if I could solve a case that the FBI and detectives couldn't solve at the time!"

"Natalie, it sounds interesting and I have a few ideas, but before I dive into this case, I'd like to read whatever cop file you have on the robbery."

"Sure I can get you that. I'll just scan it here and email you shortly."

"Besides the glory, why else are you interested in this case?"

"It's the mystery of it, I suppose. I remember the case at the time and thinking it would be solved quickly. Our best detectives were on the case and were joined by the FBI. Surely all of those smart and talented people would solve the case. But the days went by and other than understanding how the robbery occurred, they never made any headway and it remains unsolved to this day."

"So what's different now that you think you can solve it?" Damian asked.

"Fresh eyes for one thing, plus I'm a good detective, and I've got you. Your talent is in putting together obscure pieces of data so that things make sense."

Damian had to laugh at Natalie's description. If one of his computer science professors heard her explanation, he would have been affronted at so simple an explanation for what a computer scientist needed to do to manipulate data so that it made sense.

"Ah right, I'll help as usual. It's nice working on a case that isn't a murder. I hate reading the gruesome details of some of your crime scenes. I'll also admit that I would like to outsmart these thieves. I'm a little fuzz brained at the moment, but when my head clears in the next twenty-four hours, I'll read the case and give you a call. Are you going to be around this weekend?"

"Of course, call me as soon as you're ready to discuss the file. It's big because a lot of work was done on it at the time, but fortunately it's already on a computer file so there's just a few written notes I have to scan for you to have the complete binder on the case."

They ended the call and Damian rubbed his face, contemplating what to do next. The call from Natalie had helped to clear some of the cobwebs from his brain. The short nap should hold him through the rest of the day and he'd go to bed tonight at his normal time to get back on California time.

He needed physical activity at the moment, so it was outside for that spot of fishing followed by finishing Hermione's room. He'd also unpack, do laundry, and catch up on any snail mail. With his afternoon and evening planned, he got to work.

While he was painting Hermione's room, he had his computer read out loud the files in Natalie's bank heist, taking notes on questions as they were raised in his mind. He'd not tried this technology before and while the computer's voice lacked human pauses with punctuation, it was a good way to do two things at once.

By the night's end, he had a full page of questions to discuss with Natalie and a small, but private space finished for Hermione. They were coming over on the week-end for dinner and to see her new space. Other than the location and the paint color, she hadn't seen the space since he initially suggested it to her.

It was nearing his bedtime and so he wrote an email to Natalie with the suggestion they talk at a set time the next day. If she was still awake, it would give her time to look up the answers now or in the morning. As he drifted off to sleep, he was surprised by the many positives in his life. In the immediate years after his family's deaths, he never thought he'd see positives in his world.

3 CHAPTER THREE

As planned, he and Natalie spoke about the Willow Glen Heist, as the police had termed it since that was the neighborhood in which the bank was located. Natalie was running down his list of questions reading and answering them as she went along the page.

"Is the bank still open? Yes, but since that time it's merged into another banking company."

"Are any of the employees still working there? Don't know, I'll visit the bank tomorrow and assess that question."

"Are any of the original cops or FBI team members still working? I think so, but I'll confirm tomorrow."

"Have any of the stolen goods shown up on eSale or some other online reseller? Don't know if we ever looked there and I'm not sure how we would."

"Has any of the money shown up that had been stolen from the bank? At the time, a trace was put on the money, but after three years that went away."

"Was there anything else in the safe deposit boxes other than money or jewelry? Yes, I must have forgotten to send you the list."

"Are there pictures of what was in the safe deposit boxes? Yes, in some cases."

"Has anyone done a recent fingerprint or DNA analysis of what was found in the vault? That's complicated. There were a ton of prints and DNA trace because customers and bank staff go in and out of the vault all day, every day the bank is open. Some of the DNA was collected but not analyzed as a decade ago it was even slower than it is now and while the bank robbery was terrible, no one was hurt or killed so it had a lower priority than some of the murder cases at the time. I'll look into the evidence to see if any of it needs processing."

Damian had Natalie pause after her response to this question of his and said, "You mean to tell me that despite the FBI and the SJPD being in on the case, that there were insufficient resources to process some of the evidence?"

"Yes that's correct."

"Wow."

"Think about it Damian, there were perhaps a thousand different pieces of trace DNA in that vault. Most employees' trace couldn't be eliminated without taking samples from them and they're well within their rights to refuse our request; likewise it was the same for customers. It was too complicated if not impossible to sort through a thousand pieces of trace to determine who the bank robbers were. Frankly if the robbers were smart, and these guys appeared to be, they would have worn protective gear to ensure that their DNA was not left behind in the vault."

"Okay let me think about that for a while and see if I have any ideas on what to productively do with the evidence."

Natalie continued down Damian's list of questions and he was quite pleased with himself on some of his questions since he felt like he'd been at half brain power the previous evening.

"Were there any similar robberies to this one? Attempts yes, successful, no. Usually they make too much noise and someone catches on."

"Why this bank? I don't know."

"Can I get you a list of the bank note serial numbers? Some of them. Why, what are you thinking of there?" Natalie asked.

"I had a vision of writing a program that would go and match every bank transaction to those serial numbers in the time since the robbery. It would be a massive undertaking as I would first have to access those systems across multiple bank systems as well as the U.S. Treasury and I would even like to look into some of the currency conversion systems that move U.S. dollars into another currency."

"That's an interesting idea. I don't recall them trying that in the case file."

"Of course they didn't; they don't have the technical expertise to do that."

"Of course, Damian, I forget what is easy and ordinary for you, isn't for the rest of the world. I always feel dumb around you but I realize that most of the world should feel dumb around you."

"Stop with the flattery or I'll refuse to help you on this case," he teased.

"I think the case has caught your interest and you feel the same pull that I do to try and solve it. I think even if for some stupid reason, I fired you from this case that you would go on to solve it on your own."

"Natalie, you might be right!" Damian said with a laugh.

"I still have more of your questions here but it sounds like you have an enormous task in front of you by trying to do a worldwide match of U.S. currency serial numbers. I wouldn't even know where to start on such a database. Where do you even find a list of every location that uses a scanning machine to look at U.S. currency?"

"I admit it's going to be a large undertaking, perhaps larger than any other data search that I've ever done. I also want to play with the trace and fingerprint data from the case, but I want to get going first on this bank list."

"Okay, will you keep me posted on your progress? I'm guessing you won't have answers for two to three weeks."

"I might have information sooner than that, but I'll keep you posted."

They ended the call and Damian sat back thinking of the huge task in front of him. Checking his watch, he decided to check in with the ladies to see if they were ready to play SF Bay water polo. He got a reply that they were and so he put his new water polo net in his boat along with the ball and his wetsuit and set off across the bay to Ariana's house. He had the fast two seater boat that would get him there in under ten minutes as long as he didn't have to dodge too many ferry boats in the bay.

Two hours later, after vigorous play and a filling lunch, he was heading across the bay with Hermione so she could see her new room and stay the night. Once school started, she'd only be able to stay with him on Friday and Saturday evenings. He would take her back to Ariana the next day especially since she was looking for some last minute school stuff.

It was the first time he would spend alone time with Hermione on his island since she'd come into their lives four months ago. Maybe by staying with him, she'd learn to trust him with more information about her parents. They spent some time fishing and cooked dinner together, then she passed time on the computer keeping up with her school friends while Damian went to work on the list of financial institutions that he'd need to search for currency serial numbers. Then he heard a gasp from Hermione and looked over to find tears running down her face.

"Hermione, what's up? What's upset you?" he asked as he walked over to the girl to look at what she was looking at on the computer.

Then he frowned.

4 -CHAPTER FOUR

He was looking at a Facebook page with a message written in symbols. He didn't know what Asian language the words represented but he guessed it was Chinese. He knew that Hermione spoke both Spanish and Chinese, but he'd been unaware she could also read it.

'我们做得很好，找你。'

"Hermione, can you translate that for me?"

The child just sat there, mute, tears continuing down her face. Damian put his left arm around her shoulder while his right hand copied the phrase into translation software. It translated to:

'We are doing fine, searching for you.'

That was a strange phrase. The English was awkward, but maybe that was just the translation software, so he asked Hermione.

"Hermione, do those words mean 'we are doing fine, searching for you'?"

"Yes," she said in a faint voice and then added, "It's proof that Mom and Dad are alive."

Great, why did he have to have this emotionally charged moment with Hermione when Ariana wasn't around?

"Are your parents native English speakers?"

"What does that mean?"

"Is English the first language they learned?"

"Yes. Why?"

"The phrase is very awkward for an English speaker."

"What do you mean?"

"If I wrote such a note to you, I would say something like, 'Honey we're looking for you and we're doing fine'. This phrase has nothing personal in it for you to know that your parents typed it and the grammar is poor and it's weird that they didn't start with the search for you rather than the fact that they were fine."

The teenager had settled a little bit after the tsunami of emotion that had hit her with the message.

"Are you suggesting that someone besides my parents wrote the message?" Hermione asked, finally understanding the point that Damian was making.

"Maybe. I don't know your parents style of writing nor what gets lost in a translation, but this doesn't sound like the two people that produced you. There's not even an 'I love you' in words or symbols."

"I want it to be from Mom and Dad," Hermione said determinedly yet acknowledging that something wasn't right with the sentence.

"I know," replied Damian quietly.

There was silence for a while and then Damian broke it by suggesting, "How about if I go back and survey your home - I'll see if the man is still there and if there are any changes that were made. I've checked periodically and your parent's trust is continuing to pay the bills so the house should be in good shape."

"Okay. Can I come with you?"

"No. If the house is under surveillance, I don't want anyone to see your new look. Is the post from your parents a reply to your post about drills being canceled that you wrote last May?"

"No."

"That's another reason to think it's not from your parents. I could use handwriting software to see if the word usage matches your parents, but then I'd need something that they wrote that you have in your possession."

"Okay, I'll find something."

Wincing, he thought this conversation with Hermione was squeezing his heart. He felt like he was slowly destroying her dream that the message was from her parents and that they were alive and looking for her. That was the ultimate thought that every child who had loved her parents, but had been separated from them wanted to hear. He looked over at Hermione and she was searching something on her phone.

Knowing that he was thrusting another dagger in the kid's heart, he added, "There's probably nothing on the phone from them since you got it after you left your house. Would you like to look at your old phone that I retrieved from the creek?"

Hermione continued looking down at her phone and Damian watched her, trying to guess at her thinking. He knew she had heard his question, but she seemed unable to respond to it.

With tears glistening in her eyes she looked up at him and said, "I have so little from my parents. Perhaps they have little from me as well and have forgotten what I look like or how good I am at swimming."

"I don't think so. I find myself imagining what my daughters would have looked like now and I think about their personality quirks and wonder if they would have gotten stronger or receded as they grew older. My oldest played in Little League and I wonder if her love of the game would have stayed with her and if she'd be heading to college on scholarship. I haven't forgotten my children after seven years and I'm sure your parents haven't forgotten you after just a few months."

Hermione went to him and hugged him tight and mumbled into his shirt, "I'm sorry I'm making you think about your daughters."

"Hey, I find myself thinking about them every day as something catches my attention and it brings back a memory, but it's okay as I honor them in those moments."

They just stood there a while, the lost teenager clinging to the adult that was keeping her safe, and then finally she leaned back and said, "Let's go look at my old phone and see if anything is there."

Damian heaved a silent sigh of relief as he felt the crisis pass.

"Okay, we can look at it on this computer as I copied the contents here," Damian said pointing to a computer in the lab. With a few keystrokes, he brought up the directory for Hermione's old phone. She stared at the file labels and decided that the best place to look was email followed by texts for a sample of her parents' writing.

"Should we look for Mom or Dad?" Hermione asked.

"We'll need both since we don't know which of your parents might have composed that message."

A short time later she had a short and long communication from each parent. Damian ran it through his software that used artificial intelligence processes to compare word usage. After entering the information, the computer suggested that there was a thirty-five percent guess that the message matched her parents' normal pattern of communication.

"Thirty five percent is better than zero," Hermione said.

"Yes, but it's much less than even odds that it's a match. I think it's unlikely the message was written by your parents. By the way, I assume they knew how to write in Chinese?"

The question made Hermione pause. Then she said, "I never saw them write Chinese, but maybe they used translation software for the message since they knew I spoke it."

"True," Damian agreed and left it at that. As a parent, he knew that wasn't a message he would have ever written his family if he was on the run and had time to drop them the shortest of notes.

"When are you going to visit my home?"

"Probably tomorrow night. I'll want to do what I did last time and that means waiting until at least nine at night so I can have the cover of darkness."

Looking over at the 'window' in her bedroom, she could see it was dark outside. She asked, "Why not go now?"

"I wouldn't leave you alone on this island," he said simply.

Hermione looked at him and judged his feelings to be resolute on the subject, so she dropped it. Tomorrow would be good enough.

"Should I respond to the message?" Hermione asked.

"That's a good question," said Damian weighing the pros and cons in his mind. Then he said, "How about if you used a single emoticon that means something to your parents, but no one else. That way it looks random if some bad people wrote the message and if your parents did, then they'll know you're also alive and well."

"Okay," Hermione said as she started looking for the right emoticon that would convey those feelings.

"I'm going to respond with a swimmer. It won't make sense to most people but it will to Mom and Dad. Can I enter it now?"

"Yes. Any computer in my lab will bounce around the world before indicating its physical location is Siberia. But let's reply in the morning as we don't want it to look like you immediately read the message, okay?"

Hermione nodded and then she changed the subject. "Do you think I'll make the water polo team?"

Damian was delighted with her change of conversation and said, "I haven't seen the other girls play, but you're a strong swimmer and that seems like half the skillset you need to play. Is the swim coach also the water polo coach?"

"Yes."

"Then you'll get on the team. He saw a lot of promise in you during the short swim year so I'm sure he'll recognize it again."

"Okay. I think I'll head to my room and read."

"What are you reading at the moment?"

There was a brief moment of glee that flashed across her face and she said, "I downloaded Harry Potter and the Cursed Child. I'm so excited to read it."

"Well don't stay up too late or Ariana and I will beat you at water polo tomorrow."

She just smiled and retreated to her new bedroom and closed the door.

Well, Damian thought, at least she's talking to me and she's not mad nor does she think I'm stupid. With a teenager that was a total win.

5-CHAPTER FIVE

Damian was cooking breakfast the next morning - pancakes with syrup and yogurt. That should give the kid carbohydrates and protein to play hard at water polo, then go shopping with Ariana for her final school needs.

"How do you like the book?" Damian asked.

"It's great and it's sad," she replied.

"Why sad?"

"Because I truly believe this is the last book she'll ever write. I want more Harry Potter books."

"You'll have to search for authors that tell similar tales then. Check out Amazon and see what else they recommend if you like Harry Potter."

"That's a good idea, I'll do that."

"We'll leave in under an hour, I just want to see to Bailey and Bella and check my supplies then we can leave."

"Ok."

"Did you respond to the Facebook comment?"

"No I was waiting for you to decide it was okay."

"As soon as we finish eating, we'll go down together and I'll watch you hit the button. Then we'll wait ten minutes and see if there's a response. If not, then we'll go about our day."

"Sounds like a plan. Why ten minutes?"

"Ten minutes may tell us if someone is monitoring the account. You might get a response right back, or there may be dead silence."

Hermione just nodded and continued to work on her pancake

stack as they ate in a comfortable silence, not rushing to finish. After cleaning up, they went downstairs for Hermione to enter the emoticon they agreed upon in response to what Damian thought was a fake Facebook comment. Hermione hit the keys and then Damian sat with his timer counting down the ten minutes.

At the six minute mark, a response came back at them again in Chinese. Hermione translated it with a note of depression in her voice.

"Hannah is that you?"

Hannah was Hermione's real name but they had changed it to cover up her identity. Hannah had picked Hermione so that she could keep the same initials and it was the name of a beloved character in the Harry Potter books. It ended up being a good choice as it was an instant ice breaker when she entered the new school.

"My parents are too smart to put my name in print like that. You're right Damian, the original message isn't from my parents," Hermione said with a sigh and watery eyes.

"Look at the positive side; it means that someone is after you."

"What's positive about that?"

"I think it suggests that your parents are alive. Why would anyone be after you unless it is to have you available to put pressure on your parents to do something? Maybe if they have you, your parents will come out of hiding to come to your rescue."

"There are a lot of maybes in that explanation, but yeah perhaps you're right. I feel like I'm back to the beginning and I still don't know if they're alive."

"Regardless, ignore the message and let's get ready to return to Ariana's. You have a busy day in front of you."

Ten minutes later they were bouncing across the waves in Damian's ultralight two seat boat. The wind and the bay worked magic on their moods so they arrived at Ariana's dock with smiles on their faces despite the stress of the last twenty-four hours.

They walked inside the house and greeted Ariana who had papers spread out on her kitchen counter. Pointing to the mess, she said to Damian, "I have things for you to sign to get your new company underway. We can do that after we play water polo. How was your sleepover, kiddo?"

"It was a grind," she replied.

Ariana hadn't expected to hear that answer and said, "What?"

with alarm in her voice while looking at Damian.

"There was a message on her family Facebook page last night in Chinese that initially appeared to have come from her parents. But I think we agree that it's not from them," he replied quietly and Hermione nodded.

Ariana asked for greater detail of the situation and was dismayed to hear of Damian's plan to re-enter her parents' house.

"Is that safe? It's been four months, what do you hope to find?"

"I don't know what I'll find. Maybe there will be something new on the security tapes that will provide a clue, maybe I'll walk away empty handed. If the house still contains a thug; then that's new information," Damian said with a shrug.

"Maybe the house has been sold," Ariana suggested softly. "It's been empty a long time."

"Actually, it's still owned by the Sherwoods. Hermione's parents' estate continues to pay all the bills."

"Oh, well that's good news."

"Yeah, and if they weren't, I'd pay the bills since it's Hermione's inheritance."

"Do you want some help? I suppose I could creep into the house with you," Ariana offered tentatively.

Damian laughed at the tone of her voice as much as the words.

"If it makes you feel any better about breaking and entering, I was very nervous about breaking into the house the last time. What if I got caught by the good guys or the bad guys? Actually, it went smoothly with no blowback on me, so I'll still be scared this time, but slightly less so since I've done it once already."

"Can we just go outside and play water polo?" Hermione asked. "This conversation is making me feel weird."

Ariana replied, "Sure honey and I'm sorry I didn't think of the impact this conversation could have on you. Let's go outside and play."

She gave Damian a look that said, 'we'll discuss this later when the kid isn't in hearing distance.'

Half an hour later, they were all breathing heavy after a rousing twenty minutes of one on one water polo play. Ariana called for a time out and the three of them sat on the dock catching their breath.

"You think you're in shape, and then twenty minutes of play

with a star swimmer has you crying for mercy," Ariana said.

"If you don't make the water polo team tomorrow, it's only because all the other athletes were on the Olympic team," Damian added.

"Thanks, guys. I can't wait to try out and see how I do when compared to my classmates. Of course the game will be different when there are fourteen people in the pool rather than three, but at least I had a little practice before playing."

"When will you know if you're on the team?" Damian asked.

"I'm guessing, we'll all be on the team this week, and he'll begin cutting players the following week as we roll into the first match," Hermione said.

Damian was impressed with her insight into the strategy of a coach. He nodded and said, "Well I'm heading home after I sign those documents for Ariana. I need to spend some time on Natalie's bank heist, and then I'll prepare for the night's excursion into your parents' home. By the way, is there anything you want me to retrieve from any of the rooms?"

Hermione thought about it for a while and then asked, "Do you think I'll ever live there again?"

Damian caught Ariana's eye, trying to read her mind; then he replied, "I don't think so. If your parents return, unless they know each bad guy that was chasing them is dead or in prison, they'll need to stay hidden and find a new place to live. At least that would be my strategy if I were them."

Hermione nodded and then asked for a few things in the house. Damian wrote the list down and the area the items were supposed to be and moved over to Ariana's counter to read and sign the documents she had laid out for him. Twenty minutes later, he was back in his boat starting the journey across the bay. He and Ariana hadn't had an opportunity to discuss Hermione's reaction to the Facebook post, but there was no immediate urgency to do so.

6-CHAPTER SIX

Damian settled into writing the program that would begin looking for serial numbers of bank notes in circulation and jewelry items that were alleged to be in the safe deposit boxes in the bank. For those items, he was using an item recognition program to see if there was an online auction of any similar items. He'd check sites like eSale, Cassim, Agave, or Beetle. Who knew whether the items were resold in the US or China or India? By choosing these four companies, he would cover sales in most of the world and he might get a sense of whether any items had been resold from the heist.

Both analyses were going to be extremely large data runs. In the first case, there were twelve serial numbers on a twenty dollar bill which equaled 479 million number combinations for just the twenty. Add the other denominations of currency and it was an extremely large database to match. Then add that the average one dollar bill moves two miles a day and changes hands at least weekly, then banks all over the United States plus the rest of the world might be handling bills from the heist. If he weren't so lazy at the moment, he'd add up all these variables to determine just how large a database would cover the scope of where the money might be now.

He'd have to use some of his rented cloud computing power. Soon he had mega capacity computers searching for his data and an estimated time of completion of sixteen hours. With that processing, he sat down to plan his visit to Hermione's home. He'd take much of the same equipment he did on the last visit including his forward looking infrared sensor and another Halothane bomb in case he needed to put anyone asleep. He had similar protective wear and would purchase clothes to change into and then discard for the night's trespass. He also had his mandatory water gun filled with pepper juice for protection.

He loaded it all into the two seater with a plan to pick up his truck from the marina once he got there. Then he just needed to hit a discount department store for the few remaining items and wait for dusk to appear. When it was an hour before dusk he steered his boat toward the marina, wondering what the night would bring for him. Ariana had demanded that he text her as soon as he finished and was safely in his truck. If he failed to do so by a preset time, she would call the police on him.

Once he had all of his supplies ready he still had another thirty minutes to kill so he grabbed a foot long sandwich and diet cola for dinner and spent the remaining time waiting for dusk to arrive eating. Finally he drove to the empty street near the house and changed into dark clothing and darkened his face. He then drove slowly by the house, close enough to register heat sources. Holding the scanner up, he noted that there were no inhabitants in Hermione's family home. He'd still take the Halothane bomb in case there were any surprises.

He parked on the empty street and then moved quietly toward the home, and opened the gate to go into the back yard. He was out of the street view in the back yard and since he might have to spend some time picking a lock, he wanted to do it where people couldn't see him. He had the codes and keys to the house from Hermione, but if the bad guys were smart, they would have changed both by now if for no other reason than to frustrate Hermione if she ever returned home.

He debated whether to block the use of the cameras before he entered the property, but it might just end up being a waste of time; or he might miss shutting one of them down which might be an alert if anyone was watching. He was carrying a fabric that resisted bullets and did much to cloak his presence. It wasn't as good as Harry Potter's invisibility cloak, but it was better than nothing. Pulling out the key, he tried the back door and he heard the latch unlock. He also heard something behind him rustle in the bushes, but he didn't turn around to look. Before he entered the property, he used his infrared scan looking for heat sources and discovered the presence of squirrels and probably a cat and he was convinced that they were making the sounds in the bushes.

Opening the door, he entered and looked at the key pad for the security system just inside the door. The word on the panel was bypass meaning the system wasn't armed. He would arm it before he left he decided, and he moved about the home still under the cloak. He went to the kitchen and opened the refrigerator. The smells were bad as the remaining food items had expired at least two months previously. He wanted to just empty the unit and unplug it. He pulled out a trash bag and emptied both the freezer and refrigerator in under two minutes and placed the trash bag outside the back door. Then he left both doors open and unplugged the unit. He stopped a moment and took pictures of each room as he quickly went through gathering the items that Hermione requested.

He approached Hermione's secure room in the bedroom and spent ten minutes looking at the computer system. It had run continuously since he was last here except for one power failure of two hours. He wrote the time of the failure down so he could verify later that it was a neighborhood blackout. He took the tapes out of the recording device and inserted new ones. He also installed a camera for the room and software so that he could manipulate the computer from his home which he should have done during his first visit. He had one final stop in the master bedroom before he left the house.

Pictures taken, objects that Hermione wanted collected, and security disks in his duffle for later viewing, he made to leave the house. He was walking firmly down the stairs when he heard the front door open.

He quickly retreated to the second floor, his heart racing. Crap. His first thought was that the intruders would discover the refrigerator wide open and the trash outside of the back door and know someone might still be in the house during their absence. He listened a while to the intruders' movements and discovered them to be neighborhood punks out to rob the unoccupied house. They must have picked the locks on the front door. He debated what to do for a few moments. He decided to place a 911 call from a house phone, which was amazingly, still working.

He dialed the number and the emergency operator answered,

"This is emergency dispatch, what is your emergency?"

Damian replied in a soft, deep voice, "There are teenagers that just entered my home and they're robbing it," He reeled off the address and then told the operator that he had to end the call as they were coming. He hung up and then quietly made his way through the house and out the back door, engaging the alarm system as he went. After a quick debate, he decided to leave the stuff he'd pulled out of the refrigerator on the back porch with the hope that the crime scene techs would discard it. He was lugging two heavy duffels, close to reaching his truck, when he saw the first police car traveling down the street. While he wanted to wait and watch the fun, he knew that returning to the marina was his wisest choice. The cool thing about the teenagers was that their visit covered up his own, if the bad guys were still monitoring the house.

Once he reached the marina, he took a deep breath and tried to slow his racing heart. He really wasn't cut out for this cloak and dagger stuff he decided. He texted Ariana that he was at the marina and heading back to his island with the stuff that Hermione requested.

She texted back one word, 'unharmed?'

'Yes, unharmed,' he replied. Then seeing is was 12:30 am added, 'I'll call you in the morning.'

She replied, 'Before 7:30,' a reminder that Ariana had to drive Hermione to school.

He put the duffle bags in the boat, shining a flashlight around the interior before he cast off the ties. Since finding Hermione in his boat four months ago, he reflexively searched his boat before leaving the marina to ensure that no other surprises were waiting for him. Five minutes later he pulled up to his island watching the water craft door open and the folding dock unfold for his use. Shortly thereafter, he deposited the duffle filled with the items Hermione requested on her bed, and dropped the other in his lab before heading upstairs. He was tempted to study the security tapes before heading to bed, but he knew that would take two to three hours and he needed to be awake by 7:30 am to talk with Ariana.

7-CHAPTER SEVEN

Damian called Ariana and replayed for her the night's work. Just before he called her, he checked the Shepard Canyon police blotter and noted that two teenage boys were arrested as juveniles for the burglary of Hermione's house. Hermione was listening on Ariana's speaker phone and cheered with the news that the boys were caught. Damian would be over sometime in the next few days and would bring the duffle with him containing the items the teenager had requested. He mentioned the contents of the refrigerator, resetting the alarm, and the security disks. Mostly good news, but still a lot to carry on her shoulders on her first day of school. It was a short conversation because they needed to get going to school.

"Hey Hermione, good luck on your first day of school and enjoy your junior year!" Damian remarked.

"The kid just rolled her eyes," Ariana said with a laugh just before they ended the call.

Damian made himself breakfast and then headed downstairs with a large mug of coffee. He briefly debated what to do first and settled on looking at the run of money and other items from the bank heist case. His curiosity was killing him as to what the massive data run would show. He spent the next hour looking at the data and thinking about how to use the information for the case. He then wrote another program that would visually display on a map each serial number. He let that run then went on to look at what the data revealed for the non-monetary stolen artifacts of the heist. He found about a twenty-five percent match and went on to look at the items.

Jewelry and coins had been pawned from all over the United States, Canada, Mexico, Europe, and some Asian countries. Then he thought to do a match of a country by country basis for both the currency, and the jewelry and coins. He found location clusters for the currency and in some cases for the jewelry as well. He studied his map and thought that it looked like the bank robbers sat on their stolen items for a year and then began frequent trips out of California to start fencing the stolen goods. He gave it another two hours of data crunching work and then sent the document and map off to Natalie.

Next, he turned to the mystery of Hermione and her parents. Looking at the disks of the security cameras over the past four months was an endlessly dull exercise. It appeared that the man stationed in the house departed about a week after Damian visited the house and since that time, the house had sat empty until he and some thieving teenagers visited the house on the same night. He made a note to himself to see if he could figure out if the house alarms were set and then he thought about how to make the house alarm on one of his computers. He could protect the house better if he knew when someone appeared to be about to rob it.

The man that had stayed behind left his image on different cameras and he ran a facial recognition scan to identify him. He ran him through several systems with no result and then he thought about the passport control at the borders. He was soon inside Homeland Security's database that contained the logs of all people entering the United States. He downloaded their database and exited their system. He then used his facial recognition to run the man against this database.

He had a match.

The man's name was Nico Thomas and he originated from Jakarta, Indonesia.

Indonesia?

Damian tried to think of a link between Hermione's parents and Indonesia, but nothing came to mind. He thought back to when she told him she spoke Chinese because her parents had lived in China. There were Chinese in Indonesia so perhaps she meant to say they lived in Indonesia rather than China. He'd ask her later though somehow he doubted that she would have been so imprecise with her explanation.

His phone rang and he looked over to see that it was Natalie.

"I got your email and map of the world and can I just say wow?! How long did it take your computer to analyze that data?"

"Eighteen hours and I had to use computer power from the cloud. The computers in my lab aren't powerful enough to handle that much data."

"How do I explain this to Detective Shimoda? He needs to see this diagram, but he knows I don't have the ability to do that."

"You could tell him that a friend of yours knew a local university was looking for a large scale data project for a student project and both you and I chatted about it," Damian suggested.

"Yes but how did they know how to reach the banks and currency changers? Was there a legal way to get this information from those institutions?"

"Whoops … good point. Let me think of a way you can use this information. I don't suppose you could say you have a secret source?"

"No."

"Don't the police have confidential informers?"

"Yes, but any average Joe could see that this data run is beyond the brain power of any CI the department has ever used."

"An average Joe, or in this case the mysterious university students, could have used image recognition software on eSale, Cassim, and similar sites worldwide to look for the non-currency items. That's perfectly legal."

"Okay, that will work. Can you re-send this to me with just those data points and insert a fake header labeled Professor Green, UC Berkeley something class."

He laughed and said he could. "Give me twenty minutes and you'll have a new chart in your hands."

They were back on the phone again looking at where goods had been disposed of and of course it was nearly all the same locations as the currency.

"This I can take to Shimoda. They fenced the items over a five year period beginning perhaps a year after the original heist. So how do I use this to find these guys or gals?"

"Get a subpoena to get information about the sellers from these websites. Once the item was sold, money had to change hands between buyer and seller and that is where I would start. I could figure that out for you in advance, but if you're looking for a way to do this legally, that would be your route."

"Thanks, Damian. What do you think this says about the robbers?" said Natalie musing about the sale pattern.

"I think it says that this robbery was done by one, two robbers at the most."

"Why?" Natalie agreed with his theory but was curious about how he'd arrived at that conclusion.

"To be able to wait a year before touching the prize of such a robbery could only happen with one person or two at the most. Any more robbers than that and they would have insufficient trust in the other team members to wait that year."

That was exactly Natalie's reasoning and she was surprised that Damian had that insight into human behavior.

"The team that worked on the robbery speculated that it had to be four or five people minimum to carry out the heist," Natalie said.

"Why?"

"They thought there were too many tasks performed during this robbery for one person or even two to do all the work."

"Describe the work," Damian requested.

"You had to lease a business down the street - two doors down from the bank. When people were questioned about the business they described more than one person at that business."

"Do you think the business owner could have worn multiple disguises so as to make it look like different people?"

"I suppose, but let me re-read the eye witness accounts."

"Was that the only reason for thinking there was more than one bank robber?" Damian asked skepticism in his voice.

"No, it was the work tunneling into the bank and the emptying of the safe deposit boxes. In the time it was done, it seemed impossible that one person could have done it all."

"Refresh my mind on the robbery timeline."

"It was that rare day when there was a three day week-end. Friday was Christmas Eve and the bank was only open until noon. It was closed on Saturday and Sunday. The robbery was noticed Monday morning when everyone came back to work. So at most the robbers had about sixty-eight hours to finish the dig from the florist shop to the bank."

"Are you sure about that time? If I were a robber, I would dig a little each day perhaps over several months. How long was the florist shop open?"

Damian could hear paper rustling as she flipped around the file to get answers to his questions.

"Nine months. Again witnesses say the owner called it quits on Christmas Eve. Even had a going out of business sale."

"How did your team come to the conclusion of how long the dig took?" Damian asked.

"They looked at the tools used for the job and decided the speed of the drilling work."

"How did they know what tools were used? Did the robber leave them behind?"

"Yes, they were found in the tunnel."

"Did anyone verify that those were the tools used or did they just assume that since they were in the tunnel?"

Natalie let out an exasperated sigh and said, "I don't know. I'll have to study the report and perhaps talk to the crime scene techs. In my experience they don't make assumptions, but rely on fact."

"Okay. I guess for the time being, I'm done with this case as there's no other analytics you want from me."

"Thanks for your help and I'll get back to you on your questions."

After they ended the call, he thought that the police got it wrong. He was convinced that there was one or two at most and he'd bet the tools were left in the tunnel as a decoy. If the robber dug for months, then they could have sliced through the vault with a diamond cutter relatively quickly. The difficult thing would have been disarming the cameras or motion detection cameras quickly upon entering the vault with technology from nine years ago. He'd have to study what was available at the time.

Switching topics, overnight he'd had an idea to point him to the identification of Hermione's parents. He was beginning to think that one or both of them had the same computer hacking skills that he did. A lot of the precautions they'd taken were what he presently did to protect his privacy on Red Rock Island. Furthermore the kid was smart and some of that genius had to come from her parents.

It was another huge data challenge, but he'd see if he could pull it off. It would all depend on how often city cameras across the east bay cities were saved. He had their pictures from Hermione and so far he'd been unable to identify them. However he thought he would use their images to match what was captured on cameras around the cities like Richmond, Berkeley, and Oakland. He wished he'd thought of this idea four months ago as the footage might have been written over or otherwise discarded by now. He would start with red light violation cameras and move on to others.

8- CHAPTER EIGHT

Ariana was running errands in town after she'd dropped Hermione off at school. She had this weird feeling that someone was watching her. She turned around quickly hoping to surprise someone, but no one was there and she felt silly. She had one more stop for Miguel, who was at the dog groomer's for his every other month haircut, and then she'd head home glad to shake this feeling that someone was watching her.

She pulled into the parking lot and retrieved the dog. The two of them were stopped at the car as she maneuvered him toward the back seat when her arm was grabbed from behind. She tried to shake it loose and turn around to yell at the person that grabbed her, but he was holding it behind her and beginning to move it upward which was painful.

With an accent that she couldn't identify, the voice said, "You will bring Hannah Sherwood to me tonight."

She felt like saying, 'over my dead body', but she was too busy wincing over the pain in her arm, then all of a sudden she was free and the man behind her was howling. She turned around to find that Miguel had sunk his teeth into the man's leg. The man backed up to get his leg out of the dog's jaws and tripped backwards. Ariana took the opportunity to throw the dog into the car and peel out of the parking lot. Driving towards her home like a madwoman, she debated what to do. Call the police or call Damian or keep driving or go to the school and get Hermione. Her mind started to find its reasoning abilities and she knocked off her options. Hermione was safe at school, so leave her there for the moment, and not call the police because she then had to explain who Hannah was.

She looked in her review mirror and noted a dark SUV following her car. She briefly debated whether this was just another citizen from her community or the creep who accosted her in the parking lot. The car was following too close and so she decided that this was a bad guy. After many twists and turns the road she was on dead-ended, so unless she wanted to make a three point U-turn on the road, her only escape was the waterfront. She decided she would speed up and run for her boat once she got home. She could speed down her street, pull into her driveway and open the garage door like she was running into the house, but detour through the side door to the backyard and her dock. The boat's ignition key was on her car key ring, she just hoped that Miguel would cooperate and run to the boat quickly.

She pulled out her camera and snapped a picture of her rear view mirror in hopes that the man's image in the driver's seat was captured. She then stomped on the gas and drove like a crazed woman. Five minutes later with the chase car about forty-five seconds behind her, she did just as she planned. Quickly opening the garage side door for herself and the dog and closing it behind them, she sprinted to the boat expecting to hear bullets flying at any moment. She had the ties untied and gunned the boat away as she saw the same man come out of her house, gun in hand. The bay was so big that he'd have no idea of where she was going even if he had binoculars and therefore couldn't catch her. Clearly he debated whether shooting at her would be effective or would alert the cops and so in the end he decided not to shoot.

Ariana continued her path across San Francisco Bay towards Red Rock Island, phoning Damian once she was safely out of gun range. She'd been so busy trying to evade the bad guy that she couldn't have handled a phone call during the chase.

"Damian, I'm on my way to your house! Put your dock out," she commanded over the rushing wind.

"Okay. I didn't know you were coming over today," he said a bit puzzled.

"I was attacked at the dog groomer's this morning so we need to talk about next steps."

Ariana had quickly calmed down between the cool crisp air of the bay and the knowledge that she was safe at the moment.

"What! What happened?" exclaimed Damian. "Are you hurt?"

Ariana held her arm out, examining it, "I may have bruises develop later and my shoulder may be sore in the morning, but Miguel bit the man for me and then he let go. The man tripped backing away from the dog. We hopped in my car and sped towards my house. I opened the garage door before I got there, and entered and went out the side door and ran for the boat. We were pulling away from my dock when the man ran out on the lawn wielding a gun."

"Did you call the police?" Damian asked puzzled.

"No, he spoke one sentence to me and it was something like, 'Bring Hannah Sherwood to me tonight'."

The sentence chilled Damian. Somehow their guardianship of Hannah/Hermione had been noticed by the thugs after her parents. First the Facebook message, and now this.

"Is Hermione safe?" Damian asked worried.

"I assume so. The school has a locked fence around it, but I think we better both pick her up this afternoon. I don't know really what to do."

Ariana was approaching his island and could see him standing on his dock as she approached in the pontoon boat. She tied one end of the boat and he the other and then he said "Hold on a moment, I think you need a hug," and he did just that. As soon as he felt her relax he let go.

"I think we should report it to the police. They'll find nothing wrong with the paperwork concerning our guardianship. I think we need to talk to her first though, just to be sure she's not surprised by some question of the cops."

"What should I do about the name 'Hannah'?" Ariana asked.

Damian thought for a while and said, "How about if we call it her nickname?" After a pause he added, "No I don't like that."

"I could say he said to bring Hermione to him tonight and just leave out the name Hannah. He did have an accent so I could use that as a defense on the accuracy of the word."

Damian sat thinking for a few moments than nodded.

"Do you know her schedule today? Does she have any breaks that she could leave school and chat with us?"

"Yeah," and glancing at her watch said, "She has one in about ninety minutes. Oh, I forgot to show you a picture I took of the car chasing me in the rear view mirror."

"Wow, you're a cool cucumber under pressure. Let's see," Damian said glancing at the phone.

"Send that picture to me and let me see if I can enhance it for facial recognition," Damian said as they turned to walk into his lab.

Ten minutes later, Ariana was able to verify the man that attacked her as being the one in the picture. Damian did a facial recognition search but came up with nothing on the first pass.

"I need to do some more work on this. Let's return to your house to see if anything is messed up and then we'll go on to school to have a quick conversation with Hermione. I've been rethinking the police thing and I'm not sure we should report this until we have a better idea as to who the man is, and once we do, then we'll look suspicious for the delay in reporting."

"I'm okay with not reporting. We've gone down the path of being surrogate parents to this teenager and I have to say I've fallen in love with her and it would destroy me to see her yanked from our care into the foster system."

It was the first time Ariana had voiced her emotions about caring for Hermione and Damian volunteered, "I've also fallen in love with the kid. I'll do what I can to help and guide her, and cheer her on in her accomplishments. I don't want to turn her over to anyone other than her real parents."

Ariana needed another hug as she squeezed her eyes shut to block out the emotion of the moment. Then she took a deep breath, wiped the corner of her eyes and said, "Let's go look at my house. Can you sweep it for bugs or something, like they say on TV? What if the man is still there?"

"That's a good idea, Ariana, I'll grab some equipment that will make sure it's safe to enter among other things," he said and the two of them went inside to his lab. She watched him put various items into his duffle bag as well as he take the time to grab the items Hermione had requested. Soon, they were ready to head over to her house. After some discussion they decided to take both boats across the bay and before they went too close to her dock, he would use the infrared scanner to see if anyone was still in her house.

Fifteen minutes later, he was running a variety of equipment around her house as she watched in silence. Afterward he invited her out to the dock to talk.

"There are cameras and microphones installed in the common rooms as well as your and Hermione's bedrooms. I wish we'd thought to do this earlier as I don't know how long the equipment's been in your house."

"I gather by having a conversation out here you think we should leave the stuff in place." Ariana said.

'Yeah, I do. We need to go talk to Hermione. I have some ideas on how to protect both of you so at the moment we're just warning Hermione about her own safety. For at least the next few weeks, she needs to stick to only riding in your car. I think we need to give her something protective that she can always have with her at school. If she has a favorite bracelet, I can modify it so that she can sound a nasty audible alarm if anyone tries to corner her. I'll also put some tiny GPS trackers in her earrings. Let's run over to the school and chat with her on her break."

Ariana sent a text to Hermione requesting that she come out to the front to chat with them on her break. A short time later all three of them were sitting in Ariana's SUV talking.

"Can I still try out for the water polo team?"

"Yes," Ariana and Damian said in perfect synchronization.

Then Damian added, "Look kiddo, I don't know who is after you, but we're going to keep you safe. We're going to leave the cameras and microphones in place, but I'm going to interject myself into the middle of those devices and provide them with a feed different from the real one. So in a few hours your conversations will be secure again. I'm also going to modify your jewelry so that you have GPS and a screaming alarm on you at all times. I know you might get in trouble if you pull out your water gun at school to defend yourself."

Hermione looked shaken, clearly worried about Ariana. So Damian added, "Ladies, do you want to swap places with me for the next few nights? I'll stay at your house and you can stay at mine? Then you can come across the bay each morning to reach school?"

"Yes, but what if someone goes after you, Damian?"

"Ladies, how can you doubt my ability to defend myself? Besides what I could do is add a lot more security to your house for the long run which is probably a good idea. So when you get home tonight, why don't you pack suitcases for three to five nights and I'll do likewise and I'll install some enhancements and surprises to your house. Then when I'm done, I'll debug it."

There was a silence for a few minutes, than Ariana said, "I can't think of another solution. We'll do that. Hermione, I'll be back to pick you up at 4:30, don't leave the safety of the campus unless you see me. If your practice is going to get cut short call me immediately. Okay Hermione?"

"Ok," said the worried teenager.

"Look Hermione, we'll keep you safe. You know that Damian has magical abilities in regards to defense, right?"

"Yeah, but maybe we should call the police to catch the guy that tried to harm you, Ariana."

"We talked about that dear, but Damian and I love caring for you, and we don't want to do anything that would risk our guardianship. Don't worry, just work hard this afternoon to win a spot on the water polo team."

The kid nodded and jumped out of the car, returning to school. Ariana watched until she disappeared into the library. Then she looked in her rear view mirror for the car that followed her earlier, but she only saw other parents or teachers in the vicinity. She put the car in gear and headed back to her house.

"Let's take your boat back to my house since it's bigger," Damian said. "I have a bunch of gadgets and equipment that I need to bring back to rig your house up. I think we have just enough time for me to load supplies before we return to pick up Hermione. Once we pick her up, then the two of you can pack for a stay on my island while I beef up your house. This is going to delay some other things in my life, but your safety is paramount."

"Do you think I should hire security for the house? Get a guard?"

"Let me put my enhancements in place first, then you can think about that decision."

Ariana nodded and chewed on her lip. Things had been going so well. She wanted the relaxed and carefree life of the summer that she'd had with Hermione. Now she felt she'd be looking over her shoulder all the time.

Damian was thinking along similar lines. How to keep them secure, but not confine their movement? Was the man that followed Ariana related to the person that posted on Facebook, or the group behind the attack in Mexico at the start of the summer? He was conflicted on what to do first - find the man that accosted

Ariana or set up all the protections on Ariana's house. In the end, he decided to set up the protections on Ariana's house first.

9 CHAPTER NINE

Ariana and Damian were waiting for Hermione after water polo practice. She looked relieved to see both of them in the car at the curb. Her hair was wet and she was carrying her swim bag in one hand and her backpack in the other.

"So how was practice? Was it anything like what we practiced at home?" Ariana asked.

"It went well and I'm sure I'm going to make the team. The hints you gave me when we played served to give me more strategy than my teammates. With that many girls in the water, I got kicked a fair amount so I'm sure I'll have bruises for this entire season. Did you get all the security set-up, Damian?"

"No, it will take me a while. I don't think we mentioned it earlier, but Ariana got a picture of the man that chased her and I also want to work on identifying who he is, so I'll be alternating between the two activities over the next couple of days. You'll stay on the island until I have everything in place at Ariana's house. We'll both escort you to and from school this week. At the end of it, Ariana will make the call as to whether to hire on- site security as well."

"There are a couple of kids in my school that get delivered by private security. Their parents are very rich but I've never heard of them and they're very paranoid about their safety. They don't get to play on any of the sports teams."

"Do they want to play or are they just not sports-minded, so it's no sacrifice?" Damian asked curious about the other kids.

"I don't know them well enough to know. Neither of them is in my grade, so I'll likely never know."

"Well kiddo, you and I and Miguel are going to pack our bags to stay at Damian's for three to five days. We need to not discuss what we're doing while we're in the house because of the microphones."

"Did you check this car as well for spy devices," Hermione asked.

Ariana looked stricken and put her hand over her mouth while Damian laughed out loud and said, "She didn't ask me to, but yes I checked for bugs and there weren't any on the car."

"Whew," Ariana said wiping her brow.

Hermione grinned in the back seat and said to Damian, "You'll have to give me instructions on how to care for Bailey and Bella. I think I'm supposed to get them fish fresh each day. Do you cook it for them?"

"Yes, I don't know why since they eat barely dead seafood all the time, but it's a habit."

"Okay, I'll fish for them every day. So we're going to go home and pack in silence then head across to Damian's house and we can talk again on the boat or by text, right?"

She got nods of agreement from Ariana and Damian. Mostly, it seemed like an adventure. She didn't know why, but she actually felt safer with these two than with her own parents. Perhaps it was Damian's ingenuity that gave her such a sense of security. Her parents relied on secrecy and the safe rooms, while Damian deployed weapons that hurt rather than killed people, thus insuring their safety.

They arrived in Ariana's neighborhood and Damian scanned her house for heat sources and it was clear. They parked the car in the garage, shutting the door upon entry to the house. As planned, the two women packed while Damian wandered around the house looking at its present security system, making a list of things he planned to install to make it difficult to get into Ariana's house. He'd probably need to leave a bug scanner at her house, so she could frequently check for surveillance.

Within fifteen minutes they were heading across the bay to Damian's home. He would change the sheets on his bed for Ariana and Hermione fortunately already had her room. Pulling out clothes and toiletries, he packed for a few days at her house. Since the house was already wired for security, he could put some fun enhancements on it to dissuade anyone from entering. Specifically, he planned to electrify the door knobs so that anyone touching them from the outside would get a nice electrical jolt. He wanted to get to work, so after securing their comfort on his island home, he took Ariana's boat across the bay to her dock. As he was bouncing on the waves, he was debating putting the cover on the boat. That was the normal way to take care of the boat and fog would be rolling in later which would cover it in moisture. However if he needed a quick getaway, messing around with a boat cover would waste valuable time. He decided he needed to plan for the quick getaway and would place a beach towel over the steering wheel and pilot seat.

He'd again checked the house before docking and there were no human heat sources around. He studied Ariana's backyard area from the dock looking for the perfect hidey-hole for the boat key. He wanted it close to the boat, but not visible. If he had to run, the last thing he wanted to worry about was looking for a key. Of course he could hot wire a boat, but he'd be long dead by the time he completed the circuit to start the motor.

Next, he knew he had to work on the house security rather than searching the internet for a facial match to Ariana's thug. Perhaps it was fortunate that he had set up a security system for Natalie several months ago when she was under attack from the Aryan Brotherhood. That experience gave him ideas on what to do to enhance Ariana's home. Starting with her property perimeter, he developed an early detection system that would sound the alarm whenever someone more than one hundred pounds or taller than four feet crossed onto her property. That way if Miguel was outside, he wouldn't trigger the alarm.

Before he escorted the ladies over to his island, he had set up a recording device for all of the hidden camera locations and taped three hours of footage. He left the lights on for the recording as he didn't have time to duplicate a full twenty-four hours. He could only hope that whoever planted the devices didn't look at them in the middle of the night and wonder why the room was brightly lit but empty. He then diverted the cameras to the recorded coverage rather than the live picture. Once he had the feed going he got to work inside the house with a few modifications. Rather than building safe rooms for Ariana and Hermione, he instead put defensive devices in the house. Ariana could disable the entire system or just parts of it when home. Starting with the doors, he electrified the outside doorknobs.

When they vacationed in Cozumel, he had set up buckets of pepper juice inside the front door colored with red dye. It was great for stopping and staining the bad guy, but it had made a mess of the interior of their rented home. This time, he put the buckets on the outside with a failsafe to prevent anyone exiting the house from getting splashed in case Ariana forgot to disarm the system before leaving. So anyone coming in through the door would get a jolt of electricity and be drenched in pepper juice. The cool thing about that was it disabled the thug from running away as they were temporarily blinded.

Outside Hermione and Ariana's bedroom doors, which were on the second level of the house, he studied what to do. The hallway was tiled and the ceiling was smooth; what kind of booby trap could he build that wasn't in the immediate peripheral vision of the thug? He decided to place a net in a quick release sling that would be triggered by anyone entering at least three feet into the hallway to the bedrooms. He also stashed pepper juice-filled water pistols in every room, so the ladies could defend themselves at any moment.

It was approaching midnight when he felt confident that he'd done everything possible to protect the ladies and contain any thugs that dared to break in. It was time to go to bed and wait for the ladies to arrive in the morning. He went to sleep with mixed emotions, on one hand he wanted someone to try breaching his system that night as a test, and on the other he wanted a good night's sleep in a strange bed. His latter wish won out as he had a quiet night.

After he and Ariana took Hermione to school that morning, he proceeded to show Ariana the details of his security enhancements. Since he was fond of pepper juice as a way to keep the criminals away, she expected it would be somewhere in his protection scheme. Due to the length of her driveway, the postman was safe from Damian's gadgets. Deliveries were another story and she'd have to make sure she picked up any deliveries for the foreseeable future. Damian planned to spend the night at Ariana's house just to make sure they knew how to operate his system and then they could go back to their normal living situation.

Damian went home to his island to get some work done with the plan to return to pick Hermione up from school. The top of his to-do list was finding the identity off the man who had attacked Ariana. He hadn't found the man in his run through the facial recognition system. He decided he didn't want to waste any more time so he tapped into the passport system. He pulled data on every active passport and anyone that entered the United States in the last two years.

He did a facial recognition search and came up with ten matches. It looked like the ten were in reality four people that had entered the United States on different passports. To be fair their appearance was changed by hair and beards, but the bone structure remained the same. He reviewed the home country of each entrant trying to see a tie with Hermione's parents. None of the ten passports represented Columbia or China, two countries that Hermione mentioned the family lived in. There were two Canadians, two Mexicans, and six faces of other countries. It could be coincidence the one man seemed to have entered on multiple passports, or Damian's eyesight might be wrong; the computer said these ten faces were possible matches, but to his eye some of the ten faces were the same face. Wasn't there a saying that everyone had a twin somewhere in the world?

He sat back and thought some more. Maybe he could trace the car? He pulled up the picture to see if the license plate was in view and it wasn't. All he could see was the word "California" at the bottom edge of Ariana's picture. He focused in on the car's windshield looking for identifying stickers or maybe the VIN, but again he found nothing. Ariana had said the man had an accent, but she'd been unable to identify what kind of accent. He dropped her an email outlining the results of his research so far, including the countries represented by the passports and asked if the man's accent might have represented any of the countries. She replied shortly that it might have been six of the ten countries with 'might' being the operative word. Damian decided it was a lost cause and gave up on the idea.

He hadn't spoken to Natalie in nearly three days which was unusual when they were in the midst of a case. He wondered how her meeting had gone with Detective Shimoda. Sometimes she forgot to update him when she got lost in thinking of strategies for identifying the bad guys. She called him shortly after receiving his email with an apology and the exact explanation that Damian had suspected.

"What did the detective say about the pattern of sales on eSale?"

"He was going to obtain a subpoena to get the seller data. The judge he wanted to tap was away until today, so I expect to hear any moment that he has it."

"Who's going to serve it and what's the turnaround time?"

"Good question. Since this is a cold case, we'll have a hard time requesting eSale turn over the information within twenty-four hours. I expect they'll be given at least a month to comply."

"I get your reasoning but that seems like a long time. With the programmers they have, they could write a program and hand over the names and addresses of the sellers within about two hours."

"I suppose you could get the information in that same amount of time?" Natalie asked.

"For eSale alone, yes. If you include the other major sites it will run me an hour for each site. I could legally run you a report with the sellers and the states or countries eSale says they reside in. That information is available to the public."

"Even for some old sales like these? Suppose I sold stolen jewelry five years ago and I never put a second item for sale on the website. Would you still find me in a public list of sellers?"

"I think so. Hold on a minute while I try," Damian said and Natalie heard keyboard keys clacking in the background. "Yes, anyone of average computer skill could reach that information. It doesn't give you any more information than name and location, but it's a starting point. For your subpoena I would ask eSale to turn over the names, addresses, banking information, and how many items they sold."

"I'll let Detective Shimoda know about your request, meanwhile my brilliant UC Berkeley students providing free computer skills will compose a list for me to go to work on. Thanks!"

"You're welcome. I'll get you that list in an hour or so."

They ended the call and Damian thought, "I would never have made it as a cop. I lack the patience to do things legally when I can get the answers so much faster by illegally accessing computer systems.' He also knew that the kind of power he had in regards to computers could be used in the most corrupt manner possible destroying financial systems worldwide or causing chaos in major systems like airline reservations, but that was not who he was. He felt like he had a duty to police the cyber world and use his skills to bring down criminals. Helping Natalie fulfilled some of this urge of his to use the cyber world against criminals.

10-CHAPTER TEN

Damian provided Natalie with the list as promised and then sat back a few minutes to think about the case. The data run he provided Natalie was helpful, but he felt that given the success of this bank robber, the authorities were underestimating the robber's technique to pull off the heist. How else could he approach the case? Then he gave himself a little slap to the side of his head.
Angus Walsh. Why hadn't he thought of him before now? Then he knew the answer; it was his distraction concerning Hermione and Ariana's safety. Angus was a man who'd spent over twenty years behind bars before being released after new technology proved his innocence. He was good with computers and Damian had met the man at Pete's Bar when he was searching for help to understand the Aryan Brotherhood's behavior on a previous case. Angus belonged to the gang in prison, but through some of the finest acting ever, had managed never to participate in their violent schemes. His photographic memory ensured that he remained untouched once he was released. Damian had hired him for his new company which he now admitted he hadn't paid any attention to since his return due to his focus on Hermione.

Checking his watch, he decided it was a good time to cross the bay and visit his company which was located in a warehouse in Richmond. When he'd taken time off for the vacation to Australia, he added the additional day for Hermione's first day of school. Now he was overdue at the office. He could be forgiven for this slipping his mind as this was the first time he owned a company.

Prior to this, he was his own inventor with his own timeline. Now he was funding his small company with his own personal wealth and he had engineers working on ideas that had languished under his sole attention.

Thirty minutes later he was walking in the door of the warehouse that Ariana had found for him. It was far larger than they needed for the start of the company, but he did not want the technologies his company was pursuing to be limited by the lack of space for experimentation. He had installed high security fearing the theft of his technology and to keep any neighborhood kids from getting into trouble if they broke into the building and unknowingly touched any of the equipment that was dangerous in ignorant hands.

After passing a series of locked doors with card keys, fingerprint and retina scans, he entered the large room to find Angus, Haley and Chris at work at their respective work counters. Haley had taken over Damian's wave energy generator since he'd been stuck on the storage aspect of the energy. She was also working with Angus on the drone guidance. At the moment he could see that it was crashing into fake buildings. Yes, that needed a little more work. He looked over to where Chris was working on his line of self-defense items. Damian designed a polymer that he used to coat a water gun. Once the polymer was in the water gun, then the user could fill it with water or in Damian's case with pepper juice. He planned to sell the items as self-defense weapons and he was looking at other devices that could contain his patented pepper juice. His current pepper juice guns were made by a common toy water gun company. If he wanted to sell them worldwide, he needed to engineer his own mold for the polymer, design machinery to make lots of plastic guns, and have a quality control process. As yet he hadn't decided whether to also sell his patented pepper juice. There would be significant shipping restrictions on such a product. He might just grow the peppers and sell them along with a recipe. There was plenty of time to decide some of these issues.

Everyone stopped working and gathered around him once they saw him enter the warehouse.

"Hello, Haley, Chris, and Angus. How's it going?"

He got a round of 'great' and then he was asked about diving in Australia. Once they got the social niceties out of the way, he had each team member update him on his or her progress. He hadn't given a resume of each employee to the other two so Chris and Haley would only know that Angus was an ex-con if he told them of his experience. In order to maintain Angus' privacy, he called him into his office. It was funny that he had Ariana put an office in the plans for the warehouse but he had so far occupied it probably for an hour in the month their business had opened.

"Hey, I had a somewhat personal question for you and I wasn't sure if you wanted me to ask it in front of Chris and Haley."

"About me being an ex-con? They know, I told them over beer one night."

"Oh, okay. Good, I guess. Did you get any hassle over it from them?" Damian asked curiously. If he knew his team, the answer would be 'no'. He waited to hear if they passed the test.

"Good God, no. I became sort of a superhero to have survived with my wits intact. It's all rather embarrassing," Angus replied chagrined. He was Irish in heritage, with short brown hair, a few scars around his face and neck and in his late forties. Damian hadn't asked Angus what the old wounds were from, but he hoped to hear the story behind them some day.

"That's good to hear as I expected that would be their response. I'm working on a case at the moment for Haley's future mother-in-law, who's a retired detective with the SJPD. It's a bank robbery. Do you know any ex-bank robbers that did time and have been released?"

Angus laughed at his question and replied, "Damian, you are such a scientist. You're wanting to do research on how to rob a bank and now you're looking for that particular skill set among the population in the bay area. Aren't you worried that the guy might be dangerous? Might want to rob you of your millions?"

"It hadn't even occurred to me that someone like that would be dangerous." Now it was Damian's turn to look chagrined. "Okay, can you find me a bank robber, who didn't murder anyone while they robbed the bank? Do you know someone like that?"

Angus was still smiling when he said "yes."

"What's his or her story?"

"She'd been robbing banks for perhaps a decade, when she found a particular bank that she wanted to rob. There were three entrances into the bank with lots of glass between her and a busy thoroughfare. So she thought she needed a team to pull off the job.

That was her mistake."

"How did you meet her? I thought they kept men and women separate in the prison system."

"I volunteer for an organization that helps ex-cons stay on the straight and narrow and she also volunteers there. She's very smart and some day you might want to hire her here."

Damian raised his eyebrows at that comment and asked, "In what role?"

"Like me, she's self-taught. I think she'd be good as our quality control person. She's spent her criminal life figuring out how to bypass a system. She's working as a waitress now, but I know she'd like to work in a job that better uses her skill set."

"What makes you so sure she won't revert to a life of crime again?"

"She's adopted a child and she wants to always be there for the kid."

"How did she adopt? I was under the impression that anyone with a criminal record is barred from adoption."

"I don't know for sure and I'd rather not give you the wrong information. I think you should meet her. Her name is Lily," Angus suggested.

It was one thing to hire an ex-con who was wrongfully convicted as was the case with Angus. It was another to hire someone who admitted their crime and served time. He was doing confidential work and he wanted employees he could trust. He also wasn't sure about her skill set and Angus' analysis of the situation.

"You took a chance on me," Angus remarked. "Now I think you should take a chance on her."

"I didn't really take a chance on you; you were never convicted of a crime."

"Yes, but what I learned about how to commit a crime could fill a two hundred page book. Lily's been straight for five years and I really think she could contribute to this company - she has an entrepreneurial mindset."

Damian leaned back in his chair and realized he had nothing to lose by meeting Lily, and so said, "Ask her to meet us when it's convenient to her schedule. Also I'll be escorting Hermione to school for a while so I can't meet her for breakfast or happy hour."

"Did someone threaten Hermione?" Angus asked concerned written all over his face.

"Yes and Ariana and I need to figure out who."

"No wonder you haven't been here for the last few days. Anything I can do to help? If they need a security escort somewhere, I can help if you're not available."

"Thanks for the offer and I'll keep that in mind if we run into more trouble. Let me know when Lily's available."

Looking at his watch, Angus said, "I'll call her now. Can you meet for lunch today?"

Damian looked at Angus and said, "You really like Lily, don't you? If she's not available right now, I won't change my mind about meeting her, so don't have her skip work just to meet with me."

"I think she'll be good on two levels - help this company and help you with your bank robbery case," Angus said as he made the call.

A few minutes later, a meeting was arranged. They would have lunch at Pete's Bar, Damian's go-to-place for confidential meetings, good food, and perfectly chilled beer.

11-CHAPTER ELEVEN

Ariana was on her way to Sunnyvale for a meeting at a start-up incubator. Driving south on the 101 freeway, she'd been watching her mirror for the signs of anyone following her. She'd purposely set out with plenty of time, planning to get off and on the freeway to check if anyone was pacing her. There were a few cars that she'd been watching in her rear view mirror, which was no easy feat considering the curves of her hometown of Belvedere and then the 101 going over the Golden Gate Bridge, then there were the streets of San Francisco which were always an adventure. She hit a big box electronics store on the southern edge of the city and purchased a camera for the back of her car. The camera was her back-up plan; she'd study the footage when she got home to see if she noticed anyone following her. She admitted to herself that she was paranoid, but what more could she do to keep herself and Hermione safe?

The traffic was so congested and the drivers so distracted that her first threat came from just the daily traffic. It was better once she got south of the airport, but she knew it would bunch up again around the exit for Stanford University. In the city of Millbrae she exited the freeway and there were several cars that went with her. A silver Chevrolet car followed her through the intersection and back onto the freeway. Yep, it looked like she was being followed. She would exit again just to verify that the car was following her. This time she hit the exit in Redwood City and the car followed her off, but then didn't get behind her back onto the freeway. Whew, thought Ariana, she wasn't being followed after all.

She reached the street where her technology start-up was housed inside an incubator building. It was the way of Silicon Valley. If you had an idea for a technology product, then you moved to San Jose and looked for space inside an incubator where you could find like-minded individuals and meet with venture capitalists. Perhaps upwards of ninety percent of companies failed for a variety of reasons. When Ariana invested, she was cautious and demanded a Board role so she could closely monitor the company. She killed two of her companies herself, because while one of them had a promising product, they were beat to market by another start-up with a similar idea; and the other company she killed, suffered from a lack of versatility in the management team. When you were starting up a company, you needed to do everything from cleaning the floor to coding to get your idea off to a good start.

She parked and looked around for the silver sedan. She blinked when she saw two of them drive down the street she'd just been on. She grabbed her phone and snapped a few pictures so that she could later identify the cars; she couldn't tell a Chevy from a Toyota and silver was a popular color. She then proceeded inside ready to return her mind to business.

Three hours later she walked out to car. The sun was bright and so she looked for anyone standing around or either of the silver cars, and then she confronted the problem of there being some twenty silver cars in the parking lots before she stopped counting. She debated going back inside and asking someone to walk her to her car, but she knew she would look nuts at that request as this was for anyone but her, a very safe neighborhood.

Then she noticed that her car looked lopsided and she wondered what was wrong. Once she got closer, she saw the problem - a very flat tire. She walked around the car to see if there was any other damage or creepy person hiding around the edges of the car and there were none.

She went to work digging the spare out of her car frequently looking around as she did. She kept the water gun filled with pepper juice within arm's reach and worked on loosening the bolts to get the flat tire off and the spare on. After she got the car rolling again, she would head over to her local dealership and have them place the appropriate tire on the car.

She sensed someone near her and she swung around quickly, tire jack bar in one hand and the water gun in the other ready to defend herself.

She saw one of the engineers she had just been meeting with backing away hands in the air. She quickly lowered both items and said, "Sorry Connor, I'm a little on edge with the flat tire."

"Yes, well I saw you starting to change your tire from the window of our offices and thought I would come down to help. Ah, would you like some help?" he said nervously wondering where this potential violent woman had come from; she was just so pleasant in meetings.

Ariana let out a deep breath and said, "I'd love some help. One of the bolts is very tight and I've been unable to turn it." She backed away from her car to give the man space and noted a silver car leaving the parking lot.

Again she took a picture of the departing car. Connor noticed her shooting the picture and he started searching for whatever had interested her enough to take a picture. Then he just shrugged to himself; he worked with lots of people that were inconsistent in their behavior like Ms. Knowles was at the moment. He'd help her get going and then maybe the next time they had a meeting, she would return to acting normal again.

Five minutes later, Ariana was thanking him before getting in her car and pulling out of the parking lot. Had this entire day been a figment of her imagination? Was paranoia getting the best of her, or had someone really been following her? Looking at the time, she saw that she had a few hours before she needed to pick Hermione up and so she dropped into the nearest dealer to have a regular tire placed on her car. An hour later, she was feeling pumped. The mechanic told her that her tire was slashed and so she bet that one of the departing silver cars had done it. He also inspected the other tires and there were no slash attempts in them just waiting to sever when she was going seventy miles an hour.

She dropped Damian an email about her experience and he replied that he wanted a copy of her pictures and footage as he had software that would identify people and objects quickly. Once she arrived home she did just that, having some time before they would jointly pick-up Hermione from school. Ariana noted that Damian's protections at her house seemed to be working as she had no intruders at home. She'd also ask Damian to bring a gadget with him that could search her car for GPS devices. She'd need to do a search every time the car left the garage.

12-CHAPTER TWELVE

Angus and Damian walked into Pete's Bar. It was a rare occasion that Pete wasn't there but there had to be a first time for everything; he couldn't work twenty-four seven. Lily was waiting at the bar for them and Angus waved at her then nudged Damian forward in her direction.

She was the first bank robber that Damian had ever met and she was pretty enough to be a Bond girl. Damian guessed she was in her mid to late thirties. Five to eight years was the typical sentence for bank robbery as long as no one was killed. Given her history he thought he had the age about right. She had short black hair, brown eyes, and Damian guessed that one black parent and one white parent created her beauty. She was small boned and slight; maybe a size four. Overall, this was not his vision of a bank robber.

"Hi Lily, I'm Damian. Thanks for meeting us for lunch."

"No problem. I'm good for a few hours then I have to pick up my boy from school."

"School? Angus told me you adopted a child, but I had in mind an infant. How old is your son?"

"He's twelve going on thirty. He wants to be that next hot rap singer but he can't carry a tune. Mayhap his voice will improve with age."

Damian chuckled at her description imagining the boy's cracking puberty voice and said, "I'm guardian to a fourteen year old who acts like a thirty something and I wish she would find her inner child."

"Aren't children wonderful?!" Lily said with a full on smile.

"Yes they are," Damian agreed not wanting to remember the two little girls that he'd lost to a murderer over seven years ago.

They moved over to a private booth and made quick work of ordering their lunch.

He cleared his throat and said, "I understand you did time for bank robbery. As Angus might have told you, I'm working on a cold case that's a bank heist and I'm trying to understand the bank robber brain."

She laughed at his description and Angus rolled his eyes. He'd met some pretty awful bank robbers during his own prison stint and really except for Lily, he hadn't liked any of them.

"Yeah we come in a one-size fits all mold," Lily said sarcastically. "You should have met some of the dumb schmucks that I met in prison claiming to be bank robbers. They were an embarrassment to us pros."

"I can second Lily's opinion on that," Angus said. "The really dumb ones got caught quickly; sometimes before they even obtained any cash."

Damian had to laugh at their classification of crooks. It seemed that even among thieves there was a rating system for excellence. He went on to explain the cold case and Lily was aware of it. She'd been in prison at the time, but there was talk among the inmates.

"Those cons that I labeled as the dumbest would talk about doing a bank heist exactly as that one when they got out. Of course our conversations were monitored and those words didn't play well with the parole board so they got extended stays."

"How would you have done that heist?"

"It's sophisticated and the con has tremendous patience. He had patience digging and patience on spending the loot. I say 'he' but it could have been a 'she'. If I had planned the heist, this is what I would have done."

She described it so completely and confidently that Damian wondered if she had pulled off a similar heist.

They paused their conversation as their food arrived. It wouldn't be good for the waitress to overhear their conversation and think they were about to rob a bank Damian thought.

"Why do you rob banks? Is it the thought of easy money?" Damian asked.

"For the dumb ones, yes, it's the thought of easy money. My motivation was the challenge of outsmarting security systems. I'd case a bank for a while and come up with a plan. I started small hauling in two to three thousand; which was a warm up exercise for me. You need to get in and out in less than three minutes to avoid the cops, so you can only focus on one teller. After successfully pulling off three heists, I decided my approach was stupid and I needed to get cash from more tellers or focus on a teller with the highest cash drawer which is usually the merchant window. Banks move the merchant teller around so you can't assume they'll be in the same position every day."

Damian found the conversation interesting as he never paid attention to bank activities; he couldn't remember the last time he'd been inside a bank. He did everything electronically and occasionally visited an ATM.

"How much did you pull from the merchant window?" Damian asked.

"When I cased a bank, I would monitor the various merchants making deposits and in time I figured out who was giving the bank the most cash and I made sure I got in line behind them."

"How could you tell?" Damian asked.

"There were two clues. One was the size of the bag they brought and the other was the time the teller spent counting cash."

Damian was impressed with her thoughtful strategy. These weren't impulsive heists like many robbers, rather they were well planned heists.

"It sounds like you did a lot of observation. Didn't the bank notice your curiosity?"

"I'd never target the same bank twice and I'd select banks where I could loiter undisturbed outside. So it would be a bank usually with a coffee shop nearby. I'd sit in the shop and watch the activity. Once I saw a merchant target that I thought was good, I'd go inside the bank in a variety of costumes and watch the merchant. When I was satisfied, I'd type up my note on a computer and print it at a Fedex shop or something like that. I would have my own merchant bag stuffed with paper and I would get in line right behind the merchant. As long as the same teller called me I would proceed with robbing the bank. If I didn't get that teller, I would approach the other teller, open my merchant cash bag and exclaim that I'd left something behind and leave. I would make two attempts and if the process failed both times, I would move on to a new bank."

"How long did you avoid getting caught?" Damian asked.

"About five years," Lily replied.

"What was your haul from the merchant teller?"

"If I did my homework right, it was ten to twenty thousand."

"Did you move around the country or stay in one city?" Damian asked.

"I moved around the state. It didn't pay to establish a pattern within one police agency."

"I thought the FBI was involved in bank robberies?"

"They are, but I would move around their jurisdictions as well."

"Two more questions? Did you use a gun or other weapon and how did you get caught?"

"No weapons, just the note. The getting caught was entirely my fault. I found a bank where the merchants were depositing a lot more cash and the teller was so busy that she was not immediately dropping the cash into the lock box near her drawer. I thought she might have nearly one hundred thousand in her drawer if I hit it right. This bank had more security. They employed an actual guard and had three doors and were in walking distance to a police station."

"Sounds like the odds were stacked against you, why'd you pursue it?" Damian asked; she sounded smarter than to go after more than she could handle.

"It was the intellectual challenge of getting it right," Lily said simply. "Unfortunately, the partner that I needed on this heist was both dumb and impatient and I was stupid for planning the heist with him."

"How did you find him? It's not like you can take out a help wanted ad for a 'bank robber'."

"In my years of observation of bank exteriors, I came across two other future bank robbers doing the same thing. I collected their names and contact information and then passed on the particular bank they were casing. I used one of those contacts. He was impatient while we planned, but I ignored it because I needed help and if the impatience was the only bad thing about him, then I could live with that. We observed and planned and named a day and time for the heist. Our target walked into the bank. My instinct at the time was to call off the robbery. I just had the sixth sense it wasn't going to work, but my partner demanded we pursue it as planned and that was my mistake. That day they were training a new guard and so they had two of them and the younger one actually tackled me before I could get away which by the way is not bank policy."

"They want robbers to just leave and not hurt staff or other customers."

"Yes, that's correct. My partner for the heist was caught a week later when he tried to spend the loot. He's still serving a sentence."

Damian wanted to ask this woman many more questions, but Angus was right, she might be fit for his company. He didn't know why he thought that considering her background, but her description of bank heists demonstrated three things to him: intelligence, diligence, and planning skills.

Completely changing the subject, Damian asked, "What are you doing now and what's your background beside the criminal one?"

Lily looked taken aback at his questions and asked warily, "Why do you want to know?"

Damian hesitated and then said, "I don't know."

Lily hesitated and then said, "I have a bachelor's degree in mathematics and I'm working as a waitress."

Wow, Damian thought, now he could see why Angus suggested that he hire her.

"Did you ever use your degree in employment after college?"

"Yeah I did. I used it to rob banks."

"How did you use math for that?" asked Damian, genuinely amused.

"Well to count the money of course," Lily said cheekily. "I also used it to place puts and calls in the stock market. I used the Black-Scholes model for derivative pricing and made a bundle."

Damian was impressed that she named a math theory that had received a Nobel Prize.

"What do you want to do employment wise in the future?"

"You mean besides robbing banks?"

"It sounds like you have a very good reason to avoid going to jail in your twelve year old son. To do that you need to avoid criminal activities for another six years until he's eighteen," Damian suggested understanding the woman's sense of humor.

"Yeah, that's my game plan. I'll send Jacob off to college as I go back to prison for a longer time. As Angus will tell you, prison is a pretty horrible place. I still have nightmares about the place and the bathrooms and I have no intention of ever going back. Back to your original question, I'd love to get a job at Google or Apple, but my record stops that. I'll probably start my own firm once I figure out what I want to create. In the meantime, I waitress as I'm required to have a job for probation since they won't let me live on my stock market proceeds."

Damian wanted to hire her then and there, but he needed to be fair to Ariana. As his Chief Operating Officer, she might have some thoughts about Lily. So again he switched gears and went back to the bank robbery.

"What tools would you have used to dig the tunnel into the bank vault?"

Lily blinked at the rapid change in discussion and said, "I don't know anything about tunnels, so the first thing I would do is research the area. I would request copies of plans from the city planning department. Depending on what I saw in those plans, I would either have to hire an engineer or go at tunneling on my own."

"How about cutting through the actual vault? Would you use this list of tools?" Damian asked handing her a piece of paper.

She read through it, complete with pictures, then said, "No, there are more advanced tools than these. I did research about ten years ago when I was giving thought to going after a vault, and at that time I read the latest information on lasers and that is what I would have used for the metal part of the vault."

"What happened? Why didn't you try breaking into a vault?"

"I looked at the risks, the need for some engineering brains, and decided that it wasn't worth it. You know that some boxes have nothing more than paper in them, so the only thing worth putting the time into is the cash in the vault and those serial numbers are recorded by bank computers. The money I was stealing was chump change and since I grabbed the merchant money, the vast majority of my money had not yet had the serial numbers traced. Besides where would I find a legitimate engineer?"

"Lily, you've been a real help. Can I have your contact information?" Damian asked. Thinking he might be calling her tomorrow with a job offer.

Thirty minutes later Angus and Damian were back at the company's warehouse. Damian hadn't talked about Lily on the drive, his mind divided into thinking about how to use Lily in the company and wanting to do work on lasers to figure out if that was the cutting tool. It had been a very enjoyable lunch.

13-CHAPTER THIRTEEN

Damian got back to the office with just enough time to read emails and run a background search on Lily before heading to Ariana's house for their afternoon pickup of Hermione. He opened the email from her and read with dismay her experience that morning. Someone was still after her. It was rare that she'd need to travel to Silicon Valley in the next few months as she was working with Damian to get his company off the ground. If he wasn't able to identify who was targeting her and Hermione by Monday, then he would hire security to keep them safe.

He did a background search on Lily and everything seemed validated. She'd left off that she graduated Summa Cum Laude from Berkeley. Yes, she was smart. In fact she was so smart that boredom likely drove her into the bank robbery business. If he hired her, he would have to be sure that he kept her challenged. He had a few ideas to discuss with Ariana when he saw her tonight.

There was a lot of mist on the bay and for the first time, he sped across the bay to Ariana's with the Bimini top on the boat to stay dry. He arrived at Ariana's in a good mood from his lunch with Lily and Angus. She gave him a zip drive with her video footage and he demonstrated the use of a GPS detector that she could use on her car. The lesson was helped by the fact that someone had already placed a detector on her car.

"Didn't you search for it when you scanned my car for bugs? I thought you didn't find anything," Ariana said.

"I didn't find anything. I'm guessing you were followed to the electronics store and the bug was placed then," Damian mused.

Damian examined the tracker to see if he could discover anything about it, but the writing was in an Asian language, so he knew he wouldn't make head way. Then he kicked himself for touching it as there might have been fingerprints he could recover. After they returned home from retrieving Hermione, he would still try dusting it and the car to see if he could find fingerprints.

"When we drop her off tomorrow, let's place the bug on another car at the school; that will confuse them hopefully for a few days."

"You don't think they'll harm the other parents?" Ariana asked.

"No, once they see the other driver's face, they'll know they've been following the wrong car. In the best of all worlds, the car that we put the tracker on will be the same model and color as yours and the driver will have a short brunette hair style. Can you think of any other parents that fit those specifications?"

Ariana gave it some thought and said, as they got into her car, "Maybe, let's look in the parking lot now and then again tomorrow. It helps that we can narrow the possibilities by focusing on only white SUVs."

Ten minutes later, Hermione opened the door and got in the back seat, hair still wet from the water polo practice, a whiff of chlorine about her.

"Hello."

"Hey kiddo," Ariana and Damian called out in unison with Damian adding, "How was practice? Are people being dropped from the team?"

"In the end, I think there will be enough players to have a junior varsity team, so I think the coach will divide us up between the two teams."

"And you'll be on the varsity?" Ariana asked.

"I scored two goals today, one more than anyone else so yes that should secure my being on the varsity."

"Congratulations on the two goals," Damian said. "Did our practice help you to play better?"

"Swimming helps the most, but I think I'm better at getting my shoulders above the water to shoot at the net better than anyone, and trying to beat you, Damian taught me that."

"Great! Glad we made a difference," Damian smiled.

"Did you guys have any problems with intruders today?"

Hermione asked.

"You know, Hermione, Ariana and I can take care of ourselves, so don't worry about us," Damian said evading answering her.

"Yeah, well that's what Mom and Dad thought as well and look where it got them," Hermione said bitterly.

"I was probably followed into Cupertino today and one of my tires was slashed. Damian and I found a tracker on the car and when we get home, he's going to try and find fingerprints," Ariana said knowing that honesty was important when dealing with a teenager.

"Oh no! Were you attacked by anyone?"

"No, but I scared one of my start-up advisees when I turned on him with a tire jack bar in one hand and the water pistol in the other. His presence may have run off the culprit who knifed the tire."

Hermione had a small smile at the vision of Ariana wielding the named weapons, then she asked, knowing they would have something in mind, "What's next?"

"Tomorrow, we thought we'd place the bug on someone else's white SUV, and, it would be ideal if they had short brown hair," Damian offered.

Hermione was quiet then added cunningly, "Put it on Mrs. Abbott's car. It's white like yours and she's a really annoying person with a bully for a daughter. Maybe a confrontation with these bad guys will scare them into better behavior."

Ariana and Damian laughed out loud at the kid's assessment. "You know kiddo, you think like a devious adult too much of the time, but we'll get there early so we can do just that," Ariana said.

They had dinner together and they reviewed Hermione's schedule putting all her significant dates on their calendars. She went upstairs to begin her school work while Ariana and Damian spent a few minutes discussing their schedule in light of the attacks and the new company.

"I met this woman named Lily today and I'd like to hire her," Damian said. "Angus suggested her for quality control, but I think we should discuss our vision for the company with her and see where she thinks she fits in."

"What's her background?" Ariana asked thinking about the projects they had underway and a potential salary for such a person.

"She's a Summa Cum Laude graduate of Berkeley in Mathematics working as a waitress and she did seven years for a bank robbery."

Ariana blinked rapidly coming to the conclusion that Damian had asked to meet her for the bank robbery case he was helping the detective with. So she asked, "Do you think you can trust someone with that background? You have technical secrets you don't want disclosed before you submit for a patent. Has she worked in a tech firm before?"

"I spent a lot of time talking to her to judge her trustworthiness as that's my one concern. I think she has the brains to move the company forward and her personality will fit with the current group. She adopted a child after she was released from jail and so I think the twelve year old boy will be her motivation for staying out of anything illegal. She works as a waitress because her probation requires that she be employed. She also day trades on the stock market and has built up a tidy nest egg there."

"How many banks did she rob before being caught?"

"She never actually said but I'm guessing maybe thirty or forty based on time and her approach."

"Why'd she do it?" asked Ariana, puzzled as to why a person with her background would resort to criminal activity.

"My guess was for the intellectual challenge. She never used a weapon, just a note and the planning and execution were the intellectual challenge. Now that she was caught, I think the game is over for her."

"You mentioned Angus, how did he know her? It's not like they house males and females together in jail."

"They both volunteer at some agency that helps ex-cons get their life in order. Why don't I ask her to meet us and we can discuss a job opportunity with her? I believe I have computer skills to track her behavior; skills I don't believe she has. So we'll be able to verify that she stays straight."

"Okay," Ariana said, thinking about all the odd people she'd met in Silicon Valley who turned out to be excellent for a particular company. Maybe this Lily would be one of those. She knew that Damian liked to surround himself with very smart people and that was likely what caught his attention.

After discussing a few other details, Damian got ready to head for the dock to begin his boat ride home. As he was untying the boat and pushing it away from the dock, he blindly steered home toward his island thinking about how his life had changed since he met Ariana and Hermione. Six months ago, he had such a small and distant, by his choice, set of friends, that he could have been dead for two months before anyone might have possibly noticed. If he had come to that end, his deceased wife, Jen, would have smacked him upside the head the moment he showed up at the pearly gates. As he did on occasion when out on the bay, he thought about his wife and children.

"Jen, I hope you would be proud of me at the moment. I've made sure since your death that no inmate has been mistakenly released, and I've formed a family unit with Ariana and Hermione. I hope you and the girls are at peace as I seem to be at the moment."

He was grateful he was driving across the bay and the noise of the wind and waves whipped the words out his mouth before even a listening device could have heard them spoken aloud. Then he put his head out the side of the boat catching the cold and wet breeze, wondering after an excellent day, what had made him so melancholy? He continued pondering that question on and off until sleep finally shut down his mind later that evening.

14-CHAPTER FOURTEEN

Again it was quiet at Ariana's overnight and they pondered why no one was attempting to get at her or Hermione while at home. They were grateful for the peace and quiet, but Damian and Ariana couldn't think of the criminal strategy that had her followed on the freeway, but left her alone at home. They arrived at the school early and Hermione suggested where Damian could stand while waiting for Mrs. Abbott to arrive. He'd be close enough to the vehicle to place the tracker on it before her car turned away. He was texted the moment Hermione spotted the car and while Mrs. Abbott's daughter was getting out, Damian attached the tracker device under the rear bumper after pretending to drop something on the pavement. No sooner did he have his hand out of the way, when Mrs. Abbott floored the car away from the school. He wished he could be a fly on the wall when the owners of the tracking device confronted Mrs. Abbott, thinking they had Ariana.

He walked over and opened the door for Hermione to get out for school, kissing her on the forehead, then said, "Fun's over for the day, be a good student and a better water polo player! And remember that as an adult, I just set a bad example for you, Hermione."

She turned and gave him the thumbs up; secretly thrilled that Mrs. Abbott was now going to be harassed by the men that had been following Ariana. Walking over to some friends, she had a small grin on her face that stayed with her most of the day at school. Ariana and Damian headed for her house and then in turn departed in Damian's boat back across the bay to Richmond. Halfway across he let the boat coast at a low speed so he and Ariana could discuss Lily. He wanted to share Lily's background with Ariana not in earshot of his other employees. He gave her his thoughts on salary and knew Ariana would do the rest of the employment stuff. A short time later, he increased the boat's speed as they headed to the marina and his truck and then on to the warehouse. Damian had arranged an interview with Lily and the two of them to discuss opportunities. After a brief discussion, they decided there was no other way to explain their plans than to have her see the interior of the building so she and they would have to suffer the glances from Haley, Chris, and Angus. Of course Angus would guess what was going on.

Damian had given thought overnight again as to how he could use her mathematical brain and he thought he might have landed on the appropriate challenge for Lily - task her to design the artificial intelligence of his DNA processor. He'd see what she said when she arrived.

Ariana worked on her areas of responsibility, ensuring the bills and employees were paid, setting up a process for each team member to manage a budget and order supplies, and developing an offer letter and package for Lily if their meeting worked out to mutual satisfaction. While she was the Chief Operating Officer for Damian's company, it was really a part-time job and she often did the work from home only venturing into Richmond once a week or so.

She was almost done with those tasks when Damian called her into his office with a sense of urgency in his voice. She arrived at his door frame and found him looking at the computer screen.

He looked up and said, "Someone's approaching your house."

She walked quickly to his desk and looked at the monitor. It appeared to Ariana that it was one of the silver sedans she'd suspected the previous day and she said so to Damian.

"We'll get images of the license plate, but let's watch and see what he or she does. I wonder why this person is on your driveway now? They must have quickly discerned that Mrs. Abbott was not you, or perhaps they've already confronted her this morning."

"I hope she's fine; scared would be ok, but I'd like her unharmed."

"I'll check that out as soon as we're done watching this; he should be hitting the pepper spray any moment."

No sooner had Damian said that, then the windows were doused in fluid. The driver had been listening for road sounds and therefore got a blast of juice through the driver side window.

Apparently, one of the driver's two eyes was hit as they saw a hand go to the face, the car stopped, and then it reversed uphill out of her driveway, after the window had been closed. They could barely see the city road given the angle of her driveway, but it appeared the driver had parked the car and was flushing the one eye with bottled water.

"Take that you thug!" Ariana said with her hands raised in the air in victory and a smile on her face.

Just then Angus appeared at the door with Lily in tow and looked quizzically at the pair of them, saying nothing.

Damian looked up, smiled, and said, "Oh, hi Angus and Lily. We're just watching an intruder being run off from Ariana's house."

"With what?" Angus asked.

"We blasted pepper juice into the driver side window," Ariana said. Then she walked over to Lily and said, "Hi, I'm Ariana, Jill of all trades here."

"Why is your house under attack? Since you had the pepper spray set-up, you must have expected the intruder."

Damian gave Ariana a look that said, 'see I told you she was smart'.

"It's a long story for another day," Damian said. "Ariana, why don't you meet with Lily first and I'll watch the screen. I think he or she is disabled, so it's just a matter of waiting for the car to leave the vicinity."

Ariana hesitated wanting to watch the thug, but Damian said, "Go ahead and chat with Lily. I'm recording this and I'll give you a shout out if any new action occurs. The thug's eye irritation should last about four hours."

After a few seconds thought, she steered Lily to the second uncompleted floor of the company's warehouse explaining, "This is for future expansion or maybe manufacturing."

Lily nodded and sat down in a little lounge they had set up. Two minutes into the conversation, she could see why Damian wanted this woman as an employee. In some way, Lily reminded Ariana of Hermione – they both had an easy confidence that came from thinking they could outsmart the world.

Forty-five minutes later Lily signed an employment contract and confidentiality agreement and agreed to a start date in three weeks. Despite the big salary increase, she wanted to work out her two week notice at the restaurant. Ariana had new found respect for Lily for that attitude. The third week, she'd take as a vacation. Lily had some ideas of her own to discuss with Damian and the team, but she'd never had the lab to experiment with her ideas, so she was excited to start this new journey of her life.

When Ariana joined Damian in his office, she found him working on something else rather than watching the camera at her house.

"Lily has joined the company. Did the thug leave the end of my driveway?"

"Great and yes the thug left after about twenty minutes. I don't know how he could see to drive nor could I see anyone arrive to help. It's nearly impossible to not accidentally transfer pepper juice from one eye to the next so kudos to the man for managing to keep the one eye free."

"I hope I don't accidentally harm the UPS delivery person or postman or just some poor pizza delivery person."

"You diverted your mail and deliveries this week, right?" Damian asked.

"Yes, but accidents happen."

"We'll add a sign perhaps ten feet into the driveway that says something like 'Halt, fresh concrete ahead' and that way if someone ignores the sign and gets hit with the juice they have no one to blame but themselves."

"Okay. I liked Lily and I think she'll fit in with your collection of impossibly smart people."

Damian grinned at Ariana's description and added, "You're part of that group as well."

"Yeah I am. Someday we'll have to introduce Hermione to Lily. They both have this confidence that they can solve the world's problems because they're so smart; I guess they're rather like you, Damian. Short of hopping a car to the moon, there's not much you can't figure out."

"Actually it's been five months and I haven't figured out who Hermione's parents are or if they're dead or alive," Damian said frustration in his voice.

"Look at the bright side, the action I'm getting is a sign that something's going on with her parents."

"Yeah I just wish we could catch these guys so we could question them," Damian said with multiple scenarios running through his head.

"Let's have a social event to introduce Lily and her son to our other staff and their spouses or partners before Lily starts. It'll be a nice ice breaker."

"What would you suggest?"

"Baseball or football game?"

"Lily's waitress schedule would be hardest to schedule around, so find her availability and then we'll see if baseball or football will fit in. I'm going to go tell the others about hiring her and her background and our plan for a sporting event." Damian said as he stood up and left his office to go chat with Haley, Chris, and Angus.

The rest of the day was quiet with everyone working on their projects. Damian heard the occasional crash from Haley working on the navigation system. Those crashes were so disruptive yet amusing that he was tempted to have her set up her test track upstairs, but there was a certain camaraderie with the sounds of failure, so he let it go. He and Ariana left in the late afternoon to return across the bay to Ariana's house and head to school to pick up Hermione. They spent a few moments searching the area that the car had been on her driveway as well as the street. They saw two plastic water bottles that the thug had used to wash his eyes out. Damian used a piece of paper to pick them up and put them in separate paper grocery bags so he could dust them for fingerprints later.

15-CHAPTER FIFTEEN

A few hours later, Damian was back in his lab dusting the water bottles for prints. It was a long shot as he was a fingerprint amateur, and surely people had touched the bottle during the manufacturing or shelf stocking process, so he didn't have high hopes that it would lead anywhere. In fact now that he thought about it, this was his first attempt at fingerprinting. Of course he read up on it and studied some videos. He would have to see if he got a match.

He practiced once by putting his own prints on a different water bottle hopefully in the position the thug held the bottle. He then sprayed the bottle with aerosolized superglue. He looked for ridges, whirls, arches, and loops in his own fingerprints. He then did a search to see if his prints matched the national database.

There was no match. That was either because he knew the database didn't contain his prints or he did a poor job with his fingerprints. Okay time to move on to the bottle, but then he paused.

Was he making a mistake by not contacting the police? He seemed to stumble from one clue to another without looking at the entire picture. He reiterated in his mind the statement he'd made to Ariana the day before - it had been five months and he was no closer to figuring out who Hermione's parents were. Was it time to bring Natalie in on this case? Were the three of them at greater risk because they hadn't reported things to law enforcement? Would the crime scene techs do a better job with evidence than Damian was doing? The answer to many of the questions was 'yes'. So why didn't he pick up the phone and talk to Natalie?

The answer was that he feared it would take longer for law enforcement to solve the case of Hermione's parents than the path he was taking. The few cases he worked on with Natalie were delayed on her end by the need to follow the laws of the police and the courts. Damian felt no compunction for walking all over those rules, especially privacy rules, in order to get to the truth. He saw those delays in action in Natalie's cold cases and he wanted to make sure he didn't see it in regards to Hermione's life and future. He felt better for taking a long look at his decision making and reaffirming the direction he was going. He put those thoughts aside and moved on to a summation of Hermione's situation. The fingerprints were put aside once again.

Since they'd met Hermione, various thugs had touched their lives. He reviewed the thugs and events in his head. Any pictures or fingerprints that Damian lifted from their home had proven to have no matches in any system. The first thug, Nico Thomas was the man who inhabited Hermione's parents' house just after her parents were kidnapped or killed. Damian had no idea what heritage or race the man represented. The thug had spoken to police officials and they had accepted his explanation, so he must have had a normal accent; one that didn't make the police suspicious. Perhaps he would go back and study the man's movement on tape and see what he touched and go back into the house and grab some prints.

Then there was the group of men in Mexico who had broken into their vacation home. The police in Cozumel seemed to have run out of leads on the men and so that represented a dead end. Then there was the Facebook message written in Chinese, and now there was the thug who attacked Ariana. Who were these people and what or who did they want? Hermione? Or something that Hermione knew? He really wished he could catch one of these guys to question him. Were they Chinese, Mexican, Indonesian, Columbian, or good ole American thugs?

Finally he returned to the plastic water bottle that he had retrieved form the road near Ariana's house and prepared the prints by spraying the bottle first with Superglue Spray, then dusted them with black carbon powder using a fine human hair brush. Fingerprints showed up on the main body of the bottle as well as the neck. He concentrated on the main body as that was how he saw the thug holding the bottle at the end of Ariana's driveway.

It looked to Damian's untrained eyes that there were four sets of fingerprints on the bottle. He studied them further for loops and arches and thought he saw the same set repeated three or four times on the bottle which was what he would expect if the guy had held the bottle while buying it or placing it into the car cup holder or picking it up to wash his eyes out. He made a copy of the print under good light with his camera and then uploaded to his computer. He then hacked his way into AFIS database to find a match.

Thirty minutes later, there was no match which meant that the thug had no criminal conviction on record in the United States. He could still be a thug but never caught or just be a foreign hoodlum. Or Damian thought, there was a third reason - maybe he was bad at fingerprinting.

He paused and thought about his processing and the clarity of the print and decided that no it wasn't in his technique, there simply wasn't a match. Damian reviewed other places to look for a match but there were too many small databases and some of them contained just thumb prints.

Damian picked up a plastic bottle; and the thumb print while holding the bottle was different from a thumb print used by many databases.

He thought about swabbing the bottle for DNA trace but he really didn't know what he was doing there, and if he couldn't find the thug's fingerprints, he was sure there would be no DNA registry that included him. There were more fingerprints on file than DNA records.

He went back and reviewed the tape and looked at the car license plate. He assumed it was a rental or a stolen plate, but it never hurt to look. Checking into the DMV database, he found the car registered to a car rental agency at the San Francisco Airport. Cool, now he might get somewhere.

The car was rented for two weeks beginning the previous Monday when Ariana had been attacked the first time. The individual renting it had a passport from Malaysia and the name on it was John Lee. Sure Damian thought, that was like John Doe in America. The individual paid cash for the rental, plus a two-thousand dollar deposit in case of damage to the car. A credit card wasn't used for the transaction. Damian checked the VISA requirements for Malaysian citizens and none were required although immigration fingerprinted visitors upon entry. He thought about what he would do with those prints; then he realized they were worth obtaining as he could look at how often the man traveled to the United States.

When he looked up that information, he discovered the man had only visited the U.S. once. Damian thought that was interesting information. Mr. Lee wasn't part of the original hoodlum group that attacked Hermione's home. Of course, he could have used a fake name and a different fake passport. Damian felt as though he was spinning in circles; he was discovering new information about the criminals, but at the end of the day he didn't know what was truthful. It was time to put this aside and move on to the bank heist.

Damian sat back and thought about what Lily had said about the bank heist. He should probably arrange a meeting between Lily and Natalie as she would eventually hear from her future daughter-in-law, Haley, about Lily's background. Checking the time, he decided it was beyond polite hours to call her. Instead, Damian emailed a message concerning Lily's background and comments and ended with a request for her not to tell Haley of Lily's background. He was sure that Lily would tell the others in time, but he wanted it to be on her timeline and not anyone else's.

He got up from his computer to head upstairs to his bedroom for the night, when his cellphone rang. Looking at the caller ID, he saw that it was Natalie.

"Aren't you usually asleep at this hour?" he asked.

"I'm finding in retirement that without an absolute need to wake up at a certain time to start my shift on time, my bedtime hours are much more flexible. So I read your email and had to call you. You have the widest circle of acquaintances I've ever met. I wonder if Haley has a secret life, since she seems to be your only employee with a traditional background."

"If Haley has a secret life, I haven't seen it yet although you may not know that she can swear like a sailor. She's been crashing her drone into fake buildings and letting loose expletives in frustration."

"I'd be worried, if she didn't swear over that activity. I'd like to meet Lily. Can you arrange that tomorrow? You asked most of the questions I would have, but I have a few more. Besides it would be good for my soul to meet a reformed criminal. I don't know if I have ever met one before let alone, one that was an extremely intelligent woman."

"I'll contact her in the morning. You will have to come to Richmond as she's balancing her time between a waitress job and a twelve year old boy."

"I can do that. I'll head north just after nine in hopes of missing the worst of the traffic. If she can't meet me until three, can I use some desk space at your warehouse?"

"Yes, I'll put you upstairs so you're not distracted by Haley's crashes. She might have more of them with her future mother-in-law in the vicinity," Damian said, amusement in his voice.

"That will do. Why is she working as a waitress? I thought she had an engineering background if she's going to work for you."

"She's quite the stock market genius, so she doesn't need the income; she works because it is a condition of her parole. She's working out her two week notice out of respect for her current employer."

"Wow. I can't wait to meet her; she sounds like such a contradiction - a criminal with morals."

16-Chapter Sixteen

While Damian and Ariana were taking Hermione to school the next morning, he told them about identifying 'Mr. Lee' and his rental car. The conversation then turned to the rumors about Mrs. Abbott.

Hermione said, grinning, "I heard this man grabbed her elbow when she got out of her car at a salon. She screeched so loudly that staff came out of the salon in response. They found her hitting a man with her purse and then the man ran off. She apparently added a massage to her salon appointment to get over the fright of the attack."

"Where did you hear that from?" Damian asked.

"One of the other kid's mother was in a bookstore next door and heard the commotion."

"So who knew that she had a massage?" Ariana asked.

"The kid's mother heard Mrs. Abbott telling the salon that they needed to provide her with a free massage since they allowed hoodlums to lurk outside their doors."

"Wow, she really is an unpleasant woman," Ariana agreed. "I wonder if Mr. Lee knows Mrs. Abbott is not me, yet."

"I think it probably depends on his ethnicity," Damian said. "In the passport picture from Malaysia, he marginally appears to be Asian, but that could be enhancements to his face. Studies show that you see facial detail better in the ethnicity you're surrounded by most. If he really is from an Asian country, then he may not realize you're different people."

"I'll keep my ears open for word of a second attack," Hermione said smirking while getting out of the car at the high school.

The door closed and Damian said, "I hope we're not setting a bad example for the kid."

"We might be," replied Ariana. "Let's remember to discuss it with her this evening. What are we going to do next week? You can't continue to escort her to school and back each day."

"I could continue to do that, but you need the protection as much as she does and driving her to school is not your only destination each day."

"Okay, you have a plan I can tell. Do you want to share it with me?"

"I'm of two mindsets. One, we hire 24/7 security for the two of you; or two, you go back to your private life with a few more protections."

"Like what?"

"I've been playing with some additional protection devices. If you don't mind wearing an ugly vest whenever you're out in public, I could give you some options."

"An ugly vest? Please explain."

"You know those vests that photographers or fly fishermen wear?"

"Yeah and I would call them ugly. What have you invented?"

"I've been working over the summer on a pepper juice water gun 2.0."

"A 2.0, huh? What does the ugly vest do?"

"The material is a lightweight, bullet proof fabric that I've used to sneak into Hermione's house both times. The vest has a variety of pockets all filled with something you could use in your defense. The base of the vest contains an air horn as a personal alarm. Each pocket is capable of spraying something twenty feet."

"What are you loading the vest with? Your standard pepper spray, or something else?"

"Actually, a variety of things. I do have my standard pepper juice, but I've also added an exploding net to tangle someone up with, and a purple smoke bomb. The vest shoots from the front or back. Ideally someone will be within ten feet of you for the items to work, although the air horn might cause you to lose your hearing."

"How many vests do you have?"

"Just so happens that I have two. I'm sure Hermione would not be able to wear it to school, but she could leave it in your car and wear it everywhere but school."

"Is the vest on your island or at company headquarters?"

"It's at home."

"How about if we head to your home now? Do you have plastic coveralls and goggles so I can try it out? I wouldn't want to spill any substance in the vest on my clothes or in my eyes."

"I do and that sounds like a plan," Damian said as they headed for her dock.

An hour later the two of them were heading in separate boats to the Richmond marina. Damian wasn't sure of his schedule and Ariana felt so comfortable with the vest for protection, she was going to pick Hermione up on her own and bring the kid to his house that night so she could try the gadgets in the vest, then have it available for her protection.

Damian made arrangements with Lily for the meeting with Natalie in the early afternoon. During a break from her shift, she'd talk with them in the diner. He knew he should work on his inventions, but part of the reason he started the company was to take some of that research off of his shoulders. So he let go and let his employees further his ideas. Instead he had a list of items to research related to Hermione. He suspected he'd have a new assignment from Natalie after their meeting with Lily this afternoon, based on some of the things she'd said in her discussion with Damian.

Top of his list was discerning if Nico Thomas and John Lee were related or even the same person. Indonesia and Malaysia were geographically so close together he couldn't help but wonder.

Next on his list that he'd thought of a few days ago and hadn't written down and so it escaped the edge of his conscious until this morning was the camera search for Alameda County. He wanted to locate all public cameras around the east bay and then do a facial recognition search for Hermione's parents starting with her likely route to school.

He also wanted to look at all the pictures of cars that followed or were otherwise near Ariana's car the previous day.

He had four hours before the meeting with Lily and Natalie in which to answer these three questions at the top of his list. The time flew by, but he had his answers.

He was convinced that Nico and John were the same person and he knew how to verify it; collecting dust at home were some twenty to thirty fingerprints that he pulled out of the Shorewood house including some he had collected expecting them to belong to the thug who had remained in the house trying to capture Hermione.

17-CHAPTER SEVENTEEN

Natalie spent the first ten minutes of their meeting trying not to like Lily, but it was just impossible. Like Damian had said, she was very smart but he'd failed to mention her charisma. That must have kept her safe in prison which was never an easy place to survive. She had cons try to manipulate her in the past, but that wasn't Lily's charm. It was the power of talking to a woman who knew where she was in the world and where she was going. They even shared a story about raising sons. At first she'd been unhappy with Damian for putting her future daughter-in-law near a convicted felon on a day to day basis, but she'd reached the conclusion that there was no danger for Haley and besides Haley could hold her own.

"Damian mentioned that the tools found at the site were not the tools you would use for such a robbery. Can you expand on that statement?" Natalie requested.

"There are pluses and big minuses to going after the cash in the vault. On the plus side, you can come away with millions of dollars and goods, and the negative side, it's very difficult and time consuming; to be successful you need to be patient and take your time along the way. I stayed away because while I understood banking systems, I had no such confidence in the engineering. I debated going after the bank vault in Santa Barbara. I discovered a utility pipe large enough for me to crawl through that ran through a series of businesses and so I got the plans from the city and studied them."

"What stopped you?" Natalie asked, fascinated by the logical method this ex-con had of looking at criminal jobs. So many of the cons she came into contact with had huge problems controlling their impulses which was what got them into trouble.

"It was a combined sewer and electrical pipe. It was very old and caused frequent power failures to the businesses located over it; that's what brought it to my notice. What stopped me was the vision of crawling on my knees in sewage and being so disgusted by it that I'd accidentally raise my head and connect to the electrical wires. The rats down in the sewer would begin gnawing on me as soon as the smoke from my burns cleared. No thanks," Lily said shuddering at the thought.

"Got to agree with you there Lily; that's about the least attractive bank heist I can think of," Natalie agreed.

"So the first thing I would do is get a list from the city of everyone who's ever checked out the plans for that street. I say street, because a smart bank robber wouldn't check out just plans for the bank; he or she would go after the entire block," Lily suggested. "Do you know the reason the florist shop space was rented as opposed to any other space on that street? Did you look at credit card payments for that store? Don't you need some information like social security numbers or business identity numbers for the credit card companies to give you billing rights? I would circle back and interview the employee that witnesses saw in that store."

Both Damian and Natalie had been scribbling notes as Lily talked. Natalie couldn't tell if Lily was speaking from the prospective of having done a similar job in her past, or if it was her logical mind putting pieces of a puzzle together.

They wrapped up their conversation on the bank heist and Natalie said, "Damian mentioned that you're going to work for him. My future daughter-in-law works there now and loves her job. I wondered if I might occasionally call on you to discuss a case? You have a very interesting mind that helps me see the way out of a dead end."

Lily experienced a range of emotions sweep over her as a result of Natalie's questions ranging from: 'help a cop?' to 'she probably already warned her daughter-in-law not to associate with a criminal' to 'I can't believe I'm giving my criminal secrets away to a cop'. It was like smoke or fog swirling in her head; and then all of a sudden it cleared and she thought of her twelve year old boy at home for whom she wanted to set an example.

"Sure, I'll help. Call me when you have questions," Lily replied giving Natalie her phone number.

They stood up to go their separate ways - Natalie to her car, Damian to his, and Lily back to work.

Damian delayed his departure by a few minutes to thank Lily for using her break to speak to Natalie. After Natalie left she asked, "How did you meet Natalie? It doesn't feel like your paths would have crossed. Did you meet her through Haley?"

"No, my wife and two children were murdered by a convict mistakenly released by Soledad prison. She solved the case, killing the guy. She also started this memorial ceremony for me each year on the anniversary of their deaths that has brought me a little more peace with each passing year."

"Wow," was all Lily could think of to say initially. Then she added, "I'm so sorry for your loss."

Damian just nodded and then she added, "I'm amazed you can stand to be around me since I'm a convicted criminal. You can take back your employment offer."

It was the first time Damian had heard anything less than her high degree of personal confidence and so he added, "You didn't use a gun or indeed any weapons in your heists. If you had hurt or killed people you wouldn't be working for me. If you violate my trust, I'll hunt you down electronically and steal every dollar you've ever made in the stock market or anywhere else for a charity of my choosing."

Lily felt a frisson of fear at his threat having no doubt he could do it. She tried to lighten the atmosphere and said, "Hey, I'll confess to you every speeding ticket and library fine I receive."

He said, "Good," and smiled at her to let her know they were back on solid ground.

After polite comments of departure, they went their separate ways Damian to the parking lot; Lily back to work. Despite the threats from her new employer, she was very much looking forward to her new job. Perhaps that had been her problem when she graduated from college, she'd been unable at the time to surround herself with very smart people. Damian had asked her to begin work on Artificial Intelligence for a DNA analyzer. She hadn't a clue where to start and planned to spend the time between now and her first day of work figuring out how to create it. She thought that Damian probably knew she was in over her head, but he suggested that algorithm and if-then sentences were used to write code so she should be able to figure it out. Maybe it would be something she and Jacob could learn together. He seemed to respond well to competitive challenges so she'd set one up around coding. One of her regular customers at the diner did coding for some tech firm. She'd bet he could point her to a website or give her instructions on how to learn coding and setting up a competition for her son and herself.

Damian was back in his office checking on the run he designed before he left for the meeting with Natalie. He gave a silent cheer as he found his first new evidence of Hermione's parents' lives. He managed to locate them on the public cameras in Shepard Canyon.

When he pulled up the pictures though the excitement bubble burst. They managed to consistently keep their faces turned away from the camera while driving, just like the pictures in the house. He thought that kind of behavior might be taught by a spy organization.

He sat back staring at the screen of results, then leaned forward and furiously typed away. He wrote a second program to map her parents movements for several months to see if that told him anything, then he walked away letting the computer chips grind away at a huge amount of data. It was one of those programs that he wasn't sure would give him anything useful but until he tried it, he wouldn't know.

He left his office to walk towards one of the experimental rooms that he set up. He was working on two additional devices for the protective vests - a strobe stun gun, and a pneumatic tranquilizer gun. He put aside the tranquilizer gun and focused on the strobe stun gun. Using an LED flashlight, he created a pulsing light that was very hard to look at. Anyone who looked into the light would be disoriented, lose their sense of balance and fall to the ground. He wanted to do a few more tests on it and then it would be ready to be added to the protective vests for Ariana and Hermione.

An hour later, he was satisfied with his testing and had the two strobe lights ready to go. Ariana was picking Hermione up from school without him and they would journey to his home tonight for Hermione to get her vest. Now it was time to work on the men that seemed to be chasing Ariana. He hadn't as yet identified the first man who had chased her and he hadn't done anything with the pictures she taken in Silicon Valley when her car tire was stabbed. Another hour of work on locating information on the man and the cars left him with little confidence that he had the right answers. It was time to head home and maybe he would see if he could chat with Natalie along the way. He wondered what her thoughts were about the information Lily had relayed.

18-CHAPTER EIGHTEEN

"So, what did you think of Lily?' Damian asked when Natalie answered his phone call.

"As a cop, I don't have much faith in people changing their lives; in fact I was trying to think of someone I arrested in the last decade that reformed and I was unable to think of a single con that turned their life around. Lily feels like she has, but I assume that you're not just taking her word for it?"

"What do you think?" Damian asked.

"My guess is that you wouldn't have hired her unless you were convinced that you could access all of her accounts - email and financial to assure yourself that she was on the right path."

"You'd be right about that plus I let her know I had the means to steal every last dime from her at the moment. She may overtake me intellectually someday, but not now. I think she's committed to staying straight due to her child and the fact that she only set out to rob banks on a lark and that song no longer plays for her. I thought she made some salient points on the bank robbery. I think the police and the FBI had it wrong from the start about multiple robbers using the equipment left in the tunnel. How do we move forward? What does your detective think about the sales of the safe deposit box stuff?"

"As you know, he thinks that the University has a smart group of kids assisting me. He used your data to get search warrants for the major auction sites. Obviously we want to trace the stolen goods. Once the judge issues the search warrant, we'll still be at least thirty and probably sixty days out to get the seller information. This is a cold case, so we can't light a fire under anyone to get information sooner than that."

"Are you willing to reconsider the tools used in the heist?"

"Yes, after talking to Lily. I'm starting to see this as unlikely to be a team attack."

"Is there an engineer mentioned in any of the documents as being consulted on the case?" Damian asked. He had the full file, but he thought that Natalie might remember some details off the top of her head.

"They didn't use an engineer at the time. It was too costly. Perhaps if they caught the perpetrator they might have used an engineer to help with their court case, but we local police departments can rarely afford consultants on a case such as this."

"How about the bank employees? I know none were suspected at that time, but it wouldn't hurt to go back and verify that. And one more question, can you give me a run of other things that were happening at the same time? Can you get a copy of whatever was called into local police and fire as needing their assistance?"

"Yeah I can do that, but I still can't afford to hire an engineer to render an opinion."

"That's okay, I'm starting to see the viewpoint of your fellow cops, just because it was possible from an engineering point of view, I'm not sure that gets us anywhere. Obviously it was possible or the robbery wouldn't have occurred."

"The bank employee names are in your file on page twenty-three. Why don't we both work those names?" Natalie suggested. "By the way, you have unusual background noises on this call, are those inventions in the background?"

Damian laughed and said, "No, we began this conversation while I was pulling into the parking lot at the marina, then you heard the wind as I crossed the bay, and then maybe you heard my dock folding up. I'm in my home office now," Damian said as he examined the page that contained the names. There were eight listed.

It made him think, "Natalie, this list must be the employees that were just at the bank that day. It seems too small to represent everyone needed to operate a bank branch. I would also want to know the cleaning service as well as any building repairs that were made in the year before the robbery."

"That's not in your file. I'll have to contact the bank tomorrow and they'll need time to research it. If their corporate offices hire those services out, it may take even longer to get the information."

"One final question and I know this one is out there. Could the tunnel and digging be a diversion for another guy simply walking in the bank after hours and opening the vault?"

"Well," Natalie paused and then continued after some thought, "Anything is possible I suppose. Let me think about your question and re-read the file. If you're right, it would be a game changer in looking for suspects and understanding the robbery."

"Yeah well it's just a thought. After talking to Lily, I read up on bank robberies and the things people have tried over the last fifty years, so that gave me some new ways to look at this case."

"Maybe I'll do the same thing and see if it shakes any new thoughts loose in my head. Let me know if you discover anything on the employees."

Damien glanced at the clock after he ended the conversation with Natalie. Ariana should be picking up Hermione from school about now. He opened his program containing surveillance cameras on Ariana's property and all looked quiet. He peered at the end of the driveway and made a note to himself to install one camera further out close to the road. He stared at the cameras, anxiety roiling inside him over whomever was following Ariana. He breathed a sigh of relief when he saw her car come down the driveway. He watched her deactivate his various traps to get the car in the garage. No one followed them and soon they were inside the safety of her house, with his gadgets re-engaged for their safety. The two women would be over soon as they wanted to cross the bay in daylight.

While he waited for them to arrive in an hour or so, he would work on doing background checks of the bank employees. As he was going through the list, he was amazed by how many employees were still working at the bank nine years later. Either they lived in the neighborhood and it was convenient or management made the job enjoyable. He'd have a hard time suspecting anyone that still worked at the bank nine years after the robbery. It was too long a time to keep up the pretense of not having an extra sixty million dollars to spend.

He thought of another angle - safe deposit boxes. Were all of the boxes opened? If not, why not? Were any empty boxes opened? If not, then someone had to have prior knowledge of box ownership. Damian went back and perused the police report on the boxes. It said that the vault contained some six hundred boxes and it was not immediately obvious as to which boxes were opened. Some boxes were left opened and still contained paper contents. Others were completely empty, still some were available for rent. The bank notified each owner of the robbery and asked them to come in and view their contents reporting to police any items that were missing. Again Damian checked the reports and all but five owners contacted the bank. He decided to focus on those five owners as well as the small percent of owners whose boxes were not broken into.

He was so intent in his research that he was startled when he heard his perimeter alarm sound and realized he needed to open the watercraft garage for Ariana's boat that was shortly arriving. Seconds later he stood at the garage entrance watching the door open and the whirl of the motor that moved the dock. Once it unfolded, he saw Ariana gently steering the boat into the dock. Hermione stood on the dock side ready to throw the ropes to him.

The dock and boat bounced off each other and rocked a little and Damian soon had the boat tied down.

"Sorry about my late arrival here, I was working on the bank heist. Did you ladies have a great day?" Damian asked with a smile on his face

"No," Hermione said and she walked past into the house and up the stairs.

The trouble with owning a small house on top of a small island inside San Francisco Bay was there were few places to hide. His head swiveled to Ariana and said, "What happened?"

19-Chapter Nineteen

"Someone started a rumor about her on Instagram," Ariana said

"She usually has a pretty thick skin. What was said that bothered her?"

"Someone posted a picture of two adults and labeled them as Hermione's parents and said they weren't dead rather they sent her away because they didn't like her."

"Wow, that's ugly. Can you show me the post? I'm wondering if the person that posted the comment on Facebook in Chinese is the same one who did this."

Ariana started and then hit herself on the side of the head and muttered, "Why didn't I think of that?"

The two of them were soon standing at his workbench looking up the comment on Instagram. Damian traced it back through a variety of servers. After the fifth server re-direction, he looked up at Ariana and said, "This is the same behavior as the Facebook post. Perhaps it will make her less depressed to know it's coming from the same source and not one of her classmates."

"It might. Let's go find her."

In a short time all three of them were seated on the rocky edge of the island near the sand beach. Bailey, Bella, and Miguel were all keeping the teenager company as she mumbled to herself and skipped rocks.

"So I think the person that left you the message in Chinese on Facebook is the same person who posted that picture on Instagram and made those snarky comments about your parents."

"What?" asked the teenager in disbelief.

"That kind of cruel comment sounded a little too sophisticated for your fellow teenagers so I tracked the message on the internet. The message originated outside the United States and I don't think any of your classmates have the sophistication to do that, do you?" Damian said.

Hermione was quiet for a long time then said, "No."

"Did your classmates say anything about the post?" Damian asked. "By the way it's gone from cyberspace."

"Yes, they thought it was weird."

"I would call it rude rather than weird," Ariana said.

Hermione had her head down and was swinging her legs restlessly. The three of them sat in silence. Finally, Hermione pushed off the rock landing on the sand and turned to the two adults and said, "I guess you better show me how this vest works."

"Hermione, I think these social media posts point out the need for you to be careful at all times. Ignore any social media posting you don't like. Pretend they don't exist and be on alert for any strangers approaching you. I think you're safe at school, but not anywhere else. The vest will help even the odds in your and Ariana's favor."

"Okay," was Hermione's discouraged reply.

The three walked back up the island slope for Hermione to try the vest and to cook dinner. She looked at the vest with pity as it was so ugly. No one her age walked around wearing a photographer's vest.

"I like your newest gadget, Damian, but you need to improve its look - I wouldn't be caught dead wearing it at school. I'll carry it in my backpack. No one will guess its power as a weapon," Hermione said with conviction.

"I'm sorry that a fourteen year old girl has to worry about being hurt or kidnapped," he replied solemnly.

"Fifteen year old, you forgot I aged over the summer," said Hermione with some humor in her voice.

"Yeah, well I'm in my fourth decade and these guys are scaring the bejeezus out of me," Ariana replied.

"Well ladies, I wish these guys would go after me, but they don't seem to have discovered me yet."

"You got enough action in the last case from the Aryan Brotherhood, so it's okay if the thugs take a pass on you this time,"

Hermione offered reassuringly.

"Actually, it is an interesting question as I am around a lot. Perhaps they don't know where the boat goes when it leaves and the security system probably hasn't allowed them to get close to the boat since that first time to plant any bugs on it. Of course they could take a picture of me and maybe figure out who I am and where I live, but I don't think so. I have a program that looks for any public information about me daily and then wipes it out if any is found. They could also go after Ariana online, but they're not. I think they're focused on you, kiddo, hoping you'll make a stupid move that will make you vulnerable to capture."

"My parents trained me too well for that. Even today with that weird post, I wasn't tempted to run away from school."

"That's an interesting thought. I wonder if they're monitoring Hermione's movements at the school?" Ariana asked.

"Do you know if your school has cameras focused on the entrance?" Damian asked Hermione.

"They say they don't, but most of the students think there are," Hermione replied.

"Okay I'll look into that too and any other cameras I can find in your neighborhood. Hermione, I don't know what your parents did for a living but they have to be connected to some spy organization. Whomever is chasing them is affiliated with some other spy organization. I tried to track your parents through the city cameras in Shepard's Canyon and every single picture of them is a side of the face shot. They managed day after day to turn their heads whenever they passed by public cameras. That's not luck; it's training that made them so good."

"Do you think they're still alive?" Hermione asked.

Ariana reached out and hugged the girl while Damian said, "I don't know. I can think of scenarios where the behavior we're seeing from strangers makes sense only if your parents are alive. At other times, I think the bad guys think that your parents must have told you something that they want to know. We have no real way of knowing at the moment, but I'd say it's reasonable for you to have hope that they're still alive."

Damian felt like a mean adult for telling the kid that her parents might be dead or alive. He probably should just stick with her parents were alive; give the kid some hope.

"That's what I think as well," Hermione said. "They may be

alive, but whatever the problem is that made them disappear may not get resolved for several more years. Meanwhile I have to plan for the future."

Damian thought how lucky he and Ariana were to be graced by this kid who was so well behaved with no teenage drama queen scenes. Maybe it was time to change the subject to move their thoughts on to something happier.

"Were you able to arrange a sporting event to introduce Lily and her son to our group?" Damian asked.

"Yes, we're attending a Giants game next week," Ariana replied. Looking at Hermione, she added, "Lily is an interesting character and she reminds Damian and I of you. We've invited her to bring her son, and so it will be an outing with everyone's significant other. She said her son's a baseball fanatic. It's a Tuesday game, Hermione, so we'll arrive at the ballpark after water polo practice."

"Sounds interesting. What project is Lily going to work on?"

"She has a math background, so I'm lining her up to work on the Artificial Intelligence I want to use on a DNA analyzer for use by the cops in the field."

"Does she have a background in artificial intelligence?" Hermione asked.

"Not at all, but her math background should serve her well so I'm not worried. Besides she's smart and if she doesn't know something, she'll just study a topic until she figures it out."

Half an hour later, Ariana and Hermione were waving goodbye wearing their matching ugly vests. Both seemed to feel empowered to take on any adversaries.

Damian found himself pausing as he frequently did, asking why he didn't contact the police and get some real protection for Hermione. Despite his faith in his computer skills, he was afraid some hole would be found in their story and the teenager would end up in foster care. Foster care had been so bad for Damian, he couldn't imagine leaving a wonderful kid like Hermione alone in that system. So again, he kept his mouth shut and hoped he'd provided the ladies with enough protection to keep them safe.

He went back inside to work on the bank heist again and its safe deposit boxes. He had five boxes in which the owners never came forward. He checked the records again to see when the police or bank last searched for the owners of those five boxes. He also looked at the size of the boxes. All were the smallest box available to rent. They would be able to hold a little jewelry as long as it wasn't stored in a big fancy case, important papers or perhaps two or three bouillons of gold. So the boxes could contain from zero to perhaps a million dollars if the box was entirely filled with raw precious stones.

The police reports showed that the last attempt to contact the owners was about four months after the heist. The bank was supposed to eventually turn the box over to the state who would attempt to find the owner and if they couldn't find the owner, then auction off the contents and hold the proceeds until the owner showed up. So what happened to the five boxes and was that number unusual for your average vault? Looking at data the number wasn't unusual nor the fact that the State of California laid claim to the five boxes three years later. So how did he find what had been in the boxes and who allegedly owned them?

To Damian's surprise, he found that all five boxes were left intact. The FBI had left a lien that said they were to be contacted when any of the owners contacted the bank. The boxes had sat in suspended animation ever since. Could Natalie get a search warrant for them? According to an FBI report, the contents were logged on an exhibit. He looked through the police file, but couldn't find the exhibit. He dropped an email to Natalie explaining his finding and asking if she could get a search warrant for those boxes.

A short time later, she responded that she could and would get it and that they could probably go look at the boxes within a few days. She also hadn't found the referenced exhibit that contained the contents of those five boxes. It must have been an error made by the original investigators at the time. Cool, thought Damian, and then added to his email to Natalie some specific items to be covered by the search warrant like a history of the box.

That done, he went back to the employee list. In doing a comparison of the police reports to the list, he determined that the list included just those employees that worked at the bank during the robbery, and not everyone that was employed by the bank. Was there a way he could determine that? The Willow Glen bank was a branch of a large national bank. He looked at that large national system and determined that they used a payroll system he knew how to hack into. Using the names of two current employees he figured out the branch code part of the payroll system. Then he had to find the archive and determine the total number of employees at that location that were paid in the week before and two weeks after the bank robbery. He had another fifteen names now to add to the list. Then he needed one more look into the system to see if they had a system wherein an employee that usually worked at a different branch might be charged to the branch in Willow Glen. After studying records, he decided either staff didn't work multiple branch locations or if they did, their payroll hours and dollars were transferred later as an accounting transaction. Well he did the best he could accounting for all employees and since he had another fifteen names than were listed in the police report, he felt pretty proud of his investigative efforts.

He stood up and stretched and called it quits for the night. Better to go to bed on an investigative high than plug away a few more hours on the additional employees. He was pleased that he'd been able to find new angles to investigate. He wasn't sure they would lead him anywhere but it was always exciting to come across new information.

20-CHAPTER TWENTY

Damian woke up to a fog shrouded island. The fog was so dense that he couldn't see the water lapping his island. He'd probably never see the sunshine that day as Mother Nature would have to work hard burning away the thick fog. When he took over the island he'd rehabilitated the United States Coast Guard fog bell and it was set to sound every two minutes during a certain density of fog. The last thing he wanted was a boat running into his island because the boater couldn't see it before it was too late. Usually in these bad conditions, only the major ferries were out on the bay, but Damian always made allowances for the stupidity of boat drivers and so he had a bell sounding from near the water's edge.

Ariana and Hermione had nothing more planned this week other than a shopping excursion into the city. He volunteered to escort them; which was quite a sacrifice on his part, but they continued to feel powerful in their protective vests and turned him down. He planned a lazy week-end, getting in a work-out, fishing, and restocking his island. Mike, from the marina, would be transporting him later over to his truck and he had a long shopping list. Mike's bigger boat was needed to transport his supplies back to the island. On Sunday, the first football game of the season was on and he was looking forward to that; by all standards, a low key couple of days.

After his workout and breakfast, he returned to the curiosity of the additional names. Were any of the additional names the same as the names of ownership for the safe deposit boxes? No. Then he did a cross search of the addresses of all employees and safe deposit box owners.

Bingo there was his first match! The box owner and employee had different names but they both had the same address on Lincoln Ave in Willow Glen. Using Google Earth he looked up the address and found it to be a donut shop. Then he went back and looked at city records and it had been a donut shop for some forty years through five different owners. The last ownership change occurred five years ago when it changed from one owner to another well after the robbery. He looked up the owners and found that during the time of the robbery a Tim Ho owned it and the new owner's name was Joey Kim. He wondered if Mr. Kim had ever received the safe deposit notices. He looked at the time and decided it was time to go visit the Willow Glen neighborhood. He went outside and the fog had lifted enough to see about two-hundred yards he estimated; safe enough for a boat. The bank would be open for another three hours and it was as good a time as any to get the lay of the land. He vaguely remembered dining with his deceased wife at one of the many restaurants located near the downtown area perhaps a decade ago; certainly prior to the bank robbery.

He called Natalie to let her know of his direction and she was interested in his new information and volunteered to meet him in the neighborhood. He rescheduled his return time with Mike and soon met him on his beach for transport to his truck in the marina parking lot. About an hour and a half later he was searching for parking in one of Willow Glen's busy side streets. After a three block walk, he spotted Natalie standing outside of the bank reading something on her phone.

"Hey Natalie, how's it going?" Damian asked as he reached over and placed a hand on her arm as a greeting.

"It's a little hot out, but I assume it's much colder at home on your island."

"Yeah there was heavy fog there this morning though it lightened enough to get off my island. I started in the high fifties temperature- wise and by the time I reached this city, it'd climbed to near ninety degree on my car's thermometer. Ugh that's too hot. So how do you want to approach the bank?"

"Since I don't have a search warrant I would suggest we walk in and ask for management, then explain that we're private detectives taking another look at their robbery nine years ago. I'll show my license and hopefully that will stop them from calling the police on us."

"I don't see a need to go into the vault, so we won't be asking to see any confidential areas which should appease them. I'd like to just sit in a chair in the lobby and look around."

"Okay let's do it," Natalie said as she reached for the bank door and they entered.

A short time later they were sitting across the street chatting over coffee as to what they observed. On the way to the meeting with Natalie, he stopped at the donut shop and casually asked the owner about the business.

"I think it's possible for someone to have walked in the vault as much as it was for them to tunnel into the vault. We know a tunnel was built but that doesn't confirm that it was used for the actually robbery. I want to follow up on the lead of this employee that wasn't on the current employee list at the time of the robbery who had a street address and safe deposit box of the donut shop. That's three coincidences that I don't like."

"What's the missing employee's name?" Natalie asked.

"Arielle Joseph, she was a teller who had worked there for a year, but quit just two days before the robbery."

"Where is she now?"

"She disappeared off the face of the earth nine years ago just before the robbery."

"Why wasn't she investigated at the time?"

"I think she probably slipped everyone's mind. She gave and worked a two week notice, and then she dropped out of sight as Arielle Joseph."

Natalie was staring at him as he described the woman, dumbfounded that this might be their robber. Why hadn't someone picked it up nine years ago, and then she knew what Damian meant with his description of a planned departure.

"Wow! I wonder if she's our robber? Wouldn't that be an amazing plan if everyone distracted by a tunnel, missed the real evidence in the robbery? I mean this sounds like an inside job with the most elaborate cover-up scheme the FBI has ever seen," Natalie said then another thought came to mind, "Wouldn't they have deactivated her security clearance upon leaving?"

"I would have thought so, but maybe she figured out how to get a duplicate."

"So what's the role of the floral store and the tunnel? Do you think this was a two person job with the second person creating the diversion of the tunnel?" Natalie had her own thoughts, but she was always curious as to what Damian thought.

"On the surface so far it seems that might be a scenario, but I think we need to do a lot more research on the woman and the shop owner. Maybe re-think how it went down and chase clues from there. For all we know, the tunnel was used for the robbery, but maybe with different tools than the ones left behind. I think the route of the robbery is not confirmed."

They both had been staring at the storefront that had once been a florist shop. The current occupant was a hair salon. According to the police report, the building had sat empty for six months as it was considered a crime scene. Eventually, it was turned back to the landlord who'd been required to seal the tunnel to the FBI's satisfaction. There had been another occupant before the present salon had begun renting the space three years ago.

"So I wonder what the deal was with the donut shop?" Natalie mused. "There must have been something worked out with the owner. There would have been employment stuff mailed to the address. I wonder if there's a room to rent on its premises? We need to talk to the prior owner, Tim Ho, and see what he remembers."

"Let's go ask the current owner if he has a spare room and if he knows anything about the previous owner," Damian suggested.

Walking two blocks south, they found the donut shop. Its hours stated it was open from five in the morning till two in the afternoon. It smelled good to Damian; he liked the scent of sugar on a deep fried bread smell. Realizing he was hungry, he ordered a few donuts for himself and Natalie and then asked a few questions.

They walked north again toward their respective vehicles munching on deliciously puffy donuts covered with chocolate and glazed twists.

"Too bad the previous owner died from lung cancer last year. I bet he was never interviewed by the cops at the time of the robbery as they didn't see the connection," Natalie said.

"Let me look into his family. In my experience, successful donut shops are operated by families. Perhaps a wife or children remember something from that time. Since you're local, do you want to question them?"

"Yes I'll take that. I have a friend who speaks Vietnamese, so I might take her with me to make sure the wife understands my questions and is not threatened by my P.I. license. I think I'll call her now as I'm excited to follow this new thread of investigation."

Damian and Natalie arrived at their cars and parted company to pursue their own chores. A few hours later, Damian and several boxes were occupying Mike's pontoon boat deck. Damian would use his drone to lift the packages up the rocky cliffs of his island home to his front door.

21-CHAPTER TWENTY-ONE

It was hours since he left Natalie and he noted that she'd managed to contact the family of Mr. Ho. His wife had benefited from the use of the interpreter that Natalie included in her meeting with the woman.

She had worked in her husband's shop off and on for twenty years. A girl had rented a room in the back for about a year. They knew she worked down the street at the bank as they sometimes saw her there. She told them she was a student with large college loans and she wanted to rent an empty room they had in the back of their shop for a year. There was no bathroom attached, but the shop had one she could use for a toilet. Mrs. Ho said she and her husband had lived there when they were trying to save money. Like Ms. Joseph, they had a gym membership that they'd used for showers. Yes, her mail was delivered to the shop. They had no complaints about her; she was quiet and paid her rent on time. They closed the shop about three in the afternoon and so had no idea what she did in the evenings, but there was never any damage in the shop. When asked to describe her, she said, 'an average woman in her twenties, brown hair to the middle of her back, about five feet six inches tall, pale skin and nothing remarkable.' I asked her if she worked with an artist could he help her draw a picture of the woman's face and she said no. Since the girl was 'American looking' she had no distinguishable features she could remember.

Damian picked up the phone and called Natalie interested in hearing more.

"What's an American looking female?"

Natalie laughed and replied, "My friend says it's the same for her - we Americans, whether Caucasian, Hispanic, or black all look alike to her at a certain age. Mrs. Ho couldn't reliably tell me if Ms. Joseph was Hispanic or Caucasian. I'm going to talk to a police sketch artist on Monday and see if he thinks he could get anywhere with her description, and I'm also going to circle back to the bank and see if any of the employees can help us on a sketch."

"If we can find a reliable sketch, then I can run it through my various facial recognition programs and see if we get a hit. It sounds like Ms. Joseph had a talent for making herself look average. The police have a sketch of the florist store owner, right?" Damian asked thinking back to the contents of the police file.

"Yeah they do. I think I'll run the picture by Mrs. Ho to see if she recognizes the florist. If this was a pair doing the robbery, then sometime during the year that the donut shop room was rented, they had to have been seen together." Natalie said.

"Can you send me another copy of the florist's picture? The one I have is too grainy for my purpose."

"Sure. This is exciting, I think we're getting somewhere!"

"We have no proof Ms. Joseph was involved in the robbery and we can't even do a fingerprint match of the prior evidence since as an employee, her fingerprint would legitimately be there."

"True, but there's just too much weirdness about Ms. Joseph for me not to think she had a role in the robbery."

"Cop instinct?"

"That's what my gut is telling me."

"Have you ever been wrong?"

"No. My gut doesn't come into play with every case, but when it does, it's always right."

"I thought you cops were supposed to chase only the facts? Isn't that what Joe Friday said?" Natalie could hear the amusement in Damian's voice with the question.

"Yeah, well, Joe Friday was a detective like sixty years ago and by the way he never said the phrase you're thinking of - 'Just the facts, ma'am', it was a spoof of detective Friday that delivered the famous line," Natalie said.

"You're kidding right? He must have said that line since it was so brilliant."

"Well, look it up and you'll see that I'm right."

"Ok. It sounds like there isn't much for me to do until you have a conversation with Mrs. Ho."

"Just keep searching for Arielle Joseph, but other than that I'd suggest you go back to trying to create that brilliant DNA analysis machine you've been promising me," Natalie said.

After the call ended, Damian sighed with frustration. He could gather significant evidence that assisted the police to solve a cold case, but he couldn't solve the mystery of Hermione. He sat back thinking about the two men identified as chasing Ariana and the countries they represented. True, their passports could be faked, but what did the two countries have in common? Then he thought back to something that Hermione had said about her parents - her dad worked in the pharmaceutical business. He remembered hearing about some problem with drugs in that part of the world. Thirty minutes later, he had a possible idea of what demons might be chasing Hermione's parents. If he chased the angle, maybe he'd find some answers.

Organized crime units referred by the term 'Triad' were involved in the illegal manufacture of prescription drugs and illicit drugs like crystal meth. Perhaps, some of the enforcers from a Triad were chasing Hermione's parents. Maybe he had some role in uncovering the production of either substance. In Malaysia, criminals caught doing either were executed as punishment. Yikes. Some drug firms in China had been caught buying from these counterfeit prescription manufacturers.

The problem with the illegal manufacturers wasn't just that they offered look-a-like drugs at a cheap price; the real problem was there was no guarantee of the chemical content of the pills which had resulted in the deaths of hundreds of patients who took them. Researching this problem, Damian found the counterfeit scheme worth seventy-five billion dollars a year. This equaled seventy-five billion reasons to get rid of Hermione's parents if her father had a role in closing down these companies. However, it failed to explain why they were after Hermione herself. Did they have a piece of evidence that they shared with the teenager or hid among her possessions?

Thinking back to the surveillance tape, he'd watched the hoodlum in the house basically sit and watch television. He couldn't recall a time that he noticed Mr. Lee doing a diligent search of the house. He went back to the electronic file that contained the footage from the house both at the time Hermione's parents were kidnapped as well as the subsequent month. There was a search that had occurred but it was obvious that it had been for the teenager and not for some small memory stick or computer component. So what did the kid have?

He thought back to the night he'd discovered her in the dinghy. What did she have on her or with her that might hold some fraudulent drug information? Her clothes had pockets in them so she could have hid something small in them. She also wore a pendant and earrings and since her parents seemed to be in the business of spying, perhaps those were data storage items. The only other thing he could think of was an implant. Surely her parents wouldn't have implanted their own child with some kind of data device? Should he ask her if she had an implant? Given that she refused to provide many answers to questions about her parents, would she be interested in telling him the truth about what secret she held? Did she even know that she had some secret information?

He sighed and sent an email to Ariana,

'I know this sounds like a weird question, but have you ever noticed an incision on Hermione's body?'

A while later, she responded,

'No, but I wasn't looking for one either. I'll look tomorrow when we go swimming. It's a weird question, but I'm sure you have a reason for asking it.'

'I'm stuck on why anyone is after Hermione. I thought back to the night I found her in the dinghy but I can't remember anything specifically on her that's worth kidnapping her for. So I wondered if she had some kind of implant that contained information. You know a little like the Jason Bourne conspiracy books.'

'I haven't read any of those books or watched the movies, but I hope her parents wouldn't have done something like that to their child.'

'Yeah, me too.'

They ended their conversation and Damian called it quits for the day.

22-Chapter Twenty-Two

Sunday arrived as one of those rare days in San Francisco where there was no fog. Damian thought of the Boudin sourdough bread factory on Fisherman's Wharf and how the bakers must be lamenting the sunshine. They needed the fog for their recipe to attain perfection with the yeast. Visitors would walk away with bread that rose a little bit less on a day like today. After he had a leisurely breakfast and coffee, reading the news and sports online, he put his wetsuit on for a swim in the bay. It was that kind of day where a resident should exploit the outdoors on one of those rare sunny days.

He paused and gave thought for the day ahead and what his schedule should be. Certainly he should get in some fishing on such a beautiful day. He could freeze the extra fish he caught and debated going out in his dinghy to fish somewhere else on the bay or even off the coast, but the winds were moderate which meant that his boat would drift toward shore and rock over the waves. He pulled in his twelfth fish and decided it was time to take his embarrassment of riches inside to clean, skin, and freeze when his cell phone rang.

"Hey Damian, how's your Sunday so far?"

"Eddie would have enjoyed my morning; I caught twelve fish in under an hour."

Eddie was Natalie's husband of nearly three decades and he liked to tell fishing stories.

"Did you use some super-duper technology to find them or

attract them?"

"No, that would take all of the fun out of fishing. The fish were just hungry for worms this morning. What's up?"

"I was able to interview Mrs. Ho again this morning and we got a few more clues. I wanted to see what you could do with the new information."

"Okay tell me what you want researched."

"Mrs. Ho said they asked her not to bring any overnight guests back to her room since she had a key to the donut shop and they didn't trust anyone but her."

"Did they ever see a guest visit her?"

"No, but she also said she was positive that she didn't come home every night as they had an alarm system that had to be deactivated to go in and out and her husband checked every morning the girl was in residence just to make sure she was locking it. Perhaps one or two in seven days she didn't come home at night."

"Did Mrs. Ho have any idea where she went?"

"No, so I asked her if she saw her with anyone around town, or did she take frequent lunch breaks from the bank with anyone in particular. You know Willow Glen can be like a small town with everyone knowing each other."

"And?" Damian was wishing Natalie would get to the point of her phone call.

"And she was spotted at times with other tellers from the bank which was sort of what you would expect. The only other person she would see her with was a florist shop employee."

"Employee?" Damian said pondering the possibilities and thinking back to the police file. "Was anyone ever interviewed who worked at the florist shop?"

"No, both the owner and the employee disappeared off the face of the earth and that's part of the reason they were assumed to be involved in the robbery."

"Do you think they might be one in the same?"

"One and the same what?"

"Was the owner and the employee the same person?"

"I think that's one of several theories they had at the time that they were unable to confirm or deny."

"Lily suggested we follow up on credit card receipts to get business information. Have you had the chance to do that?"

"No, mostly because I'm not sure where to start since it was nine years ago."

"I would think the credit card companies could look up the florist by the street address and time period specified. But I suppose you would need a search warrant for that."

"I'll add it to my list of search warrant needs. Would you be able to find that information out of curiosity?"

"Maybe," mused Damian. "It depends if they have swept that information into an off-line archive computer. If they have, I can't reach it. Did you look through the records to see if your guys looked for those records nine years ago?"

"Yeah they didn't think to look at that particular piece of data. They looked for records of ownership, but the names lead to dead ends."

"Could anyone describe the owner? I mean what if the employee and the owner were one and the same person?"

"That's a good question; let me flip back through the file and see what I can find."

"I assume the FBI fingerprinted the florist shop?" "Yeah, they did, but like the bank, the difficulty was the wide number of prints in a public business."

"Do you have the prints collected by location?"

"Yes, as part the chain of custody documentation, we indicate where the fingerprint has been collected from at a location."

"Is there a bathroom door, computer mouse, or backdoor on the list? I would think those areas would most likely have the owner's prints."

Damian could hear Natalie shuffling paper in the background as silence reigned on the phone. Then she said, "Looks like they have prints from those surfaces, perhaps about twenty to thirty in total. Again how do we weed out the prints we don't care about?"

"Do you think we could get into the donut shop and take prints off the surfaces there and then see if there are any matches? I understand that prints can live on some surfaces for up to forty years."

"You and I could probably do it, but I won't get the crime scene team there I don't think. I haven't done prints since I was in the police academy. Do you have access to the Live Scan program that matches them?"

"I do. You get us in and I'll help you collect prints off the surfaces."

"Okay, I believe the shop is open for another hour, so I'm going to go talk to the owner now. I'd love to get prints when the business is closed, which might be soon. Can you get here quickly if the owner agrees to let us do it today? Like you might have to leave in the next fifteen minutes."

"Yeah, I can help today. Traffic to get there will be much worse tomorrow so right now is good. I'll collect the items we need and be ready to leave when you call. If you could come pick me up at a marina in Redwood City instead of me traveling to the Richmond Marina, I could cut perhaps thirty minutes off my commute."

"Let me see what the owner says and I just might be picking you up there soon. Life is always an adventure with you, Damian."

"Back at you, Natalie."

The call ended and Damian walked through his lab gathering supplies. He'd been playing with fingerprints on different surfaces and so he thought he was as prepared as he could be. Then he had a new idea for Hermione's identity. What if he tried to match her DNA to a database? Her parents had managed to erase their existence from all databases, but maybe he could find a match in an aunt or uncle or cousin. Once he got beyond Natalie's quest for prints in the donut shop, he'd see what he could find in Hermione's bedroom that might contain DNA - perhaps a hair was on the floor in her bedroom or his bathroom. It would be so much simpler if the kid would just trust him, but he guessed she was working against a lifetime of training to trust no one but her parents.

A short time later, he had word from Natalie that she was on her way to Redwood City to pick him up if he would provide an address. He did that and hopped aboard his speedy two seater boat and bounced across the bay, likely over the speed limit, towards the marina he scouted out in Redwood City. He tied his boat up as a guest dock and let the harbor master know he'd be back in a few hours. As he walked out of the harbor master's office, he saw Natalie pulling up. He jumped in the car and she turned around to head south to Willow Glen. The owner would be closing in fifteen minutes and he generally stayed an hour tidying everything up so it was ready the next day. He indicated he was willing to wait for them to finish. Damian decided to order a couple of dozen donuts from the man to be sent to the closest police department by way of thanks for staying behind for them.

They arrived back to find the owner waiting for them to enter before he locked the door behind them and put the closed sign in the window. They introduced themselves to Mr. Kim and after a few questions asked and answered by both parties, he returned to closing his business for the day while Natalie and Damian went to work finding fingerprints.

Shining a ultra-violet light, their area of interest had a surplus of prints. They discussed what they found as Damian shined the light on the various knobs and surfaces inside the small bedroom. Natalie relayed the furniture set-up that Mrs. Ho had seen in her tenant's room. Fortunately when Mr. Kim took over they had not used the room for anything other than storage. Because of the room's purpose, he hadn't bothered painting it like he did the more public areas including the bathroom she'd used. They had already decided not to try and find prints in the bathroom as it seemed that potentially thousands had used the room and it had been painted so the likelihood of finding Ms. Joseph's prints was next to nil. After discussing the placement of the furniture, Natalie pantomimed where she might have touched the wall if she lived in the little room.

An hour later, they thanked the owner for access to the room, bought all his unsold donuts that day and left. They made two sets of fingerprints - one for Damian to take home and analyze, and the other for Natalie to send to SJPD for fingerprinting once she got Detective Shimoda's approval for the analysis. She expected no issue with the detective, it was just that it would take time to go through the official steps. Natalie had built her consultant reputation by solving two, twenty-year old cold murder cases; if she solved a nearly ten year old bank robbery that the department and FBI were unable to solve, then she'd have her retirement gig reputation cemented as an excellent detective and consultant.

They dropped the donuts at Natalie's car and then had a conversation about the hair salon. In the end, they decided not to try and get prints there as they had painted and changed door knobs with each ownership change, so the odds were against them getting any quality evidence.

Natalie pulled into the parking area at the marina and Damian got out, bag in hand. He promised to call her as soon as he had anything interesting. As he wasn't an expert, they would still have to wait on the official results, but it would allow the investigation to move forward if they could identify who Arielle Joseph was and where she was located now.

22-CHAPTER TWENTY-THREE

It was late in the afternoon when he returned to the island, unloading his supplies and the fingerprint evidence. He was settling in to work at his lab when he heard the alarm go off for Ariana's house. He quickly looked at the monitors and discovered a man walking up from the bay towards the house and one parked at the end of her driveway.

He called Ariana's cell and when she answered, asked, "Are you home?"

"No, Hermione and I met up with a friend of hers and her mother in town at my favorite tea house. Why?"

"There are two men trying to get into your house. One is at the end of the driveway and the other docked a boat. I'm going to call the police as one of the men should shortly be trapped in a net."

"I'll call them, hold on," Ariana said and placed him on hold while she called 9-1-1. She told the police that her security system alarmed and she could see burglars trying to break into her house from both the road and the bay. They collected her particulars and said they would dispatch officers immediately. She deactivated the driveway safeguards as she didn't want her local police hit with a pepper juice shower.

Connecting back to Damian she said, "The police are going to dispatch a patrol car. So I think I'll head home. Did the man end up in a net?"

"Yes, and he's fighting his way out with a knife. I'm going to hop in my boat and head over as well. I'll bring a new net to reset your system."

They ended their call and Ariana stepped back inside the café to collect Hermione and head home. After a brief explanation to the other girl and her mother, they left. Ariana wanted to make sure the police arrived before she and Hermione did so they cautiously approached their road hoping to see the police in front of them. She looked down the street and saw nothing, but then she looked in her rear view mirror and saw a patrol car approaching with its lights on, but no siren. She pulled to the right side of the road to let the car pass, but held her hand out to stop them. Once they stopped, she told them she was the one who called and they proceeded forward with the patrol car in the lead.

"If I had been thinking, I probably should have left you with Megan's mother rather than expose you to the danger here. Sorry about that," Ariana said.

I'm safe with you here and I might have been in danger with Megan's mom. What if this burglary was just a diversion to get you to run home but I was the real target in town?"

Ariana looked at Hermione and let out a small laugh, "Nice try, kiddo, I can see you'll excel in a creative writing class."

Hermione just grinned in response as they pulled up to the house behind the patrol car.

They got serious as they approached the backyard. They found a net sitting on the ground that had been shredded by a knife, but was now empty and a boat just a few yards out from the dock, a man looking back over his shoulder. Ariana aimed her phone at the boat and took a picture, zooming in for a second picture as the man turned his back to avoid being photographed. Hermione called Damian to give him a description of the boat leaving their dock in hopes that he could follow it and find out more about the man.

One of the patrolmen walked over to Ariana and said, "You're the owner who called us?"

Ariana nodded and said, "I received notice that my security system was being breached and I knew there was a man stuck inside that net," pointing to the cargo net with an obvious hole in it. "I knew he'd arrived by boat and there was supposed to be a second thug at the top of my driveway."

"That's a very sophisticated alarm system. Were you expecting trouble?" the officer asked.

"I have a daughter who I'm trying to protect and it appears I was right to take precautions. Did you take a picture of the retreating boat so you find out who the assailant is?"

"Ma'am, can you tell me what was stolen from your property today?"

"I don't believe anything was stolen as according to my alarm system, he didn't make it into the house."

"Maybe he was a boater who ran into trouble and was seeking aid," the officer suggested.

Ariana couldn't believe what she was hearing, "And he ran away from a clearly marked officer of the law because why? I'm just not following your line of thinking."

"Ma'am, there's more than meets the eye here. This is a wealthy town with fancy security systems, but not one of them has cargo nets to capture suspects. Why do you want to meet these criminals?"

Ariana was becoming exasperated with the cop's questions and well, yeah he was right there was more going on than she planned to admit to.

"I don't want to meet them, I was planning on having you release them from the net into your capable hands so you could arrest them for trespassing. I don't want to meet them rather I want to make sure they never come back," Ariana said. The statement was partially true, she did want the cops to meet them and take them away, but she wanted to know their identity first.

The cop gave her a blank stare indicating he wasn't buying what she said, but there would be no further questions. Instead he mused to his fellow officer, "I've never seen an attempted burglary by boat, have you?"

The other officer shook his head indicating he also had never seen a trespasser leave by water.

"Have you had any word back from anyone on the identification of the boat and its occupant?" Ariana asked.

"No ma'am that may take a few days as we put word out to the various marinas around the bay."

The other officer then said, "I suppose we could look for prints on the cargo net, but I don't know how we would distinguish between your perpetrator and the security person who installed it for you or the people who made or sold the cargo net."

Ariana had also thought of that and came to the same

conclusion, “Sadly I agree with you. Will you let me know if you find information about the boat?”

"Yes ma’am,” and the two officers soon wrapped things up and departed.

Hermione had been monitoring her phone during the exchange and Ariana looked over at her and asked, “Has Damian caught up with the boat?”

“He caught sight of it and was following it, but it ducked into one of the many marinas across the way in Marin and he lost track of it. He wants to know if you have a name on it and can send him the picture you took.”

Ariana looked at the pictures she snapped of the departing boat, forwarding them to Damian once she confirmed they were in focus. She tried enlarging a few of them to see if she captured the name of the boat or its call letters or the driver’s face. The first shot had the best picture of the driver’s face as he apparently noticed her camera and turned his head away after that. She couldn’t read the name of the boat or its call letters as the water churned up by the motor covered it.

After sending him the pictures, she called him knowing he was likely going slow enough to have a conversation.

“Sorry my pictures weren’t better.”

“Kudos to you for thinking quickly enough to take the pictures and maybe I can identify the guy in the first picture. At least, I know the boat’s color and engine as I look for it through these series of berths in the marinas.”

“How many marinas are you going to have to look through?”

“I saw the boat just as it was rounding Peninsula Point and I lost sight of it until I rounded the same point and there are a lot of boats out here today so it may be as few as one or as many as twenty docks. Then I’ll need to add restaurant docks where boaters tie up as well so this might take me a while.”

“Are you safe?”

“What do you mean?” Damian asked puzzled. “My boat isn’t going to overturn or anything, the water is calm in this area.”

“I mean do you think he saw you chasing him and he might try to shoot you or something?” Ariana said lamely.

“I don’t think he looked back once he cleared the point because there were enough boats to try and fit in with and he didn’t see you jump in your pontoon to chase him; so he doesn’t realize anyone is following him. So no, I don't think he'll be standing on the edge of a dock looking for me and then try shooting me."

"Ah, okay. Keep us posted here. The police left suspicious of my security system."

"Are you both wearing your vests?" Damian asked and then checking something on his cell phone said, "I see the system is still disarmed. Why don't you two go inside and re-arm it until I get there."

"We're wearing our vests. We could join you in the search," Ariana suggested.

He hesitated, thought about the offer, and then said, "Okay, hopefully I'll find the boat before you get here, but if not we'll plan our strategy then. We have about three hours of daylight left, but I don't think it will take me that long on my own to search the berths for the boat. Fortunately, so many people have sailboats, yachts, or pontoon boats that I'll be able to rule out the boats as I drive by. Call me when you reach this area and we'll meet."

Ariana ended the call and said to Hermione who had been listening to her side of the story, "He's agreed to have us help. I didn't expect him to agree as he's always so overprotective of us."

"Cool," Hermione replied, ready for an adventure.

"We need to leave before he changes his mind. Let's run inside, use the bathroom, grab some drinks and snacks, and jackets and be back at this spot in say three minutes," Ariana said as she sprinted into the house.

True to her word she was seconds faster than the teenager in returning to the spot with her items in hand, but Hermione got bonus points for thinking of bringing her binoculars which would aid in the search.

Covering their heads and adding jackets gave them a little bit of a disguise. As Ariana was tooling the boat over toward Marin, she asked Hermione, "The man might have noticed this boat, before he left our dock. Let's hide the canopy so the boat can't be identified." Stopping the boat, the two women folded down the canopy. Fortunately the pontoon was a plain white color and so would blend in well with other pontoons out on the bay.

Fifteen minutes later they were pulling aside Damian's boat just outside one of the marinas. Ariana passed him water and a few snacks and then indicated that Hermione had binoculars. He hadn't spotted the boat yet, so they would start at the far end of the continuous community of yacht clubs and marinas. An hour later they met and admitted they hadn't located the trespasser's boat.

"If he was smart, he would have watched me approach the first marina and once I was out of view, blocked by the height of other boats, he could head out on to the bay and fit in with all the boats out there," Damian said. "We could make a second pass but we'd probably be wasting our time."

The women nodded and then Adriana said, "The police didn't dust for prints on the cargo net as they said there were likely too many prints on them from manufacture and set-up. What are your thoughts about that?"

"Having just gone through a fingerprint exercise with Natalie on the bank robbery case, I would tend to agree with the cops of the likelihood of the prints being of little use."

"They were kind of snarky about the trespasser and the cargo net."

"Why?" Damian asked.

"I think they thought I was hiding something given the sophistication of my alarm system. He said he'd seen a lot of security systems throughout Belvedere and no one had a cargo net to capture suspects and therefore I must have something to hide."

"That is kind of snarky. Oh well, he was there when we needed him," Damian said. "Speaking of which, let's head back to your house and I'll get a new net set up. Once I return home, I'll see if I can identify the guy from either the security camera or from your camera shot."

A short time later, Damian was putting the pieces in place for a new cargo net. He stopped and surveyed her lot. One guy had tried to enter from the driveway, and now another thug had come from the dock. That left the two side yards as the next avenue of access to the house. He had traps in place there and he hoped these guys had learned their lesson having first been sprayed with pepper juice then hauled up in the air by a cargo net. He really wished he knew what they were after. Did they want Hermione dead or alive?

He went inside the house and spoke with Ariana about the changes. Both women continued to feel empowered by the vests and while concerned about the intruders, they weren't fearful for their lives.

"Do you want to join us for dinner?" Ariana asked.

"I'm tempted but I'm anxious to see if I can find an identity to your intruder and it's going to take me several hours," Damian said. Then looking at Hermione he asked, "Do you have any scars?"

The teenager looked at him confused. How had the conversation gone from dinner to scars?

"Huh?"

"I just wondered if you have any scars from injuries - you know like falling off your bike or cutting yourself accidentally somewhere?" Thinking about his own daughters he added, "Do you have scars from chicken pox?"

Hermione still wasn't following the change in conversation, but she thought about his question and replied, "I have a scar on my knee from a fall and a scratch mark on my arm from a friend's pet cat that I got in China when I was around six or seven," Hermione said showing him the two scars.

"Okay, then your parents would know that if they ever came across you with your changed appearance, they could verify your identity by the two scars, right?"

"Right," Hermione said still puzzled by the conversation.

Ariana knew why Damian was asking and wanted to turn the conversation to a new topic. Searching her head she said, "Just a reminder that Hermione has a water polo match at four tomorrow and then on Tuesday we're going to the ballpark to watch the San Francisco Giants. Hermione will have the chance to meet Lily and her son. Everyone else is also booked to attend."

Damian knew all this and appreciated Ariana's effort to change the conversation as he'd gotten the information he wanted from the kid. Maybe he would come up with some answers regarding Hermione and the bank robbery once he got back to the island and spent time on the pictures and fingerprints. He also knew he wanted to bring back a scanner to see if she had something implanted in one of those scars. Was it a tracking device or some kind of memory stick? He hoped to find it was neither, but rather just ordinary scars.

Damian arrived back on Red Rock Island with a list of things to do. He wanted to find out how good he was at fingerprinting as he now had several samples to run. Thankfully, Natalie hadn't called to ask where her results were since he didn't want to explain why he tried to chase a boat through the multitude of docks in Sausalito.

He grabbed his duffle from earlier and took all his evidence down to his lab for processing. Three hours later he had some answers on both cases. Arielle Joseph was probably also Ashley Carrington, someone with a sealed juvenile record according to the fingerprints that he'd retrieved from the donut shop. Ariana's thug was John Lee again. On his first visit, he was sprayed with pepper juice while on the second visit he ended up in a cargo net; what was making the man try to break into Ariana's house? He leaned back and thought about Hermione's mention of the two scars. Could either of them be an implant? What kind of sensor did he need to use to detect if she had some kind of data device on her? He leaned forward and searched for tiny implantable memory devices. It could also be a simple GPS chip so they would always know where she was, but that didn't explain why someone else wanted the kid.

He'd leave the Hermione mystery alone and take a look at her scars tomorrow, before giving much more thought to a Hermione scanner. One thing he did know was she wasn't setting off routine metal scanners that one faced at large events. When he traveled with Hermione, they'd only flown on private charters so she hadn't had to go through airport screening, but her school had a metal screener that she hadn't set off. Neither scar sounded like it might be a source for a tracker, but he really didn't know.

Focusing on Ashley Carrington, he decided to see what he could find about her juvenile law encounter. He'd never tried to look at a juvenile court record before so first he explored why records were sealed and it actually seemed pretty routine. If a kid did time and followed his or her probation requirements and their crime wasn't horrible, then the record was sealed and the crime erased from the child's background. The juvenile offense occurred in the State of Washington which had different rules for sealing the record than California. His real question was whether sealed or not, was the record at one time online? Given that the offense was perhaps fifteen years ago, it was entirely possible that several online logs of the record were accessible to Damian's inquisitive mind.

He was yawning as he dug through several Washington databases. It was closing in on midnight and he wasn't at his sharpest anymore. It had been an intense day and he'd carried an adrenaline rush for a while when Ariana and Hermione were threatened. He'd been doing boring coding work since he got home and both it and the day were wearing on him. It was time to go to sleep and start on the process again when he was refreshed.

24-CHAPTER TWENTY FOUR

John Lee was treating the skin on his arms for an injury from yet another encounter with that Knowles woman. This time it was rope burns from that damn net. He also torqued his neck when the net took hold and flung him upward. He was just grateful that he had a knife on his person that he could use to hack his way out of the net. Thankfully he escaped across to the marina although it had been close for a moment as he sought items to cover the boat's name and call sign and put the cover on it. He hid behind a dock pillar when the man in the boat came looking for him, or at least he thought he was looking for him based on the way he scanned the boats. He waited until he departed, then added another fifteen minutes and then he hopped in the boat and headed out to the marina across the bay from where he had rented it. No one gave him chase.

He wanted the kid, and his employer was upset that he hadn't captured the girl in four months. The kid's parents had been taken out of their home tied up and in bags, but had eventually escaped. His employer was now convinced that the only way to bring her parents to heel was to grab the kid. After the parent's escape, they had been unable to track their present location. The kid he found purely by accident. He'd been at a bar in Oakland contemplating how to find the kid when she walked in for a private party. He followed the woman she came with and was able to identify where the kid was being housed, but despite knowing where she slept, he'd been unable to steal her.

Fortunately his employer was patient and only wanted the kid stolen in a manner that the authorities would be unable to detect her abduction. He tried reaching her through Facebook, but that hadn't worked. The only two things that had made him feel better about this assignment was he hadn't lost the kid's parents and the parents were still in hiding and hadn't contacted the girl. The men charged with the parent's kidnapping had been abandoned by his employer. They were in America with illegal documents and no funds. Yes, John Lee was glad he wasn't one of them.

The girl's father, Brad Jones, as he called himself at the time, had worked for his employer, Mr. Lin who was the CEO of a pharmaceutical company in Kuala Lumpur for over five years. One day, the Jones family left Malaysia on a vacation and they never returned. It seemed that Brad took with them evidence of the chemical compounds used to manufacture some of the drugs that Mr. Lin produced and sold. Mr. Lin was a wholesaler and offered good prices to distributors in China and Africa. His prices were cheap because the medications were sold at a reduced potency since he diluted those chemical compounds. Of course, the consumers taking the pills had no idea that their medications were weak.

Things were quiet for a time after the family left the country and Mr. Lin decided he had nothing to worry about. Perhaps he'd been mistaken that Brad Jones had evidence of his manufacturing process. Then about two years later, Mr. Lin received a message that unless he wanted his manufacturing process exposed to the world, he'd pay Brad to keep his mouth shut. The payments had gone on for over three years when John Lee had finally traced the family to the United States and California in particular. He'd been following the money for months before he found the final resting place of a fifty thousand dollar payment each month; to a bank account that belonged to someone by the name of Sherwood who lived in Shepard Canyon, California. There were a series of bank transfers that bounced around the world and all those decoys had taken him forever to run down. The payments had continued and would continue until the evidence that Brad Jones had walked away with was found and returned to Mr. Lin who'd wanted this matter handled in the quietest manner. John Lee would have handled it differently if he was Mr. Lin. He simply would have killed the entire Jones family when he'd located their address, but Mr. Lin warned him not to do that. He said that Brad had set up a security system that immediately released information about his poor manufacturing if he didn't log in on a certain website every three days. Should Jones fail to do that then the evidence would be immediately sent to a certain official in the Chinese Government as well as to the United States' Food and Drug Administration. It was far cheaper to pay off Mr. Jones than to lose the permanent business of those two countries.

When the couple was captured, Mr. Lin had worried about that issue but the couple escaped before the deadline and he received no bad news from either government so it was either a hoax or Mr. Jones visited the website by the deadline.

Mr. Lin hated to threaten a child but he'd do that to stop the blackmail from her parents. Thus John's sole job at the moment was kidnapping the child and taking her back to Malaysia, but they were sort of in a quandary at the moment. John Lee wasn't sure the parents knew where the child was nor she where they were, and Mr. Lin had lost track of the parents once they escaped. So if he kidnapped the child, how would he tell the parents? What a mess of a job! He was tempted to quit and return home, but Mr. Lin would see that he never had another job as a private investigator in Malaysia if he did that, and he had his parents under house arrest somewhere. So he was back to trying to kidnap the kid.

Where else could he take her from? She was well protected at home and at school. Maybe he'd spend a few more weeks watching her and see if she attended movies or some other social outing with kids her own age. That was when he'd have the most success at taking her. He'd just keep up surveillance of her home and school to figure out where else she might be.

25-CHAPTER TWENTY-FIVE

Normally on a Monday morning Damian would be heading into Richmond to the warehouse to work on his projects or see what advancements his employees were making. His business and his life were somewhat freewheeling at the moment as he had no deadlines in either. He'd been at work on the fingerprints since arising that morning and he still needed more time. So he let his crew know he'd be arriving after lunch while he worked on something at home. His butt and his back were beginning to ache from sitting on rather hard seats and he couldn't believe they hadn't bothered him before. He'd been so busy in his lab over the last twenty-four hours that his cats had been given dry kibble as he didn't have time to fish.

He thought back to six months ago before Ariana, Hermione, and his new company had entered his life. What had he done with his days? What had he done with his life over the past seven years since his family's murders? He had his Red Rock Island home to build, and he'd helped Natalie with a few cases, he applied for additional patents, but if Jen and the kids were watching from heaven they must have been sadly disappointed in him. Well ok, they would be proud of his efforts to prevent any other murderous felons from being released. They'd be proud of him adopting the cats, they'd also be proud of him for rescuing Hermione, but that was pure fluke; she hid in his boat, he hadn't sought her out for saving. It was the second time in as many weeks that he wondered what Jen and the kids would be thinking of his current life. Why was he having these thoughts?

Okay time to move his morose thoughts beyond his late family and back to the job at hand which was figuring out who was involved in the robbery in Willow Glen. He stood and stretched, took a few deep breaths then refocused.

Damian managed to hack into enough files to learn that Ashley was convicted in juvenile court of stealing money from the fast food restaurant that she was employed at in Spokane County in the State of Washington. That gave him a location to look for more information on Ashley. She went on to graduate high school then seemed to walk off the edge of the earth; he could find no further mention of the girl.

Damian went back to Arielle Joseph to look for information on when she appeared. He would have thought that the bank did a background check on her prior to her employment; they certainly needed enough information to search her background for thievery. He dropped an email to Natalie that she request a subpoena for the woman's personnel file. It would be full of lies, but he was sure there would be a few truths mixed in. He smiled when Natalie replied to his email that she already had thought to do that and it was pending before a judge that afternoon. He then read the guidelines for hiring employees. Several federal agencies recommended that banks fingerprint employees as a part of the background check. Nine years ago it wouldn't have been that different, so how did she get past the fingerprint check? He'd wait until Natalie got the personnel file. He then thought of something else to ask Natalie and knew it was just easier to call her.

"I had another question and decided I would just call you," he said once she answered. "Can you get a picture of Ashley Carrington? I'd like to run it through software to see if she's the same person as Arielle Joseph. Ashley did juvenile time in Spokane or she may have a driver's license."

"You really think she's our bank robber?" Natalie said.

"I would have made a terrible detective as I have no proof. It's just my mathematical mind not liking all the strange facts related to her profile."

"Where do you think she is now?" Natalie asked.

"I hadn't thought that far ahead. We know she sold items from locations all over the United States in years one to five after the robbery and that currency was introduced in heavy amounts in cities around the world. So if you had sixty million dollars to launder, how would you exchange it?"

"That's a good question. I'd probably hit casinos and use it to buy chips then cash the chips out. You could also buy cars and then resell them, I suppose. I'm trying to think of what big ticket items you could use cash for and there aren't many items even eight or nine years ago. I guess the other thing you could do is open a business and run it through as receipts."

"Let me do some research on how drug cartels and other groups like that launder cash," Damian said. "From a brief calculation though, if I spread sixty million dollars over three hundred sixty-five days of five years, I would have to launder about thirty-three thousand each day. Say you walked into a casino with cash of five thousand dollars, you still have to visit between five and six casinos a day to not be noticed by one in particular. It would be an exhausting five years."

"Yeah, but what a way to earn thirty-three thousand dollars each day! I'll ask the guys in our organized crime area what they know about it," Natalie said, amused that Damian would look for a sociological study of how criminals disposed of money. It was always a revelation as to how a scientist's mind works.

"I would have thought she'd have to have a lot of new addresses. She'd have to have a physical address to be listed on most websites I believe. So if you move every two weeks to a new town that would be a lot of hotel stays or one month apartment leases. Maybe you rent a bunch of locations for a month and move around all of them. Apartment rent would be a nice way to place money into circulation but you wouldn't get anything back. You usually need a physical address to sell stuff on the internet; if you use a post office box to sell, then it limits you to the Postal Service for delivery rather than UPS or Fedex which in the end isn't a big deal I guess."

"Remember that some of the cash showed up internationally; you could hide it in a car and drive it across the borders to be exchanged in Mexico or Canada. Border security is generally more worried about what you bring into the United States than what you take out."

"Yes, but what would you do with the money once you exchanged it? You'd have to deposit it into a foreign bank or drive back to the United States and re-exchange it back into dollars. It would no longer be marked, but you'd have a hard time accounting for it. I would think that once the bank sent you a tax form for interest on thirty million dollars that you would have to account some day for its origin," Damian mused and then added, "I guess I make a lousy criminal."

Natalie laughed and said, "That you do, you're talking yourself out of committing a crime before you even try! We don't have the law enforcement resources to watch you that closely, and every hardened criminal thinks he or she is smarter than us, when actually they are far from it, but you truly are smarter."

Damian chuckled and then said, "I'm still stuck on how to launder sixty million dollars. It just seems impossible to me. I'd love to talk to a drug lord to understand how they do it. Though I think I've read about the complex empires they manage, so they're probably running it through legitimate businesses. I guess I don't see this woman doing that given the map of where we saw her exchanging money and goods."

"I agree with you, that the distribution of dollars points to her sitting low for a year and then traveling for the next several years across America and even the rest of the world. I wonder what she did in that year of down-time?" Natalie questioned. "Maybe your mega computer could look through all the public cameras of the bay area to see if Arielle Joseph showed up in any of them in that year of waiting out the robbery."

"It's a thought, but I can't imagine that there are many online sources storing those images that are eight to nine years old at this point. Why don't I look for her now? Maybe start with passport control and if we see no activity, move on to cameras focused on the busiest intersections in the United States? Locations like Time Square in New York, major airports, and places like that?"

"You can do that? I wish you had suggested that weeks ago," Natalie said.

"Yes, but we didn't figure out who she was until this past week-end so I'm not sure who we would have been looking for…."

"You're right, of course."

They ended their conversation shortly after that and both went to work. Damian monitored the time as he needed to be over at Ariana's later for the afternoon's water polo match. He thought about the effort he needed to make to hack into the Immigration department's passport control. It would likely take him at least a full day, so he sent out a few emails to department personnel hoping to trick them into giving up their access, then he put that aside and headed across the bay to the marina and drove his truck to the office. Lily would start the following week and he was looking forward to hosting the baseball game the following evening.

He thought about his employees and decided to have a staff meeting once he got there to discuss the goals of the firm to make sure that everyone was on the same page as he was. He wanted the drone ready to go in less than six months, and the wave powered technology sooner. He also wanted to discuss the protective vests he'd made for Ariana and Hermione with the gang and discuss the possibility of commercializing them – who would be the target market and could he manufacture them cheap enough to meet their price point. He had a lot to look forward to with the company.

Minutes later he arrived at the warehouse and greeted Haley, Angus, and Chris. After a thorough discussion concerning their problems and solutions since the last meeting, Damian proposed the idea of the protective vests. Haley loved the idea, but thought that the team could make them more fashionable, while Angus and Chris wondered who would buy them, totally missing the female market. The conversation was very telling and he decided it was a project that he and Haley would work on together perhaps with a little help from Lily once she started with the company.

He reminded himself that the company was there to pursue his passions for better technology and not every idea would be liked by every employee. When he saw Ariana later at the water polo match he would ask her to do a market assessment and see if they had a market. It seemed like it was a good idea if a woman wanted to hike alone, had an evening shift job, or just lived in a shady area. Of course then he'd need to make it affordable and legal, not that he could think of any laws against the vest but he'd have to research that.

After spending several hours at the company, he headed for his island. Truth was he was more productive in his home lab than when surrounded by the nice people that worked for him. He reminded everyone about the gathering the next day and left. He stopped at home to feed the cats and then was off again to Ariana's house. He docked his boat behind hers pulling its sun deck and side window covers in place. Heavy drizzle was expected later and he didn't want the interior of his boat drenched.

Soon he and Ariana were on their way to Hermione's school pool which was hosting the first water polo game of the season. They were anxious to see her do well and it was a new challenge for her. She'd been a competitive swimmer for years, but had never tried to play water polo until their summer vacation. It was true for all the players so the playing field was even. Damian had found coverage of an Olympic water polo game and studied it to understand the strategy and rules of the game. After the match, they were going to grab a pizza to take home to Ariana's house before he headed back home to the island. When the match first started he explained the positions and rules and then they were both quiet as they watched and cheered whenever Hermione's team scored. In the end, the final score was eighteen to five in favor of Hermione's school and she scored five of the points. Hermione was exhilarated when she met them at the car after coming out of the locker room.

"Congratulations, Hermione, that was an excellent performance," Damian said. "You guys looked so much better than the other team so hopefully the rest of your games will go this well."

"Coach was pleased with our performance and several of the older players said we have a better team this year than last year and we won our league last year."

"Did you have fun playing the game?" Ariana asked.

"I've got a few bruises on my legs and hips from all the kicking that occurs under water, but I had a blast. It's so different from swimming, I like the teamwork aspect. Even the locker room was louder as people were remarking on plays. When you're a racing swimmer, you don't have this camaraderie."

"Glad you enjoyed it!" Damian said as Ariana pulled into the parking lot of the pizza restaurant. "Are you hungry?"

"Yes, very. I'll need a big meal after every game. I feel like my stomach is touching my spine since it's so empty and I can eat a whole pizza all by myself!"

Damian chuckled and exited the car to pick up their order. Soon they were back at Ariana's house sitting at her center isle eating pizza. Hermione hadn't been kidding that she was starving as Damian watched her plow through four large slices of pizza without slowing down. Soon he was saying good bye to the two women and getting in his boat to head back across the bay. As he expected, it was drizzling when he opened the side canopy to get in the boat and he had to keep it closed up on his way home.

Damian sat down at his computer cracking his knuckles and his shoulder joints before he planned his deep dive into the cameras at immigration checkpoints across the nation. It was a massive undertaking and might not yield any new information. If Arielle or Ashley or whatever name she was going by hadn't left the country in the last month, then it would be all for naught. With all the airport, bus, train, boat, and car entry points, the first thing he needed to do was create a list of all locations. He was amazed to learn that Canada had about one hundred twenty entry points between itself and the U.S. and the Homeland Security Department listed three hundred twenty-eight border crossings. From there he had to figure out which had cameras and fortunately it seemed that it was all of them. Some ports of entry were larger than others; busy ports included California-Tijuana, Detroit-Windsor, and El Paso-Juarez. The California location had over one hundred thousand visitor crossings every day. In a month's worth of footage, he would be looking at nearly four million faces for a match to Arielle Joseph in that one location alone.

He thought about how to put the computer through its paces and decided to do several runs to speed up the facial recognition match. He'd do the coastal airports as one group, all other airports plus ports as a second group, each of the three largest car and pedestrian borders as their own search, and then one final run of the other three hundred twenty-five entry points as one run. Total incoming immigration was one million visitors each day. Of course he could probably ignore half of those since he was looking for females, but then again every human that looked like a man wasn't necessarily one and vice-versa so he'd design the program to scan all faces.

He planned to search several levels on the scan. The first round would be measurements of the relative position, size, and shape of the eyes, nose, cheekbones, and jaw. He expected to get multiple matches for Arielle so from there he'd add 3D recognition which examined the mountains and valleys of the face and even skin texture if he could find it in the resolution of the photos. Finally he had everything in place and he was awaiting success with his hack which was just a single employee in a certain area of Homeland security giving up his or her user name and password while seemingly being unaware that they just did so.

Looking at his watch he thought it was unlikely that he'd catch a Homeland Security employee asleep at the switch, no pun intended, at this hour, but he'd try. He'd have far more opportunities for success during the day shift when thousands of employees were on the job.

Fifteen minutes later to his surprise, he was in their system searching for footage of the border cameras. After an hour's work, he found trouble. Only about half of the locations were on the main server; other locations hadn't been upgraded to transfer video to a central storage facility. Now he'd have to rethink his strategy. He'd start with running a search with the photos he could access and see what that showed him and worry about the other locations later.

A couple of hours later, he had his Arielle Joseph search going and he left the lab and went upstairs to his bedroom to get some sleep. It was one in the morning and he was exhausted from several busy days. Tomorrow he'd check the program when he awoke, spend some time at the warehouse, and then head over to the ballpark where he was hosting the small party at the San Francisco Giants baseball game.

26-CHAPTER TWENTY-SIX

After the night's rest, he was anxious to see what the searches revealed and as he suspected, they came up with many matches. He had the software err on a more inclusive side knowing that many of the cameras were not great and they didn't always capture a full frontal view of a face. He looked at the report and thought oh-no! There were over one thousand names produced by the search and that was just a month's video footage. He had a new appreciation for the people trying to protect the United States.

He settled down and put the thousand or so faces through his 3D software. It was a far slower program than he expected and it would likely take twenty-four hours to go through the data. He dropped Natalie an email with his findings and then thought of something to add, 'Have you gotten a subpoena to search for seller addresses for what had looked like the stolen property of the safe deposit boxes, the five unopened safe deposit boxes and for Arielle's personnel file?'

Natalie must have been working on her email as he got an immediate response, 'Yes to all, will call you after they are executed.'

Cool, thought Damian, progress at last. He had nothing else to do with the Willow Glen heist for at least a day. This case had so far been full of serious data crunching, but he felt as though they were finally making progress in the nine year old bank robbery. He fed his cats and got ready to head over to the marina and on to the warehouse. He planned to spend the rest of the day there and then go early to the ball park for the game. Natalie's son Trevor was accompanying Haley, Chris was bringing his date. Angus and his girlfriend were giving Lily and Jacob a ride. Lily had warned them that if the game went into overtime, she and Jacob would need to go home as he had school the next day and this was going to be a late night for them without additional innings. His little group was what he called mild baseball fans; they knew the rules of the game, some of the players and whether they were in or out of the playoffs, but they didn't pay enough attention to the game to get the strategy or understand when or why you would use a pinch hitter. Ariana was actually the biggest fan among them and she'd be arriving with Hermione after school.

When he arrived at his company's headquarters, he held his usual conversation with each member of his team checking on their progress. Haley was upstairs with the drone and Chris and Angus were pleased with not having their concentration interrupted by her drone's crashes. They were all making progress faster than Damian had been doing on his own which was his first measure of success. Once he was done with their projects, he entered his office to begin sourcing fabrics for his self-defense vest. The model that Hermione and Ariana had was a photographer's vest. He looked online at hunting and utility vests deciding on one of them based on the pocket placement. Now he wanted to take it to another level in terms of protection and fashion. In its present style, he had to agree it was ugly.

Overall, it was one of the most uneventful and quiet days that he'd had in a while. In the late afternoon, he left, preparing to head home and then on to the ball park. He looked at the computer search and it was still going though it was estimated to be eighty percent complete; maybe by the time he returned home tonight it would be finished.

He was soon heading across the bay to the marina that was nestled close to the ball park. He paid the berthing fee and admired the beauty of his 'parking space'. He could view the ball park and the Bay Bridge and he'd passed the Golden Gate Bridge and Alcatraz Island on his way. What a commute! After a short two block walk, he was entering the security for the ballpark. Looking at his watch, he figured he was a good thirty minutes in front of everyone else. So he grabbed a beer and stared out the window down to where the players were warming up. While he watched he thought about Hermione and her problems as well as Natalie's bank heist. It was a great place to think with the background noise of bats making a ping sound when they made contact with the ball and the thud of the ball caught in a leather glove. There was also the increasing ambient noise as people filtered into the stadium.

There was a knock on the suite's door and then it opened and the catering crew entered with a cart to set up the food. They left after a few last minute questions and Damian went back to contemplating the world from his perch above the ball park. As was often the case when he relaxed and let his brain drift, he imagined his wife Jen and their two girls alongside him at this game. He thought his oldest would have developed into an athlete and so perhaps she would have enjoyed this setting. The younger one would probably be watching people down on the field and entering the stands. He startled when the suite door opened and Angus and his friend Nikki entered with Lily and Jacob. The boy was the only person wearing any garment with the San Francisco Giants logo on it.

"Are you a Giants fan?" Damian asked.

"Yeah, I play catcher for Little League and so Buster Posey is my favorite player," Jacob replied.

He seemed tall for a twelve year old and a real baseball enthusiast. Damian bet he was a good player and so he asked, "Do you know the game strategy yet? Do they teach it at your age?"

He saw a smirk on Lily's face at his question and thought, I guess I just proved I was stupid about the game.

Jacob gave him a look that said, 'I thought you were smart, man', but said "Yeah I know strategy, what would you like to know?"

"Maybe once the game starts you can explain a little of what is going on between the pitcher, catcher, and batter."

"Sure I can do that. Thank you for inviting me to the game."

"Thank you for coming. Maybe after you explain the secret code of the three positions, it will look more like a strategic sport to me," Damian said with a sincere smile.

The kid nodded then moved over to the window to watch the warm-up down on the field. He brought a mitt with him, but sighed with the realization that he wouldn't catch any balls in this suite.

Haley and Trevor arrived next with Chris and his friend behind them. Ariana and Hermione slipped in minutes before the National Anthem. They all stood at attention, hands over hearts. Between the anthem and the first pitch, Damian introduced Lily and Jacob to everyone. The visitors were up first and Jacob explained what the strategy was with the lineup and then with the first five hitters. The kid was smart and soon had the attention of the entire suite explaining what was happening. He continued to the bottom of the first inning and then he and Ariana continued discussing the players on their own while the others looked on amused.

Damian said to Lily, "Jacob knows baseball and he's a good teacher. I had no idea all of that strategizing was going on. He's given me a new appreciation for the game."

"He's an awesome player! If he continues to develop, he'll end up with a farm team or a college scholarship," Lily said.

"Is that what you want for him?" Damian asked.

"I want him to have a future. He's smart and will be college eligible. He's gifted in baseball but he hasn't tried other sports like football and soccer yet so maybe he's just got athletic genes. The nice thing about baseball is it's less violent than football or soccer as long as he doesn't stand between a runner and home plate."

"Do you play catch with him at home?"

"Yeah I do," Lily said and added, "Someday I may need Tommy John surgery since the kid has an insatiable need to play catch."

"I'd buy a pitching machine and save my elbow. He'd then be able to catch one hundred mile an hour fastballs by the time he enters high school."

"I'll think about it," Lily said. "There's actually a used one for sale online, but the listing says it doesn't work; there's an electrical short in the motor and I'm not sure I could fix it."

"If the price is good, buy it and bring it to work with you. We're a bunch of engineers and I'm sure someone can fix it."

"I'll do that. Jacob's a great catcher, but if he practices, he could also be a great hitter and that will be his ticket to the majors or college."

A roar went up in the stadium and they broke off their conversation to try and figure out what happened. It was a home-run hit into the bay by the Giants catcher and Damian knew Jacob must be the happiest kid in their suite.

He had Ariana and Hermione speak to Lily about the vest and

soon they had her excited on what would be one of her projects in addition to the artificial intelligence for his DNA field analyzer. He chipped in about his fabric search that day and soon had the ladies laughing at his plunders inside the fashion world. He'd design the self-defense items and it was up to Lily to make the vest cool and fashionable, and she and Haley would work on the applicator switches that would release the various self-defense items.

Lily wanted to head home at the seventh inning stretch, but pleading by Jacob found her staying to the end of the game. Damian was pleased that the Giants won and Jacob's hero had hit a homerun; it had been a great night with his employees bonding and Lily getting to know her future teammates. It was approaching eleven as he slowed down and waited for his dock to unfold. He was anxious to see what his database run had turned up. After bringing his boat and dock into their watercraft garage and thus sealing up his island, he walked over to his lower level lab to check on the search.

It was finished and he leaned in to review the results.

Damian stood looking at the names and pictures and it presented an interesting pattern. Arielle or Ashley, he couldn't make up his mind which name to call the suspected bank robber, entered and exited the United States on a weekly basis. Her favorite points were San Francisco International and Peace Arch between Washington and British Columbia. She had a few visits to Mexico traveling through a variety of immigration points and she hit Sault Saint Marie and Windsor on occasion.

He debated what to do next. If he studied the data would he notice a pattern that might help them locate her presence at a particular time and place, or did he look for financial transactions looking for the sixty million dollar stash in a number of bank accounts in Canada and Mexico in addition to the United States. He decided that he liked looking for patterns and went after the first question.

He spent two hours on the detecting of her travel pattern then decided he was dead tired and seeing patterns in more places than he should and he called it a night.

27-CHAPTER TWENTY-SEVEN

Ashley Carrington silently sighed with relief as she passed through another passport control station. She'd been doing this for more than five years and she continued to marvel that she hadn't been caught. Each time she passed through the border, she feared that someone finally figured out who committed a robbery at a bank in California nine years ago. Her current home was more than a thousand miles away from the robbery location, but she knew she needed to renounce her citizenship and disappear into the world once and for all. One person knew her secret and she wasn't going to tell on her; but Ashley knew that over the past year her anxiety had been notching up with each weekly border crossing. If her anxiety got much worse, border guards would be pulling her aside for suspicious activity as they would be able to see the sweat on her brow.

She'd planned the robbery for two years including one year working at the branch to make sure she had the best plan in place. Michelle, her sister, was her partner in crime, creating the florist shop as a cover to what really occurred. At night and on weekends, they dug the tunnel, while all along developing an elaborate plan to hit the vault.

After their success in stealing nearly everything in the vault, they'd moved across country in a rented truck containing their haul. It was weird driving the van knowing that if anyone pulled them over and inspected it, they'd be arrested. A ten thousand dollar used moving van was transporting sixty million dollars' worth of stolen cash and safe deposit box contents. Of course before they filled the van up, they'd had the vehicle checked for a cross-country journey.

Ashley was convinced that the way to stay hidden from authorities after their robbery was to fade into life in the Midwest. The two sisters worked different minimum wage jobs for the first year. More recently, they'd settled in as waitresses at different diners in a city with a population of 40,000 people. Waitressing didn't require fingerprints. Ashley and her sister wanted to avoid jobs that would entail any kind of background check or fingerprinting. As near as she could tell, she wasn't on any police short list of who robbed the Willow Glen Bank. They had forgotten her completely; she knew this because she created a fake forwarding address and no one from law enforcement had made any attempt to reach her. She also read the weekly announcements from the FBI. Each week they sent her 40-50 emails detailing the various arrests, convictions, or ongoing searches for federal criminals. The details of her bank robbery had not been cited after the first three years. She spent an entire year being a steady but boring co-worker at the bank and the pay-off now was no-one associated her with being remotely connected to the heist.

She continued through the inspection area on the American side of the border. She'd been through a variety of passport control ports since the heist with a variety of documents. She had two American names and passports as well as two Canadian. So far, no border guard had been the least bit suspicious with her documents. She had a three hour drive home. This latest trip had been to mail an item she'd sold online from a safe deposit box and to exchange twenty-five thousand in robbery bills into Canadian money and deposit it into a Canadian bank. She had opened bank accounts in many places across the world with the largest dollar amounts in the Cayman Islands and Switzerland. She and her sister had another million to exchange in currency and about fifty items from the boxes. They'd been able to sell the deposit box items much faster than the currency and at the rate they were going, they'd have another year to go before they had exchanged all of the currency.

She texted her sister that she was through the border and settled in behind the wheel. After the Sault Saint Marie Border crossing, soon she was in the rural area of the Upper Peninsula of Michigan. Ashley debated discussing with her sister the possibility of exchanging the final million in five years from now but the slow exchange of currency and safe deposit box contents had put a strain on her relationship with her sister and she suspected that once they fully split the proceeds, they would each go their own way perhaps never to see each other again. She couldn't pinpoint why they were no longer close other than they each had dreams of what to do with their money and there was little common ground. It was really quite sad.

Ashley was tired of the travel involved with laundering the proceeds of the heist. She planned to purchase a house somewhere outside of the United States perhaps Australia or an island in the Caribbean and not travel. Australia was at the top of her list as she felt like it was a big enough continent to lose herself in; the Caribbean on the other hand, had an illusion of being close to the United States. Once there, she would work on a few pet passions of hers like literacy and animal rescue. Hopefully, in time, she'd find a man to settle down with and children would come later. She had more money than she thought she could spend in a lifetime. Wasn't that a good problem to have!? Then why was she depressed?

Growing up in a small town in Washington, Ashley and her sister had sworn that someday they would have it all – enough money to be who they wanted where they wanted. A big house and no more living paycheck to paycheck as her mother had done sweating out each month's rent. They deserved better than that. She was gone now and couldn't appreciate what her two daughters had achieved thanks to a well-executed bank robbery.

"Well, Mom, would you be proud of us now? Or would you be ashamed?" Ashley said to an empty car.

Nine years ago when they planned this bank robbery, they were giddy with delight during that drive across the country in the used van. The adrenaline high had stayed with them for nearly the first year. Now the stress of time and many trips across the border was weighing Ashley down. They both hated their jobs as waitresses and the strain of living a low income life since the robbery was depressing for the soul. So was the worry about getting caught; she thought that fear would decline over time as they heard nothing from law enforcement. Instead, more and more, she felt a sword over her head was waiting to drop on her at any moment.

Ashley thought back to when she conceived of the idea of

robbing a bank with Michelle. They were sharing an apartment in an area affectionately known by the name 'silicon valley'. Rent was expensive and the region was still recovering from a technology bubble. Ashley was working at a different bank than the one they eventually robbed, but it was where she got the idea. She noticed the ebb and flow of currency throughout the day and the work week. Those currency swings were due to merchant deposits. She knew if she timed it right, that she could get a lot of money out of the bank. There was a particular time of the calendar year where banks had the most money on their premises - Christmas. Bank customers withdrew more money in the weeks leading up to Christmas for gift buying and banks might increase their cash holdings by up to twenty-five percent to account for that. Additionally, merchants were seeing more cash come in and making bigger bank deposits and since it was difficult to balance the two on an hour to hour basis, the bank simply held more cash.

After she figured out the best time of year to rob a bank, she went to work evaluating methods to get into the bank without setting off alarms. For another year, she and Michelle worked at another four banks to determine security set-ups. They decided it was best to go after an old bank by digging into it and set out to find the oldest bank buildings in their area that had an empty retail space in the same block. An old bank often had a structural defect that rendered its security less effective. Their plan was to spend a year digging through to the bank from that retail space while sleeping in a cheap bed space at a donut shop and plowing all their savings into maintaining the façade of the florist shop, as well as for buying tools for digging.

Ashley thought the strain of their plan would end when they reached their new home in the Midwest, instead they endured another nine years of managing their small budget, neither able to move on with their lives. It was such a big ongoing secret that it had interfered with their relationships with other people. Well, she could walk away from the final million and the safe deposit box items. Either her sister could have it, or they could drop the money in charity buckets. She would announce her decision when she got home.

She felt immediate relief to know she was moving on. So she spent the remainder of the drive deciding where she would move the next day and what she needed to do to make a run for it. She could be in Australia in two days starting a new life down under. It was a big country and she would do research on a remote but livable area. Maybe head for Sydney, head north to Thursday Island and see how life close to the equator was or perhaps Kangaroo Island to the south. Both islands had enough tourism that she could fit in.

28-CHAPTER TWENTY-EIGHT

It had been a late night for everyone Ariana and Hermione groaned at the early wake-up alarm to get her to water polo practice. Likewise Lily was pushing Jacob to get ready for school. Damian didn't have set hours for his employees, rather he wanted to see progress on his projects and he did that by both formal and informal meetings throughout the week. Therefore, he didn't worry about when his employees got to work or when he arrived at the warehouse so he opted for more sleep that morning. He wanted a sharp brain when he tackled the data about his bank robber's movements.

Damian awoke, anxious to get a swim in before the day took over. He donned his full wetsuit and mask and was soon doing laps around the island. Even at the peak of the summer, the water temperature only reached sixty degrees so the bay was too cold to swim in comfort without a wetsuit. Forty minutes later, he'd completed his swim and showered, arriving at his computer with coffee in hand to look at last night's work.

He looked again at what the 3D search had done and saw it had reduced the total to about one-hundred faces from the thousand plus faces of the first search. Last night, he sorted by location and found the concentration at the Washington border crossing and the San Francisco airport. However, he hadn't looked at the faces yet to assure himself they were all of Ashley. He knew they couldn't be as the number represented three to four border crossings a day. He started pulling up the faces to see if he thought they matched what they had on Ashley. He studied the first ten, looking for some distinguishing feature that screamed this was or wasn't Ashley.

He supposed he could hack and log into the video to watch movement of these hundred subjects but he wasn't an expert on how women moved when walking down the street so it likely wouldn't give him any additional information. He'd probably drive himself crazy looking for similar gestures on video feed as well. If he wasn't able to focus their search on the actual entry points where she might be, then this information was almost worthless. After more thought, he decided he would analyze the entry points for the three most common border crossing sites in this month's worth of data. He had Peach Arch, San Francisco, and Brownsville Texas. He created a spreadsheet with the date and time of each entry and then noticed another problem with his analysis - there were two dates with times too close together for one person to have carried them out. So Damian's only conclusion was that his 3D software was matching people other than Ashley Carrington. He decided to put this search aside while he went to work on something new. Sometimes if he just walked away from a database search, a thought would come to him that would make it look logical.

So he tackled Hermione's problems instead. He checked on her parents' finances and the mortgage, utilities, and taxes were still being paid on their house. He was amazed that he'd been unable to trace who was filling their account with money so the bills could still get paid. He could see deposits made to their bank account; he just couldn't source them. Well, he could source them but it didn't lead him anywhere. Maybe it was time to try doing another mega search for her parents - combine all public cameras in the Bay Area to see if they were sighted on them in the last month. Damian started his computer grinding through that data and left for the warehouse.

When Damian arrived, he sat down to review the strategic plan that Ariana had developed. It gave timelines for project completion, patent application, product sale or production as well as other metrics and recommendations. After living a life of randomness, especially in the past seven years, he was surprised to see it all laid out on paper with deadlines driving the company's behavior. He knew in the back of his mind that this was how a well-managed corporation was run, but it signaled the end of childhood for his inventions. He'd now have to be a responsible adult with employees depending on him and his guidance.

Oh well, time to get to work and with the strategic plan in mind, he went out and discussed the projects and projected deadlines with his employees as a group. He had to give Ariana credit for nailing the timelines. Even without an engineering background, she nailed it to perfection. Each project due date was a slight stretch for each of them which was the way it should be. He called her to discuss the plan with her.

"Hey, how's it going?" Ariana said as she answered the call.

"Good. I'm calling to compliment you on your strategic plan. I don't think a Big Five consulting firm would of nailed the projects so accurately. Each one is enough of a stretch to keep people's noses to the grindstone without working them to death. Kudos to your brilliance."

"I told you months ago when I suggested you incorporate that I did this kind of thing for companies."

"Yeah but you're not an engineer, and yet you broke down each project's components and gave them appropriate times to completion; that's brilliance."

"Okay thanks. I spoke with each of your employees on their projects and got a sense of what had been done and what was still needed, then I planned it out. Do you have any changes to the plan?"

"I want to add Lily's projects to the spreadsheet. She'll be working on the Artificial Intelligence for my field DNA analyzer as well as the self-protective vest. Add those and we'll be good to go."

"Sounds like a plan. Not to change the subject, but have you made any progress finding Hermione's parents? It's odd that you're so talented with computer searches yet can't find them."

"Yeah, it is odd and I have no explanation. I have another search going at home. I'm checking every public camera in this region in the last month for their appearance. They're still paying their bills for the house - mortgage, utilities and taxes. I thought over time that Hermione would learn to trust us more, but she seems determined to keep these secrets to herself."

"Yeah, I know. I think she visits another place on occasion and thinks about her parents and their conversations and she thinks about telling me something. Then she pauses and seems to remember a different conversation and she bites her tongue. There seems nothing to do but wait her out or hope that we find the parents soon. Meanwhile we make admirable surrogate parents and she's safe."

"Okay."

"When are you going to the warehouse next?"

"Probably next Monday as soon as I drop Hermione off at school. I want to meet with Lily and go over our pay and other processes and procedures. Then at the end of the day when she's oriented to everyone's projects, I'd like to have a conversation with her on the timeline to complete her projects. It'll be a long day and I'll probably have you pick Hermione up from school so I can stay longer in Richmond."

"I can do that Monday and any other day you need help. She has a game tomorrow, right?"

"Yeah, I presume I'll see you there."

"Wouldn't miss it. She's one of the stars of that team! Do you want to do dinner after?"

"Yeah, I'll talk with her and see where she is homework wise. If she has a lot, we'll do something at my house. If not, we can grab a bite to eat out."

"Sounds like a plan. Thanks, Ariana, and I'll see you tomorrow."

29-Chapter Twenty-Nine

Natalie was excited that her police contact, Kevin Shimoda, notified her that he'd be getting the personnel record of Arielle Joseph as well as the data from the auction houses. Now she had to put together a list of the pieces they thought were involved in the bank robbery and those auction houses would have fifteen days to provide names and addresses of the sellers. Damian had earlier supplied her with a list of the items he matched and fortunately, she understood the spreadsheet software well enough to sort by auction house and submit to Detective Shimoda within the hour.

Detective Shimoda had already contacted the bank and they indicated that Natalie could stop by to pick up the copy of the file. She was on her way there as soon as she hit the send button on the spreadsheet. She was anxious to see what was in the file that might be of use to them in figuring out where their person of interest was now and if she was their suspect.

While Natalie was embarrassed that several law enforcements agencies hadn't solved such a large bank robbery in more than nine years, she was pleased that they seemed to be homing in on a suspect. With her resources she'd put together a profile on Arielle Joseph. She had her juvenile criminal record, her family tree laid out, and some of her employment history. She hoped that once she got the personnel file that it would fill in the remaining holes.

After she collected the personnel file and reviewed the information, she was fairly certain the SJPD would be able to name Arielle as a Material Witness and the local Washington State police would have reason to search the family property in search of Arielle. Hitting the send key on the spreadsheet of auction items for the detective, Natalie grabbed her coat and purse and was out the door five minutes later.

A short time later she was shown into the bank manager's office. After verifying her identity and the copy of the warrant from Detective Shimoda, he released a copy of the personnel file to Natalie.

"Is this everything in her file?"

"Of course," said the bank manager.

"I wouldn't want you to leave something out that you thought was irrelevant. It might be key to this investigation, so I'll ask you again, is everything in this file?"

"Yes," said the bank manager with obvious affront at Natalie's question.

"Good, and thanks for your quick response. Detective Shimoda will be by later today to witness the opening of the five safe deposit boxes whose owners the bank was unable to contact after the robbery."

Natalie turned and left the manager's office and exited through the bank's lobby to the street. She walked a block to her car, unlocked it and got in. Then she sat with the file braced against the steering wheel looking at the papers inside. She noted the address was different than the donut shop on her initial employment application and she would check that out. Her next of kin was listed as her sister, not a parent. That was curious. She'd have to go research the parents as she didn't remember that they were dead.

Then she looked at the references and noted an interesting fact, Arielle had worked at several banks. If she needed more information on the suspect she would have to research those banks. She would bet that Arielle had been observing practices of the various banks as part of her planning process for the big heist. She skimmed through the remainder of the file and decided she'd go back to her office. She needed her bigger computer to do a little research and she wanted the police to check on Arielle's sister and parents. They could look them up in the driver registration system faster than she or perhaps even Damian could do.

She wondered if the sister was involved with the heist. Should they be looking for two suspects - two sisters rather than one? She thought back to her relationship with her sister and it was a love-hate relationship in their teen years that settled into love in their twenties. She could count on her sister for joining her in an adventure and maybe when they were young and foolish, a crime.

On her short drive to her office, she thought about the sister more and what the experts had said during the initial investigation. They hadn't thought one person could do this on their own. It was simply too much work - both the dig and the emptying of the safe deposit boxes in the time period in question.

Back at her office, Natalie called her contact at SJPD to have a look at the driver's license registries. The sister was listed as Mary Joseph. The name made Natalie search way back in her memory banks to Catholic High School. It would seem that if your last name was Joseph, that you would avoid naming your child Mary. It was just a little weird to name your child after the mother of Jesus and her husband, but if you were not aware of biblical stories she supposed it could happen. As a parent if you gave one child the name of 'Arielle', it seems unlikely that you would name another child 'Mary'. Regardless it sounded to her like a fake name. She would also look under the Carrington name and see what the sister's name was purported to be. Arielle Joseph would have to have a driver's license as proof of identification, but the sister's name wouldn't be verified on Arielle's employment application.

Her contact called her back with Arielle Joseph's information. There was no driver's license issued to an Arielle Joseph, there was an old license issued to an Ashley Carrington in the State of Washington which Damian had already found, but it wasn't renewed after its expiration date four years later. Natalie looked at the picture of a California driver's license in the personnel file and decided it must be a good fake. That also meant there were no fingerprints on record that could be matched to other state driver's licenses, not that Arielle was still in the United States. If she faked a license once, she could probably do it again, so this was a dead end. Natalie looked over the file to search for another thread to follow in the investigation.

She tried another angle that was amazingly accurate and a very old-fashioned way to track young people; she pulled up their middle school and high school yearbooks. There were websites that contained old yearbooks and while you could change your name throughout your life with both legal efforts and fake names, it was impossible to go back and change your name in a long since printed yearbook.

Natalie looked up Ashley Carrington and was shocked and excited by what she saw. She picked up the phone to call Damian.

"Guess what?" she asked when he answered the phone.

"What?"

30-CHAPTER THIRTY

"Ashley Carrington has a twin sister. Her name's Michelle."

"Where did you find that?" Damian asked wondering how he missed that fact about the girl.

"Old fashioned detecting. I pulled up Ashley's high school yearbook and noted the picture next to her; what looks to me to be an identical twin."

"A print yearbook that's been digitalized and put on the web? I'll have to remember that in the future."

"Yeah before we had the internet, you would be amazed at two of our favorite sources - telephone books and yearbooks. Now the telephone books are worthless as so many people no longer have landlines, but printed yearbooks are still good."

"Do identical twins have matching fingerprints?"

"No they don't surprisingly."

"Do you know the twin's location?"

"I haven't started looking, I just had to call you with that piece of information."

"So the twin's name is Michelle Carrington and you think they might be accomplices? Or is this just a FYI."

"I'm back to that original theory put forth by the FBI that it would take a minimum of two people to carry out that robbery and perhaps this gives us a potential second person."

"Wouldn't someone notice twins in the area and mention it like 'hey is that your twin working at the flower store' or something?"

"That's a good point since we haven't figured out who leased the flower store. How about if that was Michelle Carrington? If Arielle never told her co-workers she was a twin perhaps no one noticed that they were twins and thought they were seeing Arielle around the neighborhood. Maybe the sister wore enough of a disguise, that people didn't pick up on the possibility of twins. It's been tried before successfully in the history of crime. Of course, twins on a crime scene were caught in the end so we police know they were twins, but sometimes we don't realize that initially during an investigation."

"Wow that's a new wrinkle. Did you find anything of interest in the personnel file?"

"That's what led me to the yearbook. She listed her sister as Mary Joseph on the next of kin question on her employment application. The name for many reasons didn't seem plausible and that's what urged me to go look at a yearbook."

"What's not plausible about Mary Joseph?" Damian said with puzzlement in his voice.

"It's my Catholic school upbringing. Mary was the mother of Jesus and the wife of Joseph. When I looked the name up online, the very few people called Mary Joseph were of a religious order. It's not a name that you would likely give a child in this day and age and besides we knew that Arielle Joseph was a fake name and Mary Joseph sounded even more fake."

"I hadn't thought of that."

"It's nice to know I can out think you on rare occasion," Natalie said with humor in her voice.

"I'm pretty good with a computer, but I easily miss things like the irony in a name like Mary Joseph for a potential suspect. I'll see what I can find on Michelle Carrington."

"Thanks. I'm looking through state driver's license registries and other things like that."

Damian had another thought, "How close are they in appearance? Did you say they were identical? Not fraternal? The camera views I have of them crossing the border might be either sister."

"If there weren't different names under each picture I would have thought them the same picture."

"When I looked at the border crossing data none of the times were spread out enough that it could be just one of the twin's crossing or perhaps they share a passport and take turns with it. So there's a twin but we as yet don't have a definitive fact that will tell us if both twins are involved."

"Certainly, siblings would explain the secret being kept of the robbery. Nothing like a twin brother or sister to keep secrets," then Natalie paused as another call came in.

"Hey, Detective Shimoda is calling and he was visiting the bank this morning to open the five unopened safe deposit boxes. I'll call you back if there's any news."

Natalie ended her call with Damian and switched over to the detective's call.

"Hi, it's Natalie. What did you find in the safe deposit boxes?"

"The box of Arielle Joseph was empty. She visited the box when she acquired it and then never again, so perhaps it was simply to have a key. Of the other four boxes, there were materials in one of them - paperwork, and the other four were empty. So no new news on the case with this thread. Did the suspect's personnel file show you anything?"

"Yes, guess what! She has an identical twin sister. I'm researching her at the moment, but perhaps she's the partner in this crime that we've been looking for."

"Identical twin?" Shimoda asked.

"Yes. My college students looked at the data they analyzed on border crossings to see if two crossings occurred too close together for one person to have been at both locations. That does not appear to be the case. So we'll need to find another way to confirm that both twins are involved."

"Involved? Is that a Private Detective term?"

"We have a lot of suspicion about this woman as there are just too many quirks with all of the information we've located about her not to be guilty of something."

"Keep me posted."

"Will do."

Natalie called Damian back and he laughed when she mentioned that she told the detective that her college students had run the data to see if they were implausible border crossings.

"Thanks for taking like twenty years off my age."

"You're welcome, can you send me a copy of the data?" Natalie said as they ended the call.

31-CHAPTER THIRTY-ONE

He leaned back and thought about which would be faster; get more footage of the cameras of the border crossings or do a deep dive on Michelle Carrington to see if he could figure out where she might be now. Knowing that it had taken all night for the first analysis, he thought it would be faster to query Michelle. Then Damian thought a little longer and decided to start with the parents - Mr. And Mrs. Carrington; it might say something about the daughters.

A minute later he hit a dead end. The parents were killed twelve years ago in an automobile accident which was apparently when the twin daughters moved to the Bay Area. They would have been about nineteen at the time. There appeared to be no siblings and no mention of an estate. He looked a little farther and found a few aunts and uncles in the northwest, but with no connection to the girls. Women, he corrected himself; they would be approaching thirty years old.

Okay then where are you Michelle Carrington? First he decided to look at her fake name Mary Joseph. Did she use that name at all or was it simply something that her sister had thrown on an employment application? Arielle had at least some identification with her name as she would have needed that for employment. Granted that identification was fake according to Natalie.

How about social security numbers? As twins their numbers should be a digit apart. He dropped an email to Natalie asking for the social security number listed in the employment application.

Maybe he might trace one or both of the twins that way.

Natalie replied with the number and he went to work. First thing he checked was the flower shop rental - had a social security number been used for that? Looking through the file he had from Natalie, they had a copy of the lease agreement for the florist shop from the landlord. Surely the landlord did a background check on the person he was planning to lease to? There was a social security number and it was a digit off from the number Natalie just gave him. He had no idea how hard it was to get a fake number but it appeared he had the twins' real social security numbers as they were a digit apart. He googled buying a fake identification, but wouldn't an employer run into problems if they tried submitting tax dollars to the federal government with a fake social security number? The answer was yes, the women would be caught with fake ID at the bank and elsewhere. So either they had valid fake numbers or they were using their original numbers.

So what could he find from the IRS? There were a few systems he'd never attempted hacking but if the Russians could do it, why not him? Of course the key to hacking was not being discovered and really all he wanted was the address listed on the tax return or just even in the IRS records. He'd been lucky so far in his phantom mode of hacking but he worried about pushing the envelope and so decided to try something perhaps easier - look through the top three tax software systems to see if he could find an address. On his third and final try he struck gold with an address for both sisters in Kalkaska, Michigan. It was only a post office box, but it was a starting point for their search.

He picked up the phone and called Natalie.

"Hey, I've got a mailing address for the twins. It's a city called Kalkaska, Michigan."

"Awesome. Where's Kalkaska? And how to tell Detective Shimoda that we have an address?"

"It's near Traverse City on the upper western side of the state. Why not tell the detective that the social security number was on the employment application that you picked up today and since your college students found one of the twins on their cameras, you thought you'd just check with the Michigan Department of Motor Vehicles."

"That will work. I'll just have to do that before telling the detective. How did you really find the address?" Natalie asked, then paused and added, "Wait don't tell me how you broke the law. I'd rather remain ignorant."

"Okay well see what you can do with the address. I'll see what I can find about Michelle. By the way, I thought most bank robberies were investigated by the FBI and I haven't heard you mention them once in the weeks we've been on this case."

"You're right that they take the lead usually, but since this is coming out of the cold case division, we don't feel a need to involve them. I figure we'll pick up the telephone once we have the suspect or suspects in custody, just before we start our press conference."

"Do I detect animosity between your two agencies?"

"When I spoke with the original detectives on the case, they relayed what jerks the FBI guys were. The department doesn't forget slights like that."

"Remind me never to anger you cops," said Damian and they ended their phone call.

Damian sat back and thought about the investigation. Various pieces were coming together to build Natalie's case against Ashley Carrington. He thought they would be done with this case within the week. He wondered what the twins had spent already and what was available to retrieve from them. Certainly they had nine years to pawn items from the safe deposit boxes. It would be a mess getting back those hundreds of items, but that wasn't his problem; Natalie's fake college students had that list for whoever's job it was to run down the items.

Damien had another question in his head about the bank robbery. Why did Ashley have a safe deposit box and how did they get the other boxes open? He picked up the file on the case and looked for the answers to his questions. The detectives at the time of the initial investigation said that it appeared the boxes had been opened with keys, but how could that be? Ashley had a key to her own safe deposit box and she likely had at one time or another used the bank's master key to assist a customer with access to their box. So even if she had a copy of the bank's master key, that wouldn't open all the other boxes in the vault.

The FBI speculated that one of the robbers had locksmith capabilities given the sleekness of the box openings. They initially hadn't realized that the boxes had been hit during the robbery. A week after the robbery, a customer came in requesting access to their box and discovered it empty of everything but paper. Reading about the locks, it was likely given the age of the bank building that the locks contained a resettable feature; bank employees could then reset the locks themselves when a customer lost a key or closed a box. Locksmiths considered these older locking systems to be temperamental with the average bank employee having difficulty resetting the lock on their own. Most of these lock systems allowed the bank to reset the renter's side. Apparently the upside of the system was that older delicate mechanisms slipped and the bank thief could wiggle a change tool back and forth to change the lock or open it up.

Ashley and Michelle targeted the Willow Glen bank for all the right reasons; they had a lot of cash from local merchants, the safe deposit box lock system made it easier to pick, and the security installed inside the vault was limited by the age of the building and the bank's occupation of that space dating back one hundred years. Modern bank security systems simply didn't work in the old buildings. Old bank vaults were made of steel which could fall victim to a cutting torch. Later copper was added to stop the cutting torch, then cast iron. A bank vault in Japan survived the atomic bomb dropped on Hiroshima. That very construction made them difficult to demolish if a bank closed. Modern day banks were made from reinforced concrete; something that couldn't simply be cut through easily.

So did the twins use a torch to cut into the bottom of the safe? Again he pulled out the file to see what the experts suspected. After shuffling through paper, he saw the notes that pieced together the story of the robbery and yes they thought someone used a cutting torch.

This bank that the women targeted was one of the oldest in northern California. It once belonged to the Odd Fellows. The women could have bought safe deposit boxes in a variety of older banks and while visiting the vault, leaned against a wall with a cotton ball or piece of gauze covered in potassium ferricyanide. If it left a green spot on the wall of the vault, then they knew the walls were made of iron, the biggest ingredient in steel. Of course, that was only if the women knew chemistry. He supposed they could have looked up historic records to determine the age of a bank and therefore the likely age and construction of its vault. Perhaps they looked at the Clay-Montgomery building in downtown San Francisco, but their scheme wouldn't play in that location, or it was too expensive to set up a fake florist shop there for the year and it was a more heavily traveled area so their digging noise might be detected. Willow Glen was quiet after the restaurants closed for the evening. The historic San Francisco building contained an original safe deposit vault dating to 1908 and was a present day bank.

Damian looked at the time and realized he'd been distracted for nearly an hour with bank construction and the question of why this bank. In the end, the answers to those questions didn't get him closer to locating Ashley and Michelle Carrington. He decided to take another look at the tax software that Michelle used as it likely contained the name of her employer which would clue them in on the city. Minutes later, he had his answer. It was the B & K diner in Chum's Corner, Michigan, another small city in the region of Traverse City. He forwarded the information on to Natalie including a suggestion of how to relay it to her law enforcement friends.

32-CHAPTER THIRTY-TWO

When Ashley got home, the feeling of premonition was so loud in her head that she began packing. She and Michelle shared an apartment. Michelle was due home in about an hour from work. Ashley packed her clothes, her computer, and had a paper copy of the various accounts around the world, and multiple pieces of identity. She didn't exactly know where she was going, but she created a Twitter handle in case her sister wanted to reach her. It wouldn't be a quick means, but it would serve. Her car packed, she awaited Michelle's arrival at any moment. She planned to drive tonight to the Detroit airport and get on the plane to Jordan. All she needed was her passport, a Jordanian VISA would be issued to her upon arrival there. On previous visits to this region to exchange money, she investigated it as a means of escape if she needed it.

Ashley heard Michelle open the front door to the apartment. Michelle took one look at her sister and knew she was leaving. Besides she had seen her things in Ashley's car.

"You're leaving?" Michelle asked.

"Yes. The final money is yours to keep and exchange, as are the remaining safe deposit box items."

Michelle had also felt the strain of their relationship over the last nine years grow. It was not deliberate on either sister's part; rather they both hoped to start a new life and that meant leaving their twin and their old life behind them.

"Okay, it's not like either of us needs it. I suppose I could just burn it."

"Yes you could," Ashley said. "You should get going too, I just have an urgent feeling that we might be identified as the bank robbers."

"After nine years?"

"Yes. I feel like someone is getting close to us so it's time for me to hit the road. I set up a Twitter handle that you can use to find me; although it won't be quick. I'll keep my cell phone on for another hour, then I'm going to toss it in the first lake I see. Thanks for your support in life, but I have to get going," with the last rapidly spoken sentence Ashley stood up and hugged her sister. It was a tight hug but a dried eye exchange. For all the lifelong closeness of being a twin, Ashley now felt she had to get away or it would be the end of her. Minutes after Michelle arrived home, Ashley was out the door in her rush to get away, certain she would never see her twin again. She felt orphaned with her heart breaking, but some strong feeling was pushing her to get away.

She swung out on to the highway and started the more than four hour drive to the Detroit airport. She was tired from the drive that morning and the emotional loss of cutting the connection to her twin. While she was waiting for Michelle, she'd looked up the flights and custom requirements. She was departing for Amman, Jordan, planning on getting lost to United States eyes once she landed. In Jordan, she would stay the night getting new identification and clothing. Then she would head to Bangkok and on through Cambodia and that region before moving on to Australia. She figured she would end up in Australia, her final destination in about a week. She hoped that changing her clothes, hair color, and passports would allow her to disappear into the seven billion people living on planet Earth. She worried that Michelle would be captured, but there was nothing she could do about that; she'd warned her sister.

She was coming up on the lake where she planned to ditch her phone. Pulling over, she got out of the car, put the phone in front of the tire and rolled over it. She'd pulled the battery out before crushing the phone as she didn't want to put mercury, no matter how small the amount, in the lake. After giving it a major league pitch, it was soon out in the lake. Ashely was back in her car seconds later continuing to the airport. She debated what to do with the car. She'd like to give it to someone that needed it for them to drive at least until the registration ran out. The trouble with that idea was she didn't know where to find such a person and she didn't have a lot of time. In the end she rented a space at a storage facility, paying ahead for a year for the unit and left the car inside. She then got a taxi to the airport, pleased with her brilliant idea. Within two hours she was boarding a plane for Amman, Jordan and she heaved a sigh of relief once the plane was at its cruising altitude. Being able to relax gave her time to think about the past decade – the hard work of planning and executing the robbery and the drudgery of their jobs while they were secretly amassing a fortune. She felt like she'd been working sixteen hours a day for a long time because she had been doing exactly that. Shifts at the diner were supplemented by trips abroad to exchange money or mail items sold through auction. Worrying every day that they would be caught by the police. Michelle had relaxed as the years went by and they heard nothing, but not her.

Ashley admitted now that perhaps she hit the panic button, but she couldn't shake the feeling that someone was about to close in on her for the bank robbery. She couldn't blame Michelle for thinking they were safe as it would soon be a decade since the initial robbery. Both of them had acquired additional identification papers so they would be ready to run when necessary and they actually used some of those passports on money exchange trips just to make sure they would work. It's was nice to have them ready to go so she could run when she needed to. Now over the noise that was the interior of an airplane, she could relax for the first time in the past week and get some sleep.

33-CHAPTER THIRTY-THREE

Michelle had been surprised by Ashley's departure. She knew her sister had been getting more agitated each week this past year. She'd thought it was because they were nearing the end of their long journey and the secret had been unusually stressful to keep. Anytime someone was less than civil to her in her day job, she had to control her temper. She'd felt like calling bad customers a variety of bad names and screaming that she was a millionaire, and she was sure her sister felt the same stress of life these past several years; combine that with the border crossings that were unnerving for the variety of fake identification documents they used and it was no wonder Ashley had bolted.

In the last week, her sister had warned her several times that someone was getting close. When Michelle had questioned her, all she would say was it was a feeling. They discussed what to do with the final safe deposit box items and money. They kept it stored in a storage facility inside the old van they'd driven across country. Ashley wanted them to pay the rent for a decade and walk away. Michelle had done research and could find no reference to their case in at least the last five years. While she had enough money for the rest of her life, her problem was she hadn't figured out where she was going next. She had a love-hate relationship with the Midwest. The people were really nice, but the weather could be miserable at times. Ashley knew she would leave the United States forever, but Michelle wasn't so sure. In fact she wanted to stay exactly where she was, she just wanted to live up to her new means.

She knew she couldn't do that but it was paralyzing her to figure out where she should go next. She'd been many places exchanging money over the past decade, but none of them had drawn in her heart.

She sighed, knowing that Ashley would have thrown the phone away by now. She checked again to see if she could find any mention of their case. Tonight she promised herself she would pay the rent on the unit for the safe deposit box contents, and burn the remainder of the cash. She hated to do that; she'd rather give it to a charity, but they couldn't risk it going into circulation. At the time of the robbery, Ashley had been clear over which money might be marked and which money had come in the day before the robbery and was unlikely recorded anywhere. They had about twenty thousand dollars which they used to buy a used delivery truck, rent the storage unit in Michigan, outfit their apartment and pay rent. They used the money they exchanged on their first trip across the border to fund their travels to exchange the rest of the cash and to mail the items. They'd also used it to buy identification.

Michelle would tell the landlord tomorrow that they had vacated and he could now rent the apartment as furnished since they would leave their possessions behind. She'd work her shift then quit and get in her car and cross the border into Canada, drop the car off at a salvage yard, and take the first available flight out of Canada to somewhere in the world. Where could she find the Midwest in the rest of the world? Maybe she'd research that question tomorrow while waiting to board the flight.

She decided to test Ashley's theory that someone was about to catch them. She looked out her window but didn't see anyone she wasn't supposed to see. She went to the library to use their computer, erasing her history when she was done. Again, watching in her rear view mirror, she saw no tail. She went to their storage locker and gathered the final stash of dollar bills. She then drove to a deserted area and took the money and a small fire pit that she purchased at the local hardware store and tramped out into the woods. She brought some tarps as well to screen the fire from anyone who should happen upon this deserted area. It took less than twenty minutes to burn all the money. Michelle sighed watching it go up in flames and then smiled; only a millionaire could fail to be distressed by burning money. She left the pit and tarps behind and returned to her car. She hadn't noticed a single car when she occasionally peeked above the tarps to where the road was.

She arrived back at her apartment two hours later making final preparations. She discarded anything that wouldn't be used by a future tenant, careful to wipe down all surfaces, erasing her and Ashley's departure. She'd tell their landlord that they had been called south to Arkansas to care for an aunt suffering from cancer and that's why they were leaving in a rush and the furnishings were for him. She was pretty sure he would be happy as he was getting a furnished apartment for free with rent paid for another sixty days. Like Ashley, she had a suitcase of clothes and toiletries, a computer with her vital information and identification in the car. She had her uniform laid out for tomorrow and she went to sleep dreaming of where she would be sleeping tomorrow night.

34-CHAPTER THIRTY-FOUR

Ariana was sitting in her living room by herself with a glass of wine relaxing with a good book. It was the latest Inspector Gamache from Louise Penny and as usual it was riveting. Hermione was at dinner then the movies with friends and was getting a ride home from one of their mothers. Ariana had checked with her before she left to make sure she had some self-defense items in her possession. They discussed wearing the vest but it caused too many questions among her friends. So she carried a small aerosolized bottle of Damian's pepper juice stained with blue dye. So not only would the perpetrator be stopped, he'd also be covered in blue dye. Hermione carried one in her jacket pocket and had a back-up unit in her purse.

Ariana adjusted the blanket covering her legs while Miguel sighed, going back to his doggy dreams. He seemed to always be chasing something; perhaps he dreamed of squirrels. Ariana read for another hour and got up much to Miguel's disappointment to refill her wine glass. Her cell phone rang and she noted it was Hermione.

"Hey kiddo, isn't your movie starting soon?" Ariana asked, looking at the clock.

"Well yes, but I'm not going in. You need to come pick me up," the teenager said in a slightly breathless voice that immediately alarmed Ariana.

Throwing on her coat and grabbing the car keys, her purse, and with the dog following, she was soon out in her garage ready to charge out to rescue the girl.

"What happened? I should be there in three minutes."

"A man tried to grab me as we left the pizza parlor to walk down the street to the movie theater. He grabbed my left arm, so I swung out my right hand and sprayed him with Damian's juice."

"Good job kiddo. Are you safe at the moment? Are your friends still with you? Are you in front of the pizza parlor?"

"Yes to all of your questions. I only managed to hit the guy in one eye and he staggered off to his car and left, so I didn't call the police."

"I bet your friends are giving you grief for that."

"Yes they can't understand why I didn't call 9-1-1, although they were impressed and want their own supply of Damian's magic juice."

Ariana could see Hermione ahead on the street and said, "Kiddo, I see you on the sidewalk, I'll hang up now, ok?"

She waited to hear the okay before she ended the call. She pulled up to where Hermione was standing with her friends and got out of her car. Walking over to her, she gave Hermione a hug while eyeing her two girlfriends.

"Ladies, thanks for helping Hermione out and staying with her until I got here."

"She would do the same for us, Ms. Knowles," Megan said.

"You ladies missed your movie. Would you like to come home with Hermione and watch another one? I'll call your mothers to get their permission if you want to do that or I can just drop you at your homes."

The two friends looked at each other indecisively, having not thought beyond the strange man that tried to kidnap their friend. Then they looked at Hermione and said, "Yes, let's do that," and in succession, each girl got their parent on the phone to give permission to the change in plans.

Once that was taken care of, the three teenagers piled into her car with Miguel between the two in the backseat. He broke the ice and the three kids were soon relaxing. Minutes later they arrived home and the three teenagers discussed what they wanted to watch while Ariana texted Damian and got drinks and snacks for the girls.

Are you home?

Yes.

Can you come over, there's been another attempt to kidnap H. She's safe

& watching a movie with her friends at my house. Oh & bring over several more of the magic juice bottles.

Be over in twenty minutes.

Inspector Gamache would have to wait until later. Once the girlfriends cleared out, they were going to have a heart to heart with Hermione. She wanted to gulp a second glass of wine, but knowing she'd need to take the girls home, she abstained. Out of eyesight of the girls, she did several neck rolls and took some deep breaths. She knew she'd need to provide a full explanation to each parent when she dropped off their kid. Keeping an eye out the window, she looked for the lights of Damian's boat. When she saw it, she called out to Hermione, "I'm going to help Damian tie down his boat, call me if you need me." The kid nodded and Miguel stayed in place providing guard duty. Ariana threw on a lightweight parka and walked down to the dock.

Damian was in his final approach and Ariana reached for the rope at the front of his little speedboat to tie in to her dock. He hopped out and quickly did the same with the back rope. Then sensing she needed it, he reached out and gave Ariana a hug. He waited for her to push back and she did shortly.

"What happened?"

"Hermione and her friends went to the pizza parlor on First Street and then they were going to walk around the corner to view a movie at the theater. As she left the pizza parlor, a man grabbed her left elbow and she swung at him with her right which contained your pepper spray. She got him in one eye so he was able to retreat to his car presumably, then she called me. She handled it well, but her friends are shook by the experience and the fact that we didn't call the police. I've been working on my explanation for the parents when I drop off each kid later."

"You look like you need a glass of wine, so I'll take the girls home in your car. I'll present it as a random attack and that I, as an inventor, provided Hermione with one of my inventions. I'll pass a bottle on to each parent with instructions and tell them we didn't call the police because it happened so fast none of the girls had much of a description of the man and that surely he would hide for a while since he's covered in blue dye. I'll tell them we'll notify the police tomorrow just to see if there's any video in that area, but I'll take a look now to see if there are cameras. Think that will pass?"

"It might. I would add that we wanted to avoid making a bigger deal of this with teenage girls involved. I bet they'll never again let their girls hang out in public alone with Hermione, poor kid."

"Let's go inside. Have I met these two friends?"

"One's a swimmer, so maybe."

Ariana and Damian entered her house and walked to the living room. Damian had his arm slung on Ariana's shoulder so they looked like a united front to the girls. Ariana could immediately see that all three kids were distracted and not enjoying the movie.

"Ladies, you look like you're bored with the movie. Have you met Damian?"

Megan seemed to be the spokesperson for the trio so she said, "Our hearts are still racing over the strange man that attacked Hermione, Ms. Knowles."

Ariana nodded and reached over to pause the movie. "Rather than worry about the strange man, why don't we talk about self-defense."

Damian opened the small bag he brought to reveal two small canisters like the one Hermione used. "I'm going to give one to each of your parents and it will be up to them to accept it and give it to you. We're going to talk to the police later, but we don't have high hopes as it all happened so quickly that all any of you know is that it was a man that grabbed Hermione's arm, right?"

The trio nodded and Damian went on, "As Hermione's father and an inventor, I insist that she carry my inventions for her own protection. Hermione, why don't you grab your ugly vest and we'll show your friends that."

Hermione gave him a pained expression but did as he asked, returning a few minutes later.

Damian distracted the girls with an explanation of the vest and what his company was doing with it. He asked for their suggestions on how to make it prettier and more fashionable. In the end, he had them convinced that it had been random and perhaps the man had meant to just ask for directions. Once he created a non-threatening vision of what had happened, it was time to take the girls home. He had Hermione join him, so the parents could see she was calm and unharmed. Doing his best to appear to be the concerned parent, he was able to convince everyone that the poor man had simply asked directions. Both parents were so impressed with the canister that they asked for additional supplies.

Damian and Hermione were soon alone in the car and on the

way back to Ariana's house.

"You know, we're going to have to have a heart to heart about your parents. If you want any semblance of a normal life, you have to help Ariana and me with an explanation."

The kid nodded and nothing more was said until they arrived back at Ariana's house.

35-CHAPTER THIRTY-FIVE

The three of them had cups of tea and sat on Ariana's sectional sofa. All remnants of the teenager movie night had been cleared. Damian had a laptop and was checking for public cameras outside the pizza parlor and there weren't any that he could find. After dropping the girls off, he went back to the scene of the crime to see if he could spot any cameras and he'd seen none.

"Did you get a glimpse of the man who grabbed your elbow?" Ariana asked.

"Not really, I so instinctively fired the pepper spray at him if the poor man had been asking directions, he won't do that ever again."

"That was a cover story to de-escalate your friends and their parents. I think the man meant to kidnap you and if you had been less prepared, he might have succeeded," Damian said.

"Hermione, for your own safety and that of your girlfriends, you have to tell us the secrets you've been harboring about your parents. You've stayed with Damian and me for six months now. You've vacationed with us. You must have plenty of evidence that we'll do nothing to harm your parents or you, but we're trying to protect you with one arm tied behind our backs. So do you know why the man wants to kidnap you?"

Hermione had known from the moment she called Ariana that they were heading to this crisis point and she'd been thinking all evening about what to do. She didn't know how she felt about her parents actions; on one hand she was pleased that they were extorting a bad company, but on the other hand, she was embarrassed about the extortion and she thought they should have reported the company to perhaps the World Health Organization. People were still being harmed by bad drugs under the current scenario.

She had nothing but positive thoughts and feelings for Ariana and Damian; she was so fortunate to have ended up in their hands. They had been honorable and trustworthy and it was time for her to trust them with this final nugget.

"My father worked for a Malaysian drug company. He discovered that they were selling medications that had less active ingredients than they were supposed to which means that people would have been taking less effective drugs. He decided he no longer wanted to work for the company once he found this out. People that snitch in Malaysia don't have protections like they do in the United States. If he just notified authorities, the company executive would have had him killed. So we took a vacation and then just disappeared off the face of the earth."

"So what were you doing living in Shepard's Canyon?" Damian asked.

"Dad couldn't find a job after he left the Malaysian drug company. We were running out of money and we were on the run. Mom home-schooled me, so despite bouncing around the world, at least I didn't fall behind in school. Then we returned to the United States and my parents bought the house in Shepard's Canyon. I didn't ask questions, I was just glad to no longer be moving every couple of months."

"So your parents told you what they were doing when you moved to California?" Ariana asked.

"No, I was afraid of the answers so I didn't ask questions. Not even when they had the two safe rooms built. It was the drills."

"The drills?" Damian repeated, puzzled.

"We had to do drills on how fast we could get into the safe room. Dad or Mom would time the drill. I went along with that until they did a drill at two in the morning. I refused to participate until they gave me a better explanation for why we were doing it. So they finally told me the truth."

"What did you think of their explanation?" Ariana asked.

"I was disappointed. It didn't seem the honorable thing to do," Hermione shrugged.

"So what exactly did your father do?" Damian asked.

Hermione had been so caught up in remembering the moment her parents had explained the situation to her that she hadn't realized that she hadn't told Ariana and Damian.

"Dad said he was blackmailing the drug company for fifty thousand a month to stay quiet about how they make drugs."

"Ah," said Damian while Ariana remained silent in thought.

"So this guy who's been trying to kidnap you is doing that for what reason?" Damian mused.

"I don't know," Hermione replied. "I've never met him or remember seeing him with my parents."

"Either he's trying to capture you to bring your parents to heel, or he's trying to kill you afraid that you know the company's secrets," Ariana speculated.

"Since he hasn't tried to kill you, I think we have to believe he's using you one way or another to reach your parents," Damian said. "That's good news as it means your parents are alive, otherwise I think they would just kill you and be done with it."

"Maybe he thinks I know where my parents are."

"Do you?" Damian asked.

Hermione reacted as though slapped and uttered a small, sad "no".

These two adults had shown her nothing but kindness and affection and she hadn't held up her end of the bargain by coming clean by telling them her father's dirty secret.

Ariana leaned forward, sighed, and hugged the girl.

Damian waited for the two women to settle down and separate.

"I think we need a plan. I think instead of protecting you, we should set about trying to capture him."

"So how do we do that?" Hermione asked a little fearful. She had felt quite strong carrying around Damian's magic juice. She didn't want to be held captive by anyone.

36-CHAPTER THIRTY-SIX

"Good question," Damian replied. "I don't think we'll see him out in public for a few days. It will take quite a bit of washing to get the blue dye off and his eye will hurt for at least thirty-six hours. Do you remember where it hit his face or body?"

"Just that it was the right side of his face. When he took off, he had his right hand on his right side of his face. So the dye would be on his right hand and it might have rolled into his neck."

"Did you see the car he got into?" Ariana asked.

Hermione thought back to the incident and said, "No, I think it was on another street."

"Really? He was going to drag you at least a block and a half to his vehicle and he thought you'd go quietly? Doesn't sound like a smart guy," Damian said.

Hermione brightened at that thought and replied with a smile, "No, he doesn't sound smart as I would have screamed at the top of my lungs the whole time."

Ariana reached out a fist to share a fist bump with Hermione and said, "That's my girl!"

"So how do we trap him, ladies?" Damian asked.

There was silence in Ariana's kitchen as they all mulled over options in their minds. Then Damian said, "Let's be more thoughtful than our man was tonight. Here are some suggestions of parameters to design an event to capture this guy. First we need to do it somewhere quiet where he can't call for help. Second, Hermione will have to be the bait and be safe at the same time, and third, we should confine him out on San Francisco bay as he probably can't swim ashore. Any other ideas?"

"Should we try following him to wherever he lives?" Hermione asked.

"I think that would take time as we would have to find him to follow him," Ariana surmised.

"Perhaps we can do both. I'll start searching for cameras in the areas where you two have encountered him. Then perhaps, starting on Monday, we need to find a place each day to leave you alone with us nearby," Damian said. "I can rearrange my schedule to do that."

"How are we going to subdue him, once we find him?" Ariana asked.

"Good question," Damian said. "If he's the same guy we got in your driveway, then we're close to damaging his eyesight with as many pepper juice hits as he's taken."

"How about a net like the one that dropped on him at my house?" Ariana asked.

"He could still yell for help." Hermione said.

"Yeah, but I don't think he'll be inclined to call for help as he's a hoodlum," Damian said. "I think that's a good option Ariana, and I'll just need to figure out how to activate the net. It would be best if it was fired from a spring loaded gun. That way we wouldn't have to be too close, just close enough for the spring to drive a net at and around him."

"I agree, I don't think he'll yell for help. I think we can tell him to be quiet or we'll turn him over to the police on kidnapping and stalking charges," Ariana suggested.

"I agree," Damian said. "I'll work on getting two net firing guns."

"Why not three? I can carry one too," Hermione said.

"No, you probably can't with school security and it might scare him off," Damian replied.

"Where should we lay the trap?" asked Ariana.

"Good question. He must be watching you, Hermione, to have known about your movie plan today. We could start delaying picking you up from school and Ariana and I will stay low in my truck waiting for his approach. He hasn't seen my truck, so he shouldn't be suspicious. Where else do you think would work?"

"I'm not sure that would work as there are other people about at school and they would see us shooting him with the net," Hermione said.

"We have some time to decide on location and I need to design the cargo net gun. I know the engineer that designed those guns used to shoot t-shirts into an arena crowd so I'll start with that. I could have it ready by tomorrow. Ladies, you are both more familiar with this city and your schedules to understand where we might entice the man to strike. Hermione, do any of your friends walk home from school towards this house? Ariana and I could tag team you on this road and see if we can entice the guy. It's generally deserted so it makes a good place to start."

"What do you mean tag team?" Hermione asked.

"Ariana and I could pace your walk and switch whether we were front or back as you walked."

"Okay," Hermione said with a lack of confidence in her voice.

"Sweetie, we're all in this together and, so far, we haven't failed to protect you yet still gave you some freedom to have a life. We could keep you safe by just moving you to Damian's island, which sounds like a lousy existence for a teenage girl, but it's up to you. Damian and I believe we can protect you; we just need a quiet place to take down this man so you can get on with your life and not be afraid of being kidnapped."

"Look if you don't like the plan we've drawn, if you don't feel safe, we won't do it, we won't push you into a situation that you don't want. Okay?"

Hermione looked at these two adults that came so late but so competently into her life and felt the tears come. How could she love these two people that weren't her parents, but felt like they were? She certainly felt safer as they had given her tools to take better care of herself than her own parents and her mom and dad wouldn't be on the run if they hadn't tried to take money from their old boss.

She stood up and gave Damian and Ariana hugs, saying, "It's been a long day, I'm going to go to bed now."

Damian called out, "Hermione, is everything okay? You understand that you're safe?"

"Yes, I do," was all the teenager said before she left the room.

Once she was out of earshot, Damian whispered, "She's okay, right?"

"Yes, she is. I think she's feeling guilty about her feelings towards us versus her parents. I think she's happy with us and at times doesn't miss her parents and so feels bad for that."

"Okay," Damian said looking relieved. "Is there anything more I can do for you two? Do you feel safe here?"

"Since you upgraded my security, I'm rather like Hermione with my 'bring it on' attitude. I'll talk scenarios over with her during the next few days on where we want to stage this baiting situation."

"Okay, I'm going to head home to see if I can find anything on our perpetrator and see if I can get my hands on the cannon gun tomorrow. Then I have to figure out how to get the net in and we'll have to practice our aim."

"Ever since I washed up on your island, it's been an adventure. Now I'll add net gun shooting to my resume."

He just smiled, leaned over to kiss her cheek and he was out the door heading for his boat. She knew he didn't need her help shoving off for his journey back to Red Rock Island. She found herself standing at the window watching his boat light grow fainter in the distance, the palm of her hand on her cheek. Where had his kiss come from?

37-CHAPTER THIRTY-SEVEN

Leon Williamson sat with his partner, Dave Kowalski, outside of an apartment in Traverse City. The Michigan State Troopers had been contacted by a police department in California regarding a woman living in their city who was a suspected bank robber. They found it hard to believe that inside this low income apartment could live a woman who robbed a bank of sixty million nearly ten years ago.

"If I robbed a bank of that much money, I would be living in some country beyond the long arm of the United States like Russia or Tonga. I wouldn't be living in a cold part of the country in what looks to be the low end of the housing options," Leon said.

"Yeah, well how would you get the money and goods out of the country? Don't you think the airport would notice that you had bricks of dollars bills in your luggage?" replied Dave.

"Okay, then, I would try across the border into Mexico and keep going until I reached some place where the authorities wouldn't check my luggage," Leon said.

"According to the report out of California, it would have taken a U-Haul trailer to carry all the cash and goods away from some city named Willow Glen."

"Okay, then, I'd rent a yacht and sail down the coast carrying extra gas supplies so I could anchor into some small port where I could buy customs officials off."

"How would you pay for the yacht? In cash? The marked bills would then come to light and you'd be caught," Dave replied.

"Maybe this woman or women were smart and laid low exchanging money and goods. Those California police said there might be twins inside this location or at least involved in the crime."

"I would think that it would be the one person you could trust to keep their mouth shut, a twin sister or brother that is. What a shame, in some ways, if we catch them this long after the robbery. They should have settled for keeping less of the goods and left early for parts unknown."

"Even that might have hurt their cause as we cops would eventually discover a thirty million dollar stash."

"Dave, you're spoiling all my fantasies here. I'm trying to enjoy the thought of splitting that money with my older brother and what a trip that would be."

"Well just keep in mind that however much you think it would work, in reality it's very hard to outrun the long arm of the law."

"Okay. On to more practical stuff. What are we doing here? Are we knocking on the door and arresting whomever opens it if they match our picture?"

"We've been asked to observe as the California cops believe they'll have a warrant issued for the suspect by the end of the day tomorrow," Dave said.

"Why the delay? Either there are twins inside the apartment or they're not."

"Those California judges are harder to please so they asked for more information from the San Jose Police which they're providing tomorrow. So they believe the warrant will be issued in the next twenty-four to thirty-six hours and in the interim they want to make sure they don't lose sight of someone they've been chasing for nearly ten years. Really quite exciting to be in the middle of potentially bringing down two infamous bank robbers!"

"Sounds like it going to be a long boring night. Is there another exit to the apartment other than the one we're looking at?" Leon asked.

"I don't think so, but let's take a look around."

The two officers paced around the apartment building and found a second exit on the side. There were cars in the parking area but they would have to individually check each plate to find the cars that might be owned by the women. After using their cell phones to take pictures of all the cars' license plate numbers, they went back to their patrol car to position it to see both exits of the apartment building. They went to work on the cars checking out the registrations to find the owners.

"The brown car belongs to one Bob Clark who has ten outstanding parking tickets. How do you get parking tickets in this region?" Leon asked.

"What county were they issued in?" Dave asked.

"Kent County. The idiot likes to park in handicapped spaces without a placard or license plate. Nearly $400 a pop for each violation. We could arrest him for outstanding tickets."

"No, we're here for the one to two women. Let's keep going and find their car."

"I think it's the blue one as it's registered to a Michelle Carrington. Wasn't that the name we were looking for?"

"That's the name. Let's go take a look through the windows," Dave said as the two got out of their vehicle again. They walked around the car, placing a hand on the hood. "Car's been driven recently, but I don't see any more than the usual car junk; a Kleenex box, tubes of mascara and lipstick, discarded drink bottles. Let's go."

The night proved to be long and boring and the two were glad to be relieved by the day crew at seven.

Laurie Mueller and Brad Brown took over and caught action within their first hour on duty. They followed Michelle to a diner where it appeared she worked. Their day became long and boring as they strictly waited for her to get off of work. She finished her shift about an hour into the officers' overtime hours. California had offered to pay some of the surveillance cost as the department was short on officers.

They watched Michelle go out to her car and instead of driving back toward her apartment, she appeared to be heading north. Soon they were passing surveillance over to another district for them to continue with the surveillance.

Michelle had been exhausted from work and the emotion of telling her boss that she wasn't serving out her notice due to a sick aunt. She then understood Ashley's feelings as she began experiencing an unease in the afternoon. She couldn't understand where it was coming from as she recognized the vast majority of her clients and didn't observe any suspicious strangers. She worried that someone was following her as she thought she was catching glimpses of a car in her rear view mirror that was on her tail. She was pretty familiar with this area as she had made many trips across the border. She also knew a couple places where she might exit the highway and see if she was being followed.

Dusk was setting in which would both help and hinder her. She'd have a harder time seeing a potential tail and they would have a harder time finding her. She decided to exit and gas up the car and see if anyone followed her.

Five minutes later while pumping gas, she had her answer when a state trooper car exited the Interstate and continued past where she was tightening the cap on her tank. She made up her mind that she would try a few maneuvers to see if she could lose the trooper. She felt she had a chance since they hadn't driven over to arrest her on the spot. Either her paranoid mind was at work or they lacked grounds to detain her.

Another thirty minutes up the road, well beyond the Mackinaw Bridge, she accelerated and got ahead of the trooper car significantly. They probably were hanging back thinking they knew where she was going, she took an exit, immediately extinguishing her lights. Using the flashlight on her cell phone, she steered the car into a tree area and was soon out of the car gathering her gear while covering the car with a black plastic tarp. Michelle didn't know where she was going to live, but she'd always had a good escape plan. Besides the necessities of a laptop and identification, she had a foldable electric bike in the trunk. She pulled it out planning to ride to the Sault Saint Marie docks and hop aboard a ship sailing out of there and hopefully on its way to Thunder Bay, Canada. It was a cold and slow ride but better to still have her freedom. She would use the bike to get to the airport, then take a flight first to Winnipeg, then Calgary, and then on to London. She tried crossing the border in this manner on one of her previous trips just to see if it was possible to evade customs guards and she'd been successful reaching the port of Thunder Bay and exiting into the main city. Once she arrived in the UK, she planned to take the Eurostar over to the European Continent where she would find a small city where she could ponder her next steps. She'd also leave a remark on Twitter letting her sister know she was okay and that her paranoia had been a correct read of their situation.

38-CHAPTER THIRTY-EIGHT

"What do you mean the judge wants more information before he'll issue a warrant!?" Natalie nearly screeched the question at Detective Shimoda over the phone.

"I think it's a mixture of your unusual sources and the thought that a set of unknown female twins could have orchestrated the robbery of the century. It is what it is."

"One of the twins is thought to be missing and the other is on the move toward the Canadian border. We're running out of time."

"Canada is cooperative with U.S. law enforcement if we have a duly authorized arrest warrant. If we don't, they may still be willing to provide surveillance. So if the one twin crosses into Canada, it's not the end of the case as the Mounties are pretty good at getting their man."

"Okay, what more do we need to get this warrant?"

"Actually, the judge wants to talk to you and assess if your sources are legitimate. If you can produce your professor even better. I think he's worried that we've crossed the privacy line in looking for this information and wants a deeper conversation about it."

"Will he see us tonight? If I can get my professor to come, it's still a two hour drive from Berkeley at this time of day."

"Let me talk to his clerk since we know the suspect is on the move towards Canada. I'll call you back in ten minutes, will you have an answer from your professor as to whether he or she can make it tonight by that time?"

Natalie sighed and said, "Yes."

As soon as she ended the call, she called Damian.

"Can you drive down to the Santa Clara Municipal Courts right now?"

"Why do I need to drive to a courthouse at three in the afternoon? I won't get there until at least five, a time by which I would guess the courts are closed. Couldn't he at least do a video call?"

"The judge that we're trying to get to issue an arrest warrant for the twins is hesitant to do so. He wants to speak to the professor that assisted us in getting data and if possible he wants to sense your mettle in person."

"Are you kidding? You want me to lie to a judge?"

"Aren't you a lecturer or some such title at Berkeley?"

"Yes, but that's not a professor."

"You're splitting hairs, close enough. Do you have a card that says you're a lecturer with the University's logo on it?"

"Yes."

"Then that's all I need."

"I can't produce the students that supposedly ran the data though."

"No but the judge wouldn't expect that. He's just wanting to have a conversation with you on your information sources."

Damian debated what to do. Could he have a conversation with a judge and not violate his personal code of honesty and integrity?

"Neither twin is at home in their Michigan apartment at the moment. One is missing in action and the other appears to be on the move towards the Canadian Border."

Nothing like putting the pressure on him with that additional comment. They might be losing the chance to capture the girl. "I'll do it. If you'll pick me up at the dock in Redwood City, I'll arrive sooner at this hour."

"Thanks Damian. Don't do anything yet, I'm waiting to hear back from the Detective as to whether the judge will stay late. He said he'd call me back in another seven minutes."

Ten minutes later Damian was in his speed boat heading for the marina closest to San Jose which would greatly reduce his commute time at this hour. He had a box of flash drives and some paper but figured he run through his laptop and do a demo for the judge on where his imaginary students got their data from. He hoped that would end the judge's concerns and he'd be on his way back in another hour. He had work to do on Hermione's case.

An hour later, he was returning to his island. The judge had questioned him on his data and in the end thanked him for teaching those skills to the next generation of computer scientists. He also complimented him for assisting the SJPD and they were out of his chambers in under twenty minutes.

Natalie had her search warrant and was transmitting it to the Michigan State Troopers. It was then she ran into another snag.

"What do you mean you lost her? How could you lose her on a fairly deserted straight highway?" Natalie knew what the area looked like as she studied it on Google Maps to familiarize herself with the geography.

"She must be familiar with the area as she accelerated on a curve, and exited the highway once she got beyond our sight. It's dark now so she only had to turn her car lights off and duck inside one of the many tree lined areas for us to lose a visual on her. In the daylight, we'll be able to see tire impressions, but in the dark, we're searching with a spotlight hoping to pick up the shine of metal," the trooper said.

"Okay. How far are you from the Canadian border at the moment?"

"About ten to fifteen miles. If she's walking it will take her all night to reach it."

"Good luck with your search and keep me posted. Can you notify the border to stop her if she tries to exit?"

"Yes ma'am. It's already been done."

"Okay, keep me posted," Natalie repeated before ending the call.

She dropped a note to the detective and to Damian on the Michigan search for the Carrington twins.

39-CHAPTER THIRTY-NINE

Damian got back to his island and went to work on his containment weapon for Hermione's kidnapper. While he'd been at the judge's chambers his friend had delivered the air guns to the harbormaster's office for Damian. Now he had the air gun that the Warriors used to send t-shirts into the stands and Damian had a variety of nets he was trying to figure out how to fold into the gun. In no time, he had the technology figured out and the weapon ready to use against their man. Now he just needed a location for Ariana and himself to catch their suspect.

He briefly thought about the twins on the run and realized he was partially cheering them on to escape detection. He supposed that it was because it felt like they hadn't harmed anyone and he liked their meticulous plan for staying hidden. He'd gotten Natalie's email about them eluding capture and decided he wouldn't offer to help. He assisted in solving the cold case and that would be enough. If the twins were brilliant enough to allude capture and leave the United States, then bravo to them. They hadn't physically harmed anyone and the actual robbery had been covered by insurance so he was satisfied at having solved the heist of the century with the two bank robbers still on the lam.

After a good night's sleep, Damian headed over to his warehouse to welcome Lily on her first day. She arrived shortly after him and he went through the routine of giving her new employee stuff and setting up her computer station with her. Then he had each of his other employees explain what they were working on so she would understand more about the company. Haley proudly demonstrated her drone which was ready for both patent processing and commercial production. Damian was of a mind to offer two models priced for his two target markets. One would be for people that needed help carrying stuff. A second model was for use by industry and could be programmed to run without an operator on repetitive tasks. Ariana would take the product forward to launch now that it was technically complete.

As it was the first product to be completed under the new business, Damian ordered in a celebratory lunch. He then had Lily begin work on his field DNA machine and the two women also had the side assignment of developing the self-defense vests. Damian checked in with Lily at the end of the day to find her intellectually challenged but excited about her future role. That was all he could ask of a new employee.

He transmitted that opinion in an email to Ariana and asked her if she and Hermione had found a location that could be used to capture their suspect and shortly received her response.

We both studied our usual route to school and back as well as the downtown area where H hangs out with her friends. We concluded that close to home is the only place we could shoot and cover a guy with a net and have the privacy to get away with it.

Okay, Damian thought he had another twenty-four hours before their man would be on the hunt for Hermione again given the time it would take to scrub off the dye and get his vision back in the eye struck by pepper juice. He decided to go back home and spend some time detecting where the guy hid when he wasn't stalking Hermione; that would be another option to go after him at a hotel depending on the circumstances.

Damian began looking for public cameras around the area where they had last seen their man. He was so lost in finding information about Hermione's kidnapper that it was nearly nine at night before his cats meowing alerted him it was time to take a break and feed them and himself. Sometimes he could depend on them to be an alarm clock for him reminding him of meal times. He sighed and went upstairs to find them and himself something to eat. He was making progress but his eyes and brain would probably benefit from stepping away from the computer for a while.

Twenty minutes later, with the cats purring in their sleep from full bellies, he planted himself back in front of his computer screen with a gourmet grilled cheese sandwich on sourdough. He was too embarrassed to lower himself to eating a quick peanut butter and jelly sandwich and thought that at least a three cheese grilled sandwich better reflected the sophisticated adult that he was. He was beginning to think that he found the guy at an economy hotel in Mill Valley. While the hotel was off of a busy street, he thought that he and Ariana could attack the guy at the entrance to his hotel room and haul him off in the middle of the night for questioning. It would be much easier on Hermione if he could arrange this event.

He looked at the time and thought, well there was no time like the present to do this. It was half past ten, which would give him and Ariana some practice time with the net launching guns before they swarmed the guy's hotel room at say one in the morning. He texted Ariana to find out if she was awake. He knew she had to get up early most mornings to get Hermione to water polo practice.

Yes.

Great, I'm going to call you.

"How would you like to be involved in some late night breaking and entering at a hotel in Mill Valley?"

"And why would I want to do that? I really don't want to have a criminal record," Ariana said amusement in her voice.

"I am about ninety-eight percent sure I found Hermione's kidnapper at that hotel. I thought we might go break into his room and shoot him with the net gun there in about three hours."

"Oh!" Ariana said while she adjusted her brain to carrying out a serious criminal activity in a few hours. Then she sighed and said, "You better come over here and I'll see if Hermione's awake and she'll need to know about our plans."

"Okay. Let me gather up my stuff and I'll be over in about thirty minutes."

Damian looked around his lab for stuff to take with him then went upstairs to change into all-black clothing. He then looked around his house for an area to secure his prisoner. He'd have to use Hermione's room as that would likely do the least damage to his house. He briefly debated holding the guy in his garden shed outside, but it could get cold at night and he had no way to watch it or heat it. He put a remote camera in Hermione's room and a new lock on her door. He then packed his supplies into the speed boat and headed across the bay to Ariana's house.

As he slowed the boat in approach to her dock, he saw the house ablaze with lights. She must have watched for his boat and both she and Hermione came outside to help him tie down the boat and carry supplies to her house. In short order, they had everything inside and he had the chance to look at the teenager and the woman's faces. He saw what he expected to see; part excitement, part apprehension on the face of the women and mostly apprehension on the face of the teenager.

After setting the last of his supplies on the kitchen counter, he opened his laptop and showed them the hotel where he thought Hermione's kidnapper was staying. After showing his process and the car in the lot, he then went back over several days of footage to show Hermione views of the man. Given his research and the camera angles, she agreed that was the guy.

"So, ladies, our plan for the night. We can see that this guy is staying in a bottom room, room twelve to be specific. So I thought we'd break into his room, shoot with the cargo net, duct tape his hands, feet, and mouth and lift him into the back of your car, return here and take the pontoon boat out to my island where I'll lock him into your bedroom, Hermione. That's an overview of what I plan. Thoughts?"

"Do I come with you to the hotel?" Hermione asked.

"I don't have an answer to that," Damian said, "but I would prefer to leave you here. If for some reason we get caught by the police it would be better for all involved if you were nowhere in the vicinity. That way you can't be an accessory to our criminal behavior."

There was silence for a few moments while all three thought about the best and safest position for Hermione to take.

Then she said, "If I come with you, I could serve as a lookout in case anyone gets close to your room twelve."

"And if Damian and I show ourselves to be completely inept at kidnapping, what will you do when the police show up?"

"I don't think the police are going to show up; you're too talented to get caught and I think this guy wants to keep his mouth shut, but if I'm wrong. I'll make my way back home to Ariana's house or if need be over to your island until you guys can return."

The two adults thought about their options. They liked her being close and helping. They didn't like exposing her to the nastiness of the criminal activity they were about to perform, but they had faith in her ability to make her way back to one of their houses if they should fail in the mission. Damian looked at Ariana trying to decipher if she was arriving at the same conclusion as he was and if he read her correctly, she agreed.

"Okay we'll set up an open cell phone line between the three of us so we can stay in communication. I brought over my magic fabric that will nearly make us invisible in the dark and I'll leave a piece of it with you, Hermione, for your safety. Let's go outside and practice with the net gun. We may need to reload on the spot if we both miss our first shot. I thought we'd try 'capturing' your pool's springboard as that represents a man lying down in bed. Let's see if with a little practice we can nail him from ten and twenty feet away and once we get perfect at that, we'll go back inside and get dressed all in black for this operation."

They went outside to practice and Damian was thankful that Ariana's backyard couldn't be seen by her neighbors as they would be wondering why they were shooting a net at a springboard at midnight. He smiled a little at the thought and Hermione caught his smile.

"What's so funny?" she asked.

"I was just thinking about how strange we look firing a gun that shoots a net at a diving board at midnight. If we were on a YouTube video people would question if we were sane."

She smiled in return and relaxed a little in the dangerous situation.

"Look at the bright side of this situation, Hermione; you're not a decoy, rather you'll be assisting us from a safe position."

"What if he's not in the hotel room?"

"Then we'll do this again tomorrow and he'll never know we entered tonight."

"Okay. How are you going to break into his room?"

"I have a card system that once I scan the hotel lock mechanism, it will duplicate it on to my plastic key card and I'll use that as a Master to enter his room. I'm also taking bolt cutters in case the guy has put a safety chain across his door on the inside."

"Oh. Some day when you're not fighting my wars, you'll have to show me some of this stuff in your lab. I don't want to be a computer geek when I go to college but I should understand the big picture of what you do."

"Tell you what, the next time you stay with me on the island, I'll give you a detailed tour of my computer lab. I'll have your eyes and brain glazed over in no time and you'll get a good night's sleep."

"Damian, you are such a nice man and I'm so lucky that I crawled into your dingy of all the boats in the Richmond harbor."

"Hermione, thank you for not subjecting me to teenage hormone dramas. You are such pleasure to take care of and support and I feel lucky you came into my life," Damian said giving her a hug.

The two embraced while Ariana continued practicing her aim at the springboard. She figured with five more shots and reload, she'd have it down to be a good partner in crime. She was glad to see Hermione and Damian getting closer as it was good for both of them.

"Okay before the two of you turn to mush over there, I think we should move on to our next stage. Hermione and I will change into all black clothing and then let's talk our plan through. Damian, do you have any grease paint in your supplies? Our faces are going to glow in the dark."

"I didn't remember to bring that but if you have dark eye shadow and some Vaseline, we can make our own."

Hermione was on her way out of the room yelling, "I've got that, I'll bring the supplies down to the kitchen and some fabric for everyone's hair."

"She seems to have bought into our plan and I think she'll be safe in the car. If the worse should happen, then she'll make her way home. It might be a long journey but the kid has the gumption to get there," said Ariana.

"Let's just hope the plan goes according to schedule," Damian said worried about Hermione and Ariana getting caught in this hare-brained scheme of his.

After Hermione returned and mixed the ingredients, they were all nicely covered in black and hard to see in the dark. Damian went through the plan one more time and demonstrated the use of the magic fabric outside in the dark so the ladies could see how well it would cloak them. After he finished demonstrating the technology they would be using and their plan to subdue the man in room twelve, it was time to pile into Ariana's car for the journey over to Mill Valley.

40-CHAPTER FORTY

They made a pass by the hotel to review the parking lot and looked at the door to room twelve. As they passed, all three were also looking for a parking spot that would be close enough for Hermione to be able to view the hotel room, but not so close as to put the car under a light or for the car to look out of place.

On the third pass they determined the perfect spot and Damian pulled in. Hermione immediately pulled the magic fabric over herself and the three of them tested their headsets before they got out of the car.

Both Ariana and Damian moved towards the hotel room. With the slight breeze coming off the bay, they occasionally appeared when the wind blew their magic fabric cloth away from their bodies but then Hermione knew what she was looking for. At this time of night, she thought that no one else would notice the occasional appearance of a human leg. They would assume they were seeing things late at night.

Pretty soon Hermione thought the two were over in front of room twelve. As they were close to the building, they weren't getting the wind they had crossing the parking lot. Keeping an eye on the door, she saw it open and then close again. They were inside the kidnapper's room. Hermione took a moment to look at the front of the hotel and saw no action going on elsewhere. One light was on in the entire hotel and she heard no approaching sirens. All good news.

About five minutes later, she saw the door to room twelve open again. Damian was still wearing his concealing cloth and it appeared there was an upside down body moving across the parking lot. She could see only feet striding across the lot toward the car and it was really freaky looking. Then the breeze hit them again beyond the protection of the building and she caught a quick glimpse of Ariana. Hermione also knew by monitoring the microphones that they had woken the poor man and had him tied up and out of the room in no time.

The car door was suddenly opened and he was deposited in the seat next to Hermione. Damian motioned her out and into the front seat and he took her place in the back seat, while Ariana climbed in, started the car, and they left Mill Valley heading for Ariana's home in Belvedere. No sound was coming from the man so Hermione assumed they had taped his mouth shut. On one hand she felt sorry for him. It must be hard to breathe given the stress of the moment and the tape, but then she wiped that out of her mind with the thought that given a chance the man in the back seat would have done the same to her.

The drive was quiet on the way to Ariana's house. When they arrived, Damian again carried the man over his shoulder in a fireman's clutch to Ariana's pontoon boat. Twenty minutes later they pulled up at Damian's dock and he moved the man inside to her bedroom. Some of the revulsion for her kidnapper sitting on her bed and on her sheets must have shown in her face as Damian whispered to her that she would have new bedding the next time she stayed with him.

Once in the room, Hermione watched Damian chain the man to a new hook that he must have installed for this purpose. She also noted the camera. Again the distress must have shown on her face as Damian whispered 'later' at her as a way of providing her with the knowledge of a further explanation. Then she shook her head and told herself to move on from these petty feelings. She was lucky to have these two adults that captured the man that likely knew something about her parents. She was about to get her first answers in months as to what was going on.

Once the man was secured in her bedroom, the two adults came outside to check on her.

"Kiddo, are you doing okay?" Ariana asked sensing the teenager's stress.

"Yes. At first I was angry seeing him in my room, on my bed.

Then I told myself to get over it as it made sense to secure him there rather than anywhere else in this house. It also makes sense to bring him to this island as if he should escape the room, he really can't swim ashore unless he has a wetsuit on and I don't see one. So I'm chill with the situation."

Damian reached over and gave the girl a hug and said, "Sweetheart you're going to fall asleep in class tomorrow from all this late night activity. Do you have water polo practice at six?" He looked at his watch as he asked the question, thinking the kid would have to be back at school in just under four hours.

"No practice tomorrow as it's a late day because the teachers have a meeting. So you picked the perfect night for me to stay up very late."

"There is no perfect day to involve a teenager in a kidnapping of another adult," Damian groaned feeling like a failing parent.

The teenager just patted him on the arm and said, "It will be okay."

Damian had a hundred emotions crossing him at once including who was the parent here and wow wasn't he an awful parent for exposing this wonderful child to the kidnapping of another adult. He should be shielding her from the violent world.

"Why don't you go upstairs to my kitchen and make our prisoner some tea? I suspect he'll want something to drink once I remove the tape," Damian requested.

Hermione frowned at him suspecting that he just wanted to get her out of earshot so he could threaten the man some more. Then she shrugged and said, "Sure, I'll be down with tea in about five minutes. Cups for everyone?"

He nodded and she left his computer lab to take the stairs to the kitchen. He had an induction cooktop and so it wouldn't be long before she reappeared with tea for all.

Damian opened the door to their prisoner's room and said, "I'm getting some tea for you, me and the ladies. I figure that after I remove the tape across your mouth, you'll want something to drink. A word of caution, as you might have guessed from the boat ride, you are on an island in San Francisco Bay. You don't have a wetsuit, so you'll die from hypothermia before you reach the shore. You've been trying to kidnap our sweet teenager so we're going to have a conversation about that in a minute. Understand?"

The man nodded and looked resigned. With a razor blade,

Damian cut the duct tape that held the man's two wrists together. He couldn't go anywhere though as Damian had handcuffed one of the wrists to a wall hook well secured into the framework of the house.

Ariana pulled out documents she found in the man's hotel room. Picking one of them up, she opened a passport and said, "This identification says you're Jack Mayang, a resident of Malaysia. This passport says you're John Lee from Malaysia, and yet a third identification says you reside in Hong Kong. Pretty careless to leave all of these conflicting passports around for anyone to read. Who are you really and maybe we should just turn you over to immigration along with your multiple forms of identification?"

He couldn't answer her as the tape was still across his mouth. Damian heard Hermione returning with a tea set and said to the man in a low and menacing voice, "I'm going to remove the tape on your mouth and you'll be provided some herbal tea and you'll say nothing but pleasant things while that teenager is in the room. Do you understand?"

The man nodded and, as Hermione was arriving, Damian began removing the tape, a relatively painful process. He paused and said to Hermione, "Hermione, this tape is really sticky. Can you run back to my kitchen and get some olive oil? It will make getting this tape off a much less painful process."

She was gone and returned moments later with the desired bottle and a paper towel. Damian used the towel to pat the oil around the tape and it began to come off with less pain for the man. When Damian finished, he was handed a cup of herbal tea which he appeared to gratefully swallow.

Finally, he set the empty cup down on the bed and said, "I'm John Lee from Malaysia."

"Why have you been trying to steal Hermione?"

He looked puzzled by the name and said, "You mean Hannah?"

Hermione spoke up from the door and said, "My name is Hermione Smith."

John Lee replied, "Your name is Hannah Sherman and I'm searching for your parents. But you don't know where they are do you?" he asked looking at Hermione.

Ariana spoke up then, "Look we're not going to argue names here. What were you planning on doing with the child if you had managed to capture her?"

"I was planning to use her to get her parents."

"Then you're barking up the wrong tree as she doesn't know where they are," Ariana said.

Mr. Lee said, "Barking up the wrong tree? What does that mean?"

"That was Ariana's way of telling you that Hermione has no idea where her parents are or even if they are dead or alive. They were kidnapped in the middle of the night. She has not seen nor heard from them since," Damian knew these were brutal words for Hermione to hear.

41-CHAPTER FORTY-ONE

John Lee had run through a myriad of emotions in the last hour. He had been sound asleep when the two people broke into his hotel room. Before he knew it, he was tied inside a net and hauled over someone's shoulder to a car then a boat. He knew enough of the geography of the area to know that he was still in the region and he was clearly not on a boat of any kind. The teenager's guardians must have figured out where he was staying and gone after him. What to do next?

He couldn't go back home as he had no job and quite possibly no life. Clearly though, the game was up in the United States. He had no weapon on him and there were none in this room, which after looking around appeared to be the teenager's room. The silvery purple paint color seemed to suit the girl, not the adults. Overpowering these people was a problem as he noted they were each carrying a spray bottle, and he was sure that acid substance was inside the bottle. He wasn't sure his eyesight would stand many more attacks. He felt that beyond the terrible burning sensation of each hit, his eyesight had been a tad blurrier. Maybe the eyes would heal in time and maybe not.

If the three of them were telling the truth, and he had seen no evidence otherwise, then the girl would not serve as leverage against her parents as she had no way of contacting them. It seemed that parents and child had been separated since last spring. Then other questions arose in his brain.

"Who are you people? Are you relatives of Hannah?"

"I'm Damian and this is Ariana and we're Hermione's legal parents."

John Lee had been in the United States for a while, but he didn't understand the term 'legal parents'. Why were they calling the girl named Hannah something else that was unpronounceable to him?

"Harmony's parents?"

"Hermione, as in the Harry Potter series," replied Hermione.

"Harry Potter? Who is that?"

"Never mind," Damian replied recognizing that the man's knowledge was limited in that area by his age and his lack of knowledge of popular icons in the western world. "What were you planning to do with Hermione if you captured her?"

"I was going to make her contact her parents. She must have a way to do that."

"I don't," was Hermione's stony reply.

John Lee stared at her finding it hard to believe the child was cut off completely from her parents.

"You and your band of thugs stole my parents in the middle the night. The last contact I had with them was watching them be restrained and loaded into a van about four or five months ago. I have no idea where they are now or even if they're alive," Hermione said ending with a sob.

John Lee watched the older woman hug the child in comfort and said, "If you were unable to communicate with your parents, my next step would be to call Mr. Lin for guidance."

"Who's Mr. Lin?" Damien asked, though he had an idea.

"He's the man who hired me to find Hannah."

"It's Hermione," the teenager said rebelliously and Ariana rubbed her shoulder and whispered to her, "Depending on what this man says we may need to change your name again, so don't love it too much."

"Did your Mr. Lin want Hermione killed at some point?" Damien asked.

John Lee looked startled at the question in front of the teenager but then answered, "Yes because he thinks she knows about the problem in his drug manufacturing. So even if he found and killed her parents, she was still a liability."

These were harsh words for Hermione to hear, but she didn't lose it as it was merely a confirmation of what she had thought all along. Her knowledge was a liability. For some reason, she found comfort in the fact that she was with Damien and Ariana rather than her own parents. She felt she was able to lead a more normal life and was better protected than just having a safe room to run into and barricade herself. Then she felt guilty for her thoughts; she loved her parents very much.

"So what are our options?" Damien asked.

No one in the room knew who he was addressing the question to and so there was silence.

"How do we get rid of Mr. Lin and his threats once and for all?" Damien asked rephrasing his question.

"I say we contact the United States FDA and tell them about Mr. Lin's corrupt manufacturing," Ariana said. "It will terminate the bribery payments to Hermione's parents account, but it will take the heat off of her."

Damien felt like he needed to think about their options and do some more research on Mr. Lin and his corporation. It was going on three in the morning and he was exhausted. He bet all of them looked miserable as they hadn't removed the grease paint yet and it was smeared on each of their faces.

Damien stood up to leave the room and said, "John Lee you are secure in Hermione's bedroom. You can't escape and I have a video camera and other alarms on this door. As I mentioned, you're on an island and you'll freeze to death before you make it ashore if you should try swimming. Let's all get some sleep and we'll decide what to do tomorrow on well rested brains."

Damian allowed the man use of the bathroom and then locked him up for the remainder of the night. He then went out into the lab and said, "Ladies, do you want to sleep here or at home for what remains of the night?"

"Kiddo, I think we should head home as you need to go to school in a few hours. We may as well go home so you can sleep as late as possible and not have to worry about the commute across the bay to get to school," Ariana suggested. Then with a worried glance, she added, "Maybe you should take an excused absence from school tomorrow."

"I can't, I have a presentation with another classmate on a science project. Remember we worked on it two nights ago?"

"Okay," Ariana said thinking the teenager didn't seem traumatized by their nighttime activities.

"Damian, are you safe by yourself alone with this man?" Hermione asked.

"Are you doubting my fighting abilities?" he asked as he faked being affronted.

"Noooo," Hermione said slowly, "But you're a genius and you would probably lose a fist fight at school."

"You're probably right which is why I have a series of traps laid out should Mr. Lee try to break out of your bedroom, and don't worry, I'll completely change everything so you won't notice his presence the next time you stay here."

"You're not going to keep him for long?" Ariana asked.

"I don't think so. I can't hold him captive for long as there's no point in doing that and he's disrupting my life at the present so I want to take him back to Mill Valley as soon as we have a plan."

"Okay," Ariana said and followed that with a big yawn. "Kiddo, let's go take the boat home and we'll sort this out tomorrow."

Damian saw them off and then checked on his prisoner. Fifteen minutes later, he got a text from Ariana saying they were safely at home.

He knew he should be exhausted, but his mind wouldn't let go of what to do about Mr. Lin and he still had the remnants of adrenaline from the kidnapping attempt. In his kitchen, he sipped tea while looking out into the fog of the night and thought about the problem at hand. He had an idea that he planned to discuss with Ariana in the morning and with that he again checked his alarms and finally, fell asleep in his own bed.

42-CHAPTER FORTY-TWO

As Michelle had projected, it was a slow cold ride to the Soo locks. Her bicycle was quiet and she aided the battery by pedaling, as well, which served to keep her warm. She knew the police were looking for her but she felt secure with her mode of transportation. She knew they would discover her car at some point and perhaps as early as daybreak. She carried her bike over the soil and onto a concrete road so they would not have tire tracks and know to be on the look-out for a bicycle. Also if they thought she was moving on foot, they knew she wouldn't reach the border for hours rather than the single hour she expected to take.

While at work that day, she called the Soo locks to get the boat schedule which they recorded each day as a courtesy to tourists. She was aiming for a ship that was traveling to Thunder Bay with road salt for the coming winter. She especially liked this ship as it would be docking at an oil refinery dock rather than the Port Authority in Canada and thus it was easier to avoid customs.

In her practice run a few years ago, she lowered the bike and then herself over the side of the lock in the dark, before the lock began to fill with water to take it to the higher Lake Superior side. Generally speaking people weren't watching the back of the boat at this time; they were looking forward to where the ship would sail and watching the water level to judge when they would be able to untie and sail forth.

She quietly approached the locks, cutting through a cyclone fence. She was in all black and had a dull black tarp over the bike so that nothing shown in the night. She was fortunate that it was the quarter phase of the moon as she might have been seen in a full moon. She was also blessed by heavy fog. Soon she was on the deck of the ship and she rolled her bike and herself underneath a heavy oilcloth cover of ropes on the deck. They would arrive under cover of darkness the next night. In the meantime, Michelle had food, water, and a jar to pee in to make the most of the slow ride to Canada. She just hoped they wouldn't hit any rough seas or she might end up tossing her stomach contents. Her patience for such a journey was supported by the knowledge that her freedom was at stake.

She heard crewmen around her at times, but she knew that a ship like the one she was on needed at most four to six crewmen on duty at any one time. Her private nest among the rope coils went undisturbed. She estimated they were an hour out from Thunder Bay and so she began preparing her escape. Unless the weather was in her favor with very heavy fog, she'd have a hard time getting both her bike and herself off the vessel without being detected. During her practice run she made her escape entirely on foot and they had docked at a different location in Thunder Bay so this was where she could make mistakes and potentially be seen by people that might want to turn her over to the police. She used her cell phone to see the geography of the dock on Google.

She felt the engine slowing but the rim of the ship railing was so high that she couldn't tell how close they were to shore. With rope she'd found under the canvas cover, she fashioned a rope harness so that she could carry the bike down off the boat; she just needed a rope to hang off the edge and slowly ease her path onto a dock. As she hoped, she had both night and heavy fog to hide her appearance. Looking to make sure the coast was clear, she crawled out and looked over the edge to see what was facing her and couldn't believe her luck. There was a small rowboat laying on its side on the dock. She could be over the edge and rowing away in less than two minutes and with the fog obscuring the front of the boat from the back, hopefully no one would be the wiser.

Her luck held and shortly she was in a tiny rowboat with her bike's front tire hanging over the front of it, gently rowing the boat away from the giant ship and to a beach she expected to be in the distance. She just needed to keep her bike battery and her laptop from dipping into the water and all would be good. Oh and hopefully no other vessels on this river would hit her tiny rowboat in the complete darkness.

An hour later, she dragged the boat up on the beach. She carried her bike and used one of the boat paddles to cover up her steps in the sand. She didn't think the Michigan State troopers could connect these footprints in sand with a missing American woman, but why take chances on anything? Once she was on the road, she followed her GPS to a Walmart Supercenter. If her bike was stolen while she was inside then she'd call for a taxi to take her towards the airport.

Thirty minutes later armed with a suitcase, duffle, snacks, and a wardrobe, she looked around for her bike and found to her delight that it was stolen. It saved her getting rid of it and she hoped that some thief would get some use out of the bike. Shortly, she was at the Thunder Bay Airport having booked a flight to Calgary via Winnipeg. If all went well, she'd be on the midnight flight to London and then free as a bird in perhaps another eighteen hours. She hoped Ashley was as successful in her travels and she admitted she was looking forward to the adventure ahead now that the die had been cast and she was on the run.

Her passport said she was Magdalena Nylund which was a fine Finnish name and there was a large Finnish population in Thunder Bay. Michelle had a white blonde wig and given that she'd been living in cold Michigan and her skin hadn't seen the sun for a while, she thought she probably had the appropriate Nordic features. Once she was beyond Canadian security and customs she took a deep breath. She had never used this passport before and felt anxious that it would have all of the embedded security in it. She'd bought it two years ago when she passed through Toronto and had taken her passport picture in the same white blonde wig that she had on now. Hopefully, if the Michigan troopers gave her information to the Canadians, the passport and changes she made to her appearance would get her out of the country unnoticed.

Nearly twelve hours later and again traveling overnight, Michelle's airplane landed at London's Heathrow airport. She managed to get some sleep on the plane and again after clearing through customs and security, she picked up her suitcase and looked for the underground so she could catch a train to the Eurostar station. Once her train finally arrived in France she was going to get off in Wimereux, a small town on the western coast, and plant herself in a small hotel with twenty-four guestrooms. She would hang out there while she tried to consolidate her assets. Then she would hop back on the train and head to Turkey. She thought she would rent an apartment or house in the town of Izmir and relax beyond the usual reach of the United States.

Sighing as she sat back in the train seat, she looked back on the last decade. It had been work, first just planning the robbery, then the actual digging while operating a florist shop, then executing Ashley's meticulous plan for exchanging the currency and safe deposit contents all the while holding down full time day jobs. They hadn't had a vacation in all that time despite sitting on a pot of gold. Now, she was about to live for the first time in her life. She could go anywhere, be anyone starting tonight in France. She didn't speak French but she was anxious to see what random strangers she'd find once she got there. Her new adventure was about to begin!

Meanwhile, Ashley Carrington was making her way on the last leg of a long journey. After Jordan, she had flown to Kuala Lumpur, Malaysia and finally Darwin, Australia. She had located a six month rental in Cullen Bay and planned to just stay in the area after she located a place to live on a more permanent basis. The wet season would start soon in this area which meant she better get used to hot and humid temperatures. Still a nice change from windy and cold Michigan.

She hoped her younger sister by two minutes had taken her advice and skipped town. They both had explored options over the years of how to escape detection and so she knew that Michelle would head north to Canada and then out of the country, but she'd been unable to say where she wanted to go once she left America behind. After she arrived at her new living space, she would unpack and check the twitter account she set up to communicate with her sister and to also see if there had been any news on the Willow Glen Heist.

There was a Tweet from an avatar she knew to be Michelle that said she was hanging out with the Flyers for the day. Good Ashley thought, Michelle had taken her warning to heart and had at least made it to Thunder Bay. The Flyers were their hockey team. Ashley tweeted good luck with the Flyers and that she had a good time with the Shamrock Eagles, a local football club. So that was good news; they both were safe outside of the long arm of the United

States.

Ashley then went to work on the bank heist to see if anything was mentioned in the press in California or Michigan, but there was no news. She'd keep checking over the next few days, but she felt relatively safe in the hot corner of the North territory of Australia. Darwin had another one hundred thousand people in it for her to get lost in. She changed her identity three times between departing Michigan and arriving in Darwin. Her story to people she met in Darwin was one of an inheritance and a desire to start over in this part of the world. From what she knew of Australians, they would appreciate her approach. She planned to try all kinds of lessons from surfing to playing the piano, to trying to paint. She planned to set up a dating profile on one of the online dating sites. A year from now, she might still be in Darwin, or she might have moved on.

43-CHAPTER FORTY-THREE

Damian woke up later than usual the next morning but still short of six hours of sleep. He checked on his prisoner who also appeared to be awake. He was examining the room and the daylight filtering through Hermione's infinite window. He watched the guy touch it as though expecting it to be a window that opened to the outside and he seemed disappointed to learn it was a plasma screen. Damian put his robe on, grabbed his bottle of pepper juice and traveled downstairs to speak with his prisoner.

Thanks to the camera in the room, he could see that the guy was away from the door, still secured to the bed. He knocked and then opened the door.

"There's nothing but rock outside that fake window. The screen imitates what's outside so you'll note that it's just another foggy day in the bay."

"How long are you going to keep me here?" John Lee asked.

"Look, holding you prisoner is screwing up my life of freedom, so I'll take you back to Mill Valley as soon as today or tomorrow. We need to make plans and so your release depends on those plans. You will not be harmed as that is not who I am. I just need to secure Hermione's safety and decide what to do with your nutcase of a boss and you. What's your suggestion?"

John Lee looked taken aback by Damian's question. He couldn't believe the guy was asking him what he wanted to do. These Americans were tricky people as they didn't always behave in the manner he expected. They were a lot more casual in their ways and that always confused him.

When John Lee provided no answer to Damian, he asked, "Do you work for Mr. Lin's company or are you independent? What exactly are you - a private investigator? That's what it says you are when I Google you."

"Yes I'm a private investigator and no, I'm not an employee of Mr. Lin's. He hired me privately to take care of the problem that Hannah's parents created for him almost two years ago. It took some time to unravel where the deposits were going from Mr. Lin. After I traced the family to California, we made a plan to capture them."

"What were you going to do with them once you had the family?" Damian asked.

"There was confusion as to what we would do. Then we finally settled on flying them out of the country to Malaysia."

"So what happened to that plan?"

"The parents escaped before we could secure them on Mr. Lin's private plane that was to have taken them out of the United States."

"What did you do then?" Damian asked.

"We put a lookout inside the house thinking they would come for the girl, but they must have known she evaded capture and somehow ended up with you and the woman. Mr. Lin's plane has long ago returned to Kuala Lumpur."

"Hermione stayed hidden in the house for nearly a week, so she would have been there if her parents had checked," Damian noted. "So, did Mr. Lin threaten you? Something like 'don't come home without this family and oh by the way you'll never work here again if you fail me'?"

John Lee looked up and at Damian when he offered his suspicions as to Mr. Lin's threats. Finally, he said "You must be a mind reader, sir, as he said something very similar to me."

"When I looked for news of you on the Net, threatening a teenager and her family seemed pretty far removed from your usual work. So how else has he threatened you? Do you have family that are within reach of this man? Has he scared you as to their safety?"

Again John Lee marveled that this stranger could guess so many of his secret dealings with Mr. Lin.

"Mr. Lee, I'm a very smart man and therefore I can guess at some of Mr. Lin's tactics, but I've also worked with my share of bullies in the past and your Mr. Lin sounds like one."

"I regret the day I answered his phone call and met him in his office," John Lee said. "Now I must see this job to its conclusion."

"Why? What's his hold over you?"

"My parents."

"Does he have your parents in custody?"

"Yes, they are but simple farmers from the island of Langkawi growing rice. For the past six months or since Hannah's parents escaped my custody, he's held my parents in a compound of his in Kuala Lumpur."

"Can't you tell the authorities there?"

"Mr. Lin is connected to an important government leader and therefore I would be shut down before I ever reached my parents."

"So we need a plan to expose Mr. Lin and rescue your parents in order for you to leave Hermione alone. Is that correct?"

"Yes."

"When is your next scheduled conversation with Mr. Lin?"

There was silence in the room while John Lee thought about his answer. The man was a stranger, but he had an interesting array of weapons and he knew more about Mr. Lin than he would have thought possible. He felt that potentially turning a child over to Mr. Lin was as lowering to his level of self-respect as doing nothing to get his parents released. Mr. Lin had wanted him to execute the family, but he'd been firm about that. He'd capture them and turn them over to Mr. Lin, but that was as far as he would go. He'd been in a quandary as to what to do. His parents were being taken care of at the moment but they didn't understand why they were being held captive and they worried about their crops rotting in the ground. John felt like the worse son imaginable.

"It's tomorrow. He knew I needed time to recover from the latest interaction with that spicy concoction you make before I could start tailing the kid again."

"How do you talk with him? Does he call your cell phone?"

"Yes."

"What kind of report was he expecting from you during the call tomorrow?"

Mr. Lee looked puzzled by Damian's question and so he added, "Does he ask you questions about your search? Does he allow you to speak with your parents?"

"Yes to both of your questions."

"Okay. I'll come up with a plan."

"Sorry? I don't understand."

"I need to develop a plan that accomplishes three things," Damian said, counting off his fingers. "One: Hermione stays safe and is no longer bothered by you or any other person associated with Mr. Lin. Two: your parents are released from captivity unharmed, and three: Mr. Lin is exposed as the terrible CEO that he is. Does that cover everything?" Damian asked.

John Lee looked at him in confusion and said, "Are you proposing to rescue my parents from Mr. Lin?"

"Yes."

"Why would you help me? You could just turn me over to American authorities."

"Yes, I'm glad you realize that. I could just call the cops and turn you over, but then Mr. Lin would just send someone new and we would start all over again protecting Hermione. So that doesn't solve my problem. I am not the type of low life human that would harm you or your Mr. Lin. I would rather beat you both with brain power."

"Who are you?" John finally asked. "You're not your average American. How do you propose rescuing my parents? That seems to be the tricky question in your scenario."

"I agree with you as I have never been to Kuala Lumpur nor do I know your country's culture or geography. With your help we can figure something out. I would like to release you to assist me in looking for answers but I'm not putting my own safety at risk. Let me warn you that this room and the lab beyond have a number of layers of security that will keep me safe, but make a mess of my lab or this room if I have to deploy them. For example, if you had tried to escape last night, the moment you put your hands on the door, you would have been doused in green slime. The slime is a combination of oil and poison oak, so you would have broken out in an awful itchy rash soon after it touched your skin."

John Lee looked both chagrined and chastened with Damian's explanation.

"So I would like your word that for the next twenty-four to forty-eight hours, you'll live in a peaceful manner in my home and on my island while we figure out how to rescue your parents," Damian said looking into the man's eyes. He considered himself a good judge of character, but this man was from a different culture and it wouldn't be the first time he made an error on that basis.

"I agree," Mr. Lee said with both hope and fear in his voice. "If your green slime is anything like that liquid that landed in my eyes, I'll be itching the rest of my life. Besides until I had this case, I never worked anything other than a missing person case or an occasional adultery case. I lack the ingenuity to get myself off this island. I will follow your lead. How can I help?"

Damian stood up and said, "I trust you but I don't. I'm going to re-lock you in the room while I grab a shower and dress. Then I'll be back to free you and offer you a shower and breakfast, then we'll get to work."

44-CHAPTER FORTY- FOUR

Thirty minutes later, the two men were outside fishing for his cats' breakfast. Damian was of a mind at times that watching a man or woman fish told you something about their character. Fortunately, during the abduction, Ariana thought to grab some of John Lee's clothing so the man didn't have to fish in his drawers which would have been a very cold endeavor. He dropped her an email that morning with the progress he had made with John and he sent word to his staff at his Richmond warehouse that he wouldn't be coming in today. He had a small smile at that thought. Less than a year ago, his body could have laid dead for months on his island, now he had people that would worry about him if he was a few hours late.

After making breakfast for his pets and chopping fish for later meals, the two men returned to his lab and Damian got to work. John Lee was amazed by the man and understood why he so easily protected the teenager; his technology was a wonder.

"What do you want to do with your parents once they are freed?"

"I don't understand your question. What do you mean do with my parents?"

"Do you want them to be able to resume their lives farming or will it be difficult?"

John Lee now understood Damian's question.

"If Mr. Lin is neutralized, they will be safe to continue farming."

"So if we shine a bright light on his practice of making diluted drugs, he'll become someone with no power, disrespected, and perhaps imprisoned by your government despite his connections?"

John thought about that for a while before giving his answer. His government was by and large ethical and would shun Mr. Lin for bad business practices, but would they contain him from doing any more harm? Then he had an idea.

"Mr. Lin brings tax dollars to the government and is revered as a businessman in addition to his family connections. He holds a position of respect. If we could figure out the names of some people inside the Malaysian government that have been harmed by his medications, that will neutralize him, but how do we do that?"

"Good question, let me look into your health care system. Do you recall if your medical record is computerized when you visit a doctor?"

John looked affronted at the question he thought Damian was asking. "Yes we use computers in our hospitals. We are not backward."

"That's not my question. When you visit your local doctor, does he or she write information by hand or do they carry some kind of computer for entry of information that you tell them."

"I haven't been to a doctor for several years, but I know from others who have been that yes they use computers in that manner."

"Okay then that makes it easier to gain information. Let me look at this company and see if I can determine the types of medications he sells and then from there that might give us some ideas of where to look for people that have been harmed."

"I can tell you since my own parents take some of his medication and now you have me worried for their health. He makes the most common pill used for diabetes that my father has been taking for at least five years. My mother has high blood pressure and she takes a drug he makes for that."

"With the help of medication, are your parents in reasonably good health?"

"No their problems have not gone away. They're probably taking diluted medications. I know their doctors are puzzled about why they don't work."

"Okay get me the names of their medication and we'll go from there. By the way, are there any other pharmaceutical companies in Malaysia?"

"I don't know, I don't follow that industry," John said.

"Do you have friends whose health conditions haven't seemed to be under control?"

"Yes. I have one friend whose blood pressure is always out of control no matter what he does. He hates going to the doctor because the doctor always accuses him of not taking his medication. His supply must be coming from Mr. Lin's company."

"Do you think you could get some of the pills from your parents or your friends that I could have analyzed? I'm thinking of contacting a popular journalist in your country as well as one here and providing them with the analysis of the medication and stories of people whose chronic diseases should be under control but are not. Normally something like this would take months to put together, but we don't have that kind of time. I'd like to get this done in under a week. If I arrange a charter plane to get you home to Malaysia, could you collect a sample of prescription drugs in say three or four hours and fly back to the United States?"

Things were moving fast for John Lee. The thought of flying on a private plane to home and back was unimaginable. He had a glimmer of hope that this American had the resources to expose Mr. Lin for all of his unethical and illegal business practices, and then he thought of a problem.

"Mr. Lin is supposed to call me at ten in the morning tomorrow. How do I take his call if I'm on a plane?"

"Your phone will work on the plane's Wi-Fi, but let's think of a reason you won't be available and for him to delay calling you by a day. I wouldn't want him to be suspicious if he hears the background noise of a jet airplane. Have you ever delayed another phone call to him? We may as well start with what has worked in the past."

"I've had to delay a few calls whenever I had Hannah or her family under surveillance and it would've been detrimental for my voice to carry while talking on a cell phone. So I could tell him I need to delay the call because I'm carrying out surveillance at the high school to make another grab for the girl," John said. Then he shrugged and said, "It's not far from the truth. It's what I would've been doing if you hadn't intercepted me."

Damian just gave him a long pained look and said, "The kid's name is Hermione, not Hannah. Can you make that correction? It's annoying me. Notify your Mr. Lin of your planned surveillance and let's get you out of here. A word of caution, once you arrive in Kuala Lumpur, you're free to disappear into your country. I won't pursue you, but your parents won't be safe either. Do you have a friend that can get you prescription medications on short notice?"

"Yes I can do that and I'll be back. You're my only hope at the moment of freeing my family."

"Okay then. We're going to take my boat over to Richmond and I'll drive you back to your hotel so that you have whatever you need to travel with. Then I'll drop you off at San Francisco International airport and you'll start your eighteen hour journey there and back. So you need to line up people now that will give you their medication or a pharmacy to dispense it without a physician's order. You can also make arrangements from the plane. Come back as soon as you have what I need. If you get that done in an hour, then the plane will fly back sooner. I need bottles with drug names on them. Got it?"

"Yes. I'll text you an image to make sure that what I have will work before I leave to return."

With that Damian had John Lee underway to collect what he hoped could be used to expose the corruption of Mr. Lin and his corporation. He also lined up a couple of reporters in New York and San Francisco to cover the story. The reporter in New York also had ties to the main Malaysian paper - The Star. As Damian steered his boat back home after dropping off John, he wondered how he had gotten tangled up in this latest conspiracy. Would his life ever revert to that of a simple inventor?

45-CHAPTER FORTY-FIVE

Natalie was kicking the side of her metal desk in frustration. It appeared as though the delay suffered by the judge wanting to chat with Damian was all the time the twins needed to disappear from Michigan.

After the one twin lost the trooper in the Upper Peninsula of Michigan, the Traverse City police interviewed the landlord and employers of the twins.

They had been model renters in the years they had lived in the apartment. The rent was always paid on time and they were quiet as church mice. They said they had to leave town on an emergency to move to the south to take care of a relative with cancer. They left the apartment paid for sixty days and fully furnished for the next renter. The landlord couldn't tell the two women apart and never knew which one he was speaking to. One of the twins had notified him yesterday that she was leaving from work to drive south and she said the other twin had already left ahead of her.

The two employers had told the same story. They had a first name for each of the twins, but to be honest the other twin might have worked. They were punctual and except for the odd day off for a flu bug, they'd been model employees. Both diner owners were upset with the short notice and sorry to lose the worker. Neither woman had been close to any other employee at their respective diner. The twins occasionally socialized with folks, but after interviewing the other employees, no one seem to know much private information about either woman.

They had shared the woman's picture with Canadian authorities, but it was now thirty-hours beyond when the troopers first lost sight of one of the twins and it appeared that the other twin left a full twenty-four hours earlier according to her employer. Was the case basically closed because the two women escaped United States' jurisdiction? Sure they could post something on Interpol, but Natalie thought these two women were too smart to be caught as they had evaded law enforcement for nearly a decade now.

There were two other options she could pursue - shutting down their assets if she could find them and having the Michigan Troopers dust the girl's apartment for prints just from a confirmatory point of view. Then she thought of a third option.

They clearly took off unexpectedly. Maybe one of them had a sixth sense that they were closing in. What if they found their stash? Maybe they hadn't had time to finish selling all of the goods or to have exchanged all of the cash from the robbery. Maybe there was something to recover for the bank and that something would also serve as further confirmation of the identity of the two robbers.

As there wasn't loot left in their apartment and they apparently left with few belongings, then their stash was likely still in the area somewhere. Natalie guessed there might be ten storage facilities in a region that size. It wasn't that large a town and several of the smaller surrounding cities wouldn't be large enough to support a storage facility. Natalie thought if there were just a few storage areas, she could pursue further questioning in hopes of locating the remaining spoils of the robbery.

Detective Shimoda basically considered the case closed with the twins' names as the only suspects of the robbery, but she'd go one step farther and see if she could find some stolen goods, then Natalie would be satisfied with the case's conclusion.

She began making calls to the storage facilities. She opened with a question of how long they were open and then asked if they had a plan for a renter to pay ahead five or ten years, then she planned to joke about as if anyone really did that and see what those conversations would shake out. She struck gold on the fifth storage facility. After her usual questions, she asked, if they had any long term clients.

"Yes, in fact, the lease was renewed just two days ago and it's paid up for the next decade. I remember it as it doesn't often happen in this rental business. Most people think they'll only need storage for a year or so and then they'll get around to throwing out stuff and they won't need it again. This woman's been our renter for at least seven years and now she wants another ten. She must be a pack-rat if she can't thin out her possessions in all that time."

Or a bank robber, Natalie thought while the clerk babbled on.

"Can you describe that renter?" Natalie asked when clerk paused to take a breath.

"Thirtyish, normal weight, black hair, Caucasian, no accent, wore glasses."

That probably described half the United States female population.

"Was it one woman or were there sisters that rented?"

"Just one woman. She is always pleasant to speak with and look at."

"Are you expecting her back at her storage unit soon?" "I don't know. People rarely tell me when they'll be visiting their storage unit."

"So she didn't say anything like see you soon or something like that?"

There was silence on the other end of the phone and then the guy said, "No nothing like that. What's this woman done? It's not like I ever saw anything illegal going on there. I'd ask her if she needed a hand moving stuff and she always assured me she was lifting lightweight boxes. When she drove past the office, I never noticed that her car was piled with boxes so I assumed it was just small stuff."

Yeah, thought Natalie, small stuff like stolen jewelry or packs of money, but she just asked the clerk one more question.

"What's the name of the renter of the unit?"

"Arielle Joseph."

Bingo. Got you.

Natalie thanked the clerk for his time and ended the call. Then she placed a call to the detective. She wanted to get a search warrant for the storage facility. Maybe they would find stolen goods inside. The detective thought they would have a search warrant for the Michigan Troopers the next day.

Natalie was so tempted to fly to Michigan to be there when they opened the storage area, but alas she stayed back in California. If the troopers opened the storage area and found any of the stolen goods, the FBI would move right in and assume control of the case. Oh well, she didn't work cold cases for the glory, rather she worked them to bring justice to those denied it for a long time. Maybe they would find some keepsake still in the storage area that's invaluable to the family or person from which it was stolen nearly ten years ago.

She notified the troopers of her search warrant ETA and ended her work for the day. Tomorrow could be exciting. If she found any of the stolen goods, her reputation as a detective would shoot through the roof and she'd likely have all the consulting cases she wanted.

46-CHAPTER FORTY-SIX

Several days later, John Lee returned as promised with the perfect cache of medications. He had a good friend in the pharmacy business who had seen so many medications fail, that the friend wondered about the potency at times, but hadn't known what to do with the idea. He had bottles sealed by the manufacturer that he gave to John for testing in the United States. Damian had contacted a couple of testing labs in the region. He then lined up his Food and Drug Administration expert and the two journalists while he awaited the outcome of the testing lab.

A day later John Lee had his scheduled call with Mr. Lin which was filled with promises that he was just about to capture the teenager. Meanwhile he was working with Damian to figure out his parents' physical location. They both hoped that while Mr. Lin was distracted by the negative press directed at his company that John could swoop in and free his parents. Over the six months they'd been in custody, they had given him various descriptions of the property where they were being held and Mr. Lee asked to speak with them during his most recent call to Mr. Lin for even a little more clarification. He'd waited while the connection was made which told him they weren't nearby Mr. Lin.

Damian searched the Malaysian property databases to determine the scope of Mr. Lin's holdings. The two of them discussed the difficulty of holding the older couple in nearby countries like Singapore or Brunei and so they focused on Malaysia. His parents heard large jets on occasion and the pinging sound of someone striking a golf ball. Damian was focused on estate homes on a golf course in one of the cities with an airport. As the couple didn't always hear jet engine sounds suggested it wasn't Kuala Lumpur's airport. There was an airport in one of the larger northern cities near one of Mr. Lin's properties and they guessed that was where the couple was being held.

John Lee's rescue of his parents was his to plan and execute. Damian didn't want to be involved for many reasons. He was willing to provide John and his private investigator buddies who would accompany him, with weapons made in his own lab. He was also willing to charter him back to Malaysia at the appropriate moment. He had two reasons for doing that - to make it easier for John to transport some of his pepper juice and for Hermione's peace of mind to know that she was safe. Damian was hoping to have the drug production exposé ready to go to the U.S. authorities and the journalists within the next twenty-four hours. Of course, the lab testing might come back with all medication being made appropriate to formulary, but from everything he had read, he should have a bombshell on his hands. His contact at the New York Times also had a contact at a newspaper in Beijing. A story about a Malaysian drug manufacturer charging the Chinese for weak medications would destroy Mr. Lin's company overnight.

A question was bothering Damian and so he asked John, "When you held Hermione's parents captive, where did they escape from? Was it your hotel in Mill Valley or closer to their home?"

"I knew about the family's boat so we took them there and then went out into the bay as I didn't want them to be able to call for help or escape."

"So what happened to them?"

"I don't know actually. One moment they were on board and the next, they were gone. I watched the news for any sign of bodies turning up but never heard anything."

"Did they have wetsuits?"

"No they were wearing the pajamas we took them in."

"How far out was the boat from shore?"

"Maybe closer than your island is to shore, but not by much."

"So did you think her parents had drowned?"

"No. They were very cunning people; I'm sure they survived somehow."

"Were they tied up?"

"Yes, we duck taped them into one of the beds in the boat and that was the last I saw of them."

"So you were still chasing Hermione on the belief that her parents had escaped the boat and contacted her."

"Yes."

"You're really a hapless criminal, John Lee," Damian said with a small smile.

"I know. I never did anything like this in my own country let alone in America. It's probably why I was so inept. In my heart of hearts, I didn't want to be successful."

"Why didn't Mr. Lin hire someone else to do his dirty work?"

"Mr. Lin had low expectations. He was for the most part pleased with my work as I had at least located where the family was hiding."

"Okay," Damian said his mind on Hermione's parents. Had they drowned or survived?

47-CHAPTER FORTY-SEVEN

It was nearly noon when two Michigan State Troopers pulled into the A-1 storage facility in Traverse City, Michigan. They had a copy of a search warrant issued by a California judge for the storage facility rented to Arielle Joseph. Retired detective Natalie Severino was quietly going out of her mind by not being with the troopers. She talked one of them into using FaceTime technology on her iPhone to give Natalie immediate access to the storage room as they opened it. Natalie could see as they approached the space that it was a large space.

The owner had gone with them to open the space, but returned to his office when he noticed the private lock on the storage room. The trooper took a pair of bolt cutters out of his trunk and cut the lock open. The door slid up to reveal a large storage room containing boxes in front. The deputy went to move the box only to find it empty and then it was clear that a row of empty boxes were blocking the view of a small cargo van at the back.

The deputy used the bolt cutters again to break the lock on the cargo van and then opened the door. Natalie had visions of stacks of dollar bills and glistening jewels. Instead there was a row of boxes along the back wall of the truck. The troopers climbed into the truck and opened the first box and Natalie got her wish.

Her voice came from the cell phone and said, "Is that a large ugly necklace in that box?"

"Yes," was the amused reply from the trooper.

Natalie had opened the spreadsheet before the trooper opened the storage door with pictures of some of the contents of the safe deposit boxes that owners supplied at the time of the original robbery. She had a smaller spreadsheet of items that hadn't shown up yet at the major auction houses. She quickly searched for a match to the ugly necklace that she was looking at via the camera.

"Got it. Those are real gemstones according to the original owner and the necklace was insured for seventy thousand dollars nearly fifteen years ago. Good thing we notified the FBI, I think we've found the robbery contents!" Natalie said while doing a little happy dance.

Looking at his watch the other trooper said, "The agent left Detroit this morning and should be here within about thirty minutes to take possession of these contents."

"If this truck was full when it arrived, your bank robbers have already fenced most of the stolen goods and cash," remarked the one trooper.

"Yeah, I can see. I'll have to take satisfaction in the fact the case has been solved, the robbers identified, even if most of the cash and loot and the robbers have disappeared," Natalie said.

"Sometimes that's all you get in this business. Congratulations, Detective on some fine work. From California to Traverse City, a pair of twin thieves, and the remainder of the loot. Hopefully the owner of that ugly necklace is still around so she may have the pleasure of wearing it again."

Natalie heard another voice and guessed the FBI agent had arrived on the scene. Natalie wrapped up the conversation with the two troopers and agent and ended the call. She then immediately called Detective Shimoda.

"Case solved!" Natalie said when the detective answered.

"Really? Great work, Natalie! Did they find the cash?"

"No it was a mostly empty storage truck with just a few boxes left. I identified a necklace in one of the boxes as one that is on our inventory and the FBI is now on the scene to handle stuff on that end."

"And the twins have disappeared?"

"Yeah, one of them disappeared the day before the other that our troopers lost in the Michigan wilderness. So we'll leave a warrant out for their arrest, but I'm not expecting any arrests."

"No one we can charge as an accessory?"

"No, those two kept the crime between the two of them. No

evidence of anyone else being involved."

"We'll have to coordinate a press conference on our end with the FBI and Michigan so stay available for that."

The two wrapped up the phone call and then Natalie called Damian. She could have sent him an email, but she was still on an emotional high for this final piece of the bank heist.

"Hey," she said once they exchanged pleasantries, "I found the loot from the bank heist!"

"You did? Great job! Where and was there much left?"

"In Michigan, of course, and no there wasn't much left. No cash, just boxes with stuff inside a cargo truck inside a storage facility," Natalie said retracing her detective work for him.

"Something must have made the women paranoid as they ran at the last possible moment to escape capture."

"At least we know who the robbers were and we have an arrest warrant in the United States and through Interpol if they ever surface again, but I think if they continue to be careful, they'll live comfortable lives somewhere beyond our reach."

"You don't seem sad about that," Damian commented, curious about Natalie's attitude.

"No one was physically hurt by their actions. Most of the losses were compensated for. I rather like how smart these women were and imagine what it would be like to start over in your early thirties with the cash to do whatever you wanted," Natalie said wistfully.

"But look what you would have given up in your case - no husband, no son, no satisfying career as a detective. I would also bet the twins never see each other again as they'll know that might blow their cover, so you would have to give up your sibling as well. Still want to move to the end of the earth and start over?"

"Do you have to be so practical, Damian? I'd fallen in love with my romantic notion of these two bank robbers."

"Well, get over it and go solve another cold case," he said, though she could hear the smile in his command.

"Yeah, okay then. I'll spend another hour or two dreaming about where I would land, then I'll probably go do a press conference about solving the case and then it's, as you say, time to open another cold case folder and see what I can do. You know it's depressing talking to you; I don't why I called."

Damian laughed out loud at the almost whining quality of her complaint. "Sure you do, you wanted me to tell you all the reasons you were not going to go out and plan your own bank robbery so your mind could move on to the next case."

Natalie laughed at his assessment, knowing he was right. "Well, thanks for your help. You found the robbers and I found the loot. Good teamwork!"

Damian smiled as he ended the call with Natalie. Then he saw the email he'd been waiting for.

48-CHAPTER FORTY-EIGHT

It was from the first of the three companies that were analyzing the drug specimens. All three had said they would have results by mid-day. He opened and read the results then shook his head. Looking at these results, he knew he was doing a favor for the people of Malaysia and China and wherever else Mr. Lin's products were sold.

Of the four medications he'd had analyzed, the pills ranged in potency from ten percent to fifty percent. He didn't know what some of the stuff was in these medications only that the active ingredients weren't there in the stated amounts. The other two companies shortly followed the first one's emails with verification. Damian wanted no public role in uncovering the pharmaceutical problem in Malaysia so he worked it out with his journalist friends that it looked like they had been suspicious and discovered the problems with manufacturing. He gave them the data and then he faded into the background while they went to work on their investigative journalism reporting. Three days later, Mr. Lin was under investigation for his company's manufacturing with Malaysian authorities holding him under house arrest pending their own investigation.

John Lee and his friends had met no resistance in freeing his parents. Mr. Lin's staff had deserted the house when word of his problems reached them. Damian sat back satisfied with his actions and that afternoon he was heading over to Hermione's school for the last water polo match of the season. If her team won, they moved on to regionals which they were expected to do.

He'd kept the two women informed on his actions in regards to her kidnapper, but hadn't relayed his conversation with John Lee to Hermione. He did a search of the news for any bodies that turned up anywhere in San Francisco Bay. Damian had looked at the tides and determined that at the time Hermione's parents went overboard, the tide would likely pull them toward shore, but it was a guess as the tides changed direction every four to six hours so if his timing was off, then the tide charts weren't meaningful.

If they were alive had they been unable to find Hermione or were they still on the run or were they dead? He didn't have answers.

He pulled up to the dock at Ariana's house and went inside.

"Hey, how's it going," she asked when he entered after a slight knock.

"It's going well. Our Mr. Lin will never again be a problem for Hermione nor will he make millions of people sick in Asia from poorly manufactured drugs. So my work is done there."

He was sitting at her counter sipping from a tea mug he brought with him from his island, while she was wrapping up some work on her laptop.

"But?"

He looked at her puzzled.

"Something else is still puzzling you. Is it the bank robbery? I think you said that was coming to a conclusion."

"No that concluded this afternoon; I spoke with Natalie about an hour ago and they found the loot in Michigan, but the robbers have very likely left the United States. You'll hear about it on the news tonight or tomorrow."

"So what else is bothering you?"

"How can you tell I'm bothered by something?" he asked with a small smile.

"Because you're about ninety percent in my kitchen and another ten percent of your brain is processing some program in the background."

Damian laughed at her explanation and said, "Are you trying to speak geek to me?"

"Just calling it like it is. So what's up?"

"Before John Lee left, I asked him about Hermione's parents escape. He and his crew took them to the boat in the marina and then sailed out onto the bay so they couldn't call for help or otherwise walk away."

"Oh. That's means that her parents had to have escaped by water or drowned in the bay."

"Exactly. I'm not sure what to say to Hermione about it. I'd like to believe they're alive, but that I've hidden her identity so well they haven't been able to find her."

"Well, she got her swimming and water polo DNA from somewhere so it would make sense that her parents are good swimmers."

"Yes, it would, but the bay is pretty cold and they were wearing pajamas."

"Did you search for unidentified bodies showing up since last spring?" Ariana asked knowing that he would have looked at that angle.

"Yes, I did but nothing fit the description of her parents from a height, age, or hair color perspective."

"Yuck. I'd hate to fish partially eaten human bodies out of the bay."

"Not my cup of tea either. So what do we say to Hermione?"

"The truth and we'll simply have no answers as to the question of where are her parents."

Nearly three hours later, after Hermione's water polo team decimated the competition, they sat alone in a Thai restaurant. Hermione was so deft with chopsticks that Damian found it mesmerizing at times to watch. She looked up at him and said, "Go ahead and tell me whatever's bothering you. This is the third time in the past twenty minutes that you've gotten lost in watching my chopsticks. That's a sure sign you're avoiding talking about something to me."

Damian gave her a small smile for her wisdom beyond her age. He described his conversation with John Lee and then let the words lie there.

"So," Hermione said slowly. "My parents either drowned or they're fine."

"Were they good swimmers?" Ariana asked.

"Yes, they met in college on their respective swim teams. I figure that's where my talent came from."

"So it's possible they were able to swim ashore," Damian said.

"Yeah, it's possible. I mean they had the skill to do it, but I'm not sure about swimming in the cold water, but people swim in the bay without wetsuits."

Damian and Ariana were silent, thinking about the teenager's response and waiting for her next question.

"So if they made it alive, where have they been all these months? Why didn't they return to the house and rescue me?"

"I don't know," Ariana said. "Maybe they ended up with pneumonia after the swim and were hospitalized and by the time they were discharged, you were gone from the house."

Hermione just stared at Ariana, clearly not buying her explanation.

Damian cleared his throat and said, "Ah, um I looked through police records for bodies that washed up and nothing matched your parents."

Hermione gulped at Damian's information.

"Do you think they ever saw your Facebook post where you used symbols to indicate you were alive and well?" Ariana asked.

"If they did, they didn't respond back to it."

They went back and forth on some other scenarios until they ran out of ideas.

"Well Hermione, you have proof of nothing at the moment so you can choose one of two paths. You can choose to believe your parents didn't survive and you're now an orphan. Or you can choose to believe they are alive and searching for you. I buried your identity and your parents would need computer skills like mine to find you. Otherwise, it's going to take serendipity for them to pass you on the street and identify you."

"Regardless," Ariana said, "I love being your second mother and Damian feels likewise. You can wait until you're eighteen and begin a public search for your parents if they don't show up in the next two and a half years and continue to make your life with the two of us. Think about it and you don't have to answer us now. Now that those men are no longer after you, we could change your name back to Hannah Sherwood."

"I already know my answer. I want to stay with you guys and I don't want to start anything that might get you in trouble for taking me in instead of handing me over to foster care, so I'll keep the name Hermione Smith. I know that I've screwed your lives up with having to go to school events whereas you were both free as birds but I love living with you."

"That's because we haven't grounded you yet or refused to let you drive at sixteen," Damian said.

"Or embarrassed you in front of a date. I promise to do all of those things in your future. You might wish not to be my child at those times."

Hermione just stood up and put her arms around both of them for a hug and they all sat with moist eyes waiting for the moment to pass and for them to find composure.

Damian held up his tea cup and said "To the Knowles-Green family" and the other two clanked their tea cups with his.

The End

ABOUT THE AUTHOR

Discover my other books:

Jill Quint, MD, Forensic Pathologist series

Vials

Chocolate Diamonds

A Breck Death

Death On A Green

A Taxing Death

Murder At The Podium

A 7th book is a work in progress for this series.

Damian Green Series

Red Rock Island

Willow Glen Heist

Connect with me:

Friend me on Facebook http://facebook.com/AlecPeche

Find me on Twitter @AlecPeche

www.alecpeche.com

email: author@alecpeche.com

Blog: www.AlecPeche.com

Made in the USA
San Bernardino, CA
12 May 2017